JB

Scraps of Paper

The First Spookie Town Murder Mystery (Prequel to ***All Things Slip Away, Ghosts Beneath Us, Witches Among Us, What Lies Beneath the Graves,*** *and* ***All Those Who Came Before****. A seventh book* ***When the Fireflies Returned*** *will be out in December 2020)*

By Kathryn Meyer Griffith

~

Why is the town called Spookie? In this murder mystery series it is a tongue-in-cheek, a tip-of-my-hat to my earlier roots as a horror writer and little else. This book is for my sweet brother Jim Meyer, who passed away on May 27, 2015. He was a great singer/musician/songwriter. If you'd like to listen to some of his songs, here they are: http://tinyurl.com/pytftzc

Scraps of Paper

by Kathryn Meyer Griffith
(1st Spookie Town murder mystery)
Originally published 2003 in hardcover by Avalon Books

Cover art by: Dawné Dominique

This is dedicated, as always, to my family.

Other books by Kathryn Meyer Griffith:

Evil Stalks the Night
The Heart of the Rose
Blood Forged
Vampire Blood (Prequel to Human No Longer)
Human No Longer (Sequel to Vampire Blood)
The Last Vampire (2012 Epic EBook Awards Finalist)
Witches
Witches II: Apocalypse
Witches plus Witches II: Apocalypse
The Calling
Scraps of Paper*-The First Spookie Town Murder Mystery*
All Things Slip Away*-The Second Spookie Town Murder Mystery*
Ghosts Beneath Us*-The Third Spookie Town Murder Mystery*
Witches Among Us*-Fourth Spookie Town Murder Mystery*
What Lies Beneath the Graves*-Fifth Spookie Town Mystery*
All Those Who Came Before*-Sixth Spookie Town Mystery*
When the Fireflies Returned*-Seventh out in December 2020*
Egyptian Heart
Winter's Journey
The Ice Bridge
Don't Look Back, Agnes
A Time of Demons and Angels
The Woman in Crimson
Four Spooky Short Stories
Night Carnival
Forever and Always Novella
The Nameless One erotic horror short story
Dinosaur Lake (2014 Epic EBook Awards Finalist)
Dinosaur Lake II: Dinosaurs Arising
Dinosaur Lake III: Infestation
Dinosaur Lake IV: Dinosaur Wars
Dinosaur Lake V: Survivors
Memories of My Childhood

***All Kathryn Meyer Griffith's books can be found here:**
http://tinyurl.com/ld4jlow
***All her Audible.com audio books here:**
http://tinyurl.com/oz7c4or

Reviews

Scraps of Paper *is an engaging story of what happens when you go digging into the past and the possible consequences. It also has an underlying story about dealing with what life hands you and finding the strength to move on. Both Frank and Abby are strong characters that have had to deal with the loss of a loved one and to learn to deal with that loss. You find yourself drawn to them and to all the quirky people who live in the little town of Spookie. In the end you want to know what happened in the old house so many years earlier. I'll be looking forward to more books about this quaint little town.* ***9 stars out of 10*** **Novelspot Book Reviews,** *Theresa. March 2006****

*"**Scraps of Paper** is a well-constructed mystery with just the right mix of good guys and bad guys, with a sprinkling of oddballs and misfits thrown in. Kathryn Meyer Griffin does a nice job of allowing the friendship of the book's two main characters to develop as the story progresses. I would recommend this book to anyone who likes a good who-done-it, set in a picturesque environment with believable characters. This is the first book in a series the author calls 'The Spookie Town Mysteries'."* ***5 Stars*** *Reviewed by* **Michael McManus** *for* ***Readers' Favorite May 17, 2013 ******

"Ghosts Leave Messages Towards Solving Murders…"

"Great old-fashioned mystery about a long ago crime…."

"Solving a heart breaking story of murder…."

"Absolutely loved it!!"

Chapter 1
2003

Abigail Sutton began driving, with no real destination in mind. It'd been years since she'd done anything as spontaneous, not since before her husband, Joel, had walked out of their apartment late one night for cigarettes and hadn't returned. She'd loved her husband more than anything in life and he had loved her just as much. Joel hadn't merely run out on her; she knew that from the first. He wouldn't have done that because he wasn't that sort of man.

They'd been happily married for twenty years and were about to begin building their dream house. They'd had the land; it'd been cleared off and the building would have commenced the following week.

Then Joel had disappeared and for two and a half years he'd been missing…until last month when the police had phoned one morning to inform her his car, and his body, had been found in the middle of a ravine in the deep woods outside of town. Joel was dead. He'd been a victim of an ill-fated mugging, the police said, left lifeless and robbed, in his stripped car in a remote place no one had found until now.

It was ironic. She'd remained alone in the cramped apartment for two years, waiting, believing he'd stroll back in one night just as he'd walked out; believing she'd get a phone call from him, a message, anything. It hadn't happened. Her life had been frozen and sad for so long, too long.

She'd lost her graphic artist job at the local newspaper last month, which was partly her fault. She'd quit that job, sick of producing ads and inserts among a group of overworked and frantic people always fighting with the out-of-date computers. There'd been too many deadlines; not enough employees. It'd been coming for a long time. Losing Joel had changed her. She wasn't easy to be around, she knew that. She was angry or melancholy all the time. Obsessed with finding Joel. She kind of went nuts. Her co-workers ended up ignoring her and it hurt. With all those people around her, she'd never been so alone. It'd taken her a while to figure it out but there was more to life than some lousy job and an empty apartment. Joel's official death certificate sealed that belief. Now, she was acting on what she'd learned.

The asphalt road before her car was shimmering in the summer's heat and the steering wheel, under her hands, felt good. She was in search of a new life because the past was unchangeable, but the future wasn't.

Traveling the main highway for over an hour she veered onto an exit, and a side road which wound into woods, and ended up in a town the map called Spookie. She was searching for a sleepy hamlet; a certain feeling or magic remembered from childhood, of summer innocence and safety, of a picturesque and welcoming village where she could start over.

Because for the first time in a long time, she was free. She was free to reach out to other people, open her heart, her life, live, and reinvent herself. She wouldn't be moody and reclusive any longer. She was going to be happy.

With her savings, she'd have enough to buy a fixer upper house, move in, and just make it for a while until she got another job–if a traditional daytime job was what she had to do to pay the bills. She had this crazy idea of being a freelance artist, of selling paintings and drawings, and not ever having to work locked up all day in an office again. But it'd been a long time since she'd drawn, illustrated anything, because computers had replaced her creative skills and she hoped she hadn't forgotten how to do those things.

How peaceful the country roads and the surrounding woods were. She stopped the car on the shoulder and tramped into the damp grass alongside an old wooden bridge, where the light, pale shades of tawny gold and delicate vermilion appeared softer.

She began climbing, using slim trees to help her upwards. At the top of the rise she paused. The countryside, all hills and tree-dotted valleys, was laid out for miles around her and the sky above was a palette of pinks, blues and wispy whites. The breeze lifting her brown hair gently about her face seemed to sing to her. *Here you will find home.*

There was a miniature town nestled in the center of a clump of woods below, pretty as a picture postcard, and so cloaked in fog it was barely visible. She studied it, fascinated. From where she was, the village appeared full of tiny houses, tiny buildings and tiny roads. But real people lived in those houses and buildings, lived their lives out among the woods, and the mist. The town was calling to her as if she belonged there. *Home is here.*

Back in the car she found herself on the town's Main Street, which was lined in Victorian frame houses and shops. Each house was well cared for, unique, some covered in climbing ivy, some surrounded by towering trees and decorated in American flags for the coming holiday. There were people sitting and chatting quietly on shady porches, or coming in and out of doorways, or strolling through a park around the courthouse. A small lake surrounded the park. Businesses, a bookstore, a modest general grocery store, a five and dime, a hardware store, a restaurant, an ice cream parlor and what had to be a library, squatted side by side with homes. A perfect little town.

Welcome to Spookie, population 558 in big white letters on a bright red board were the words on the sign on the side of the road.

Abigail couldn't help herself and laughed. It was a peculiar name for a town. But the drifting fog, the darkness huddled beneath the trees and sky, partially hidden by leaves and branches created an eerie ambiance to the place. It was a little spooky. She liked it though. It reminded her of an English village, tranquil and mysterious, or a town right out of the1950's. It was much like the town she'd grown up in and had loved. Penny candy at the corner confectionary, books dragged home from a musty library, playing hide and seek at twilight and riding her bike through tree lined shady streets with her siblings were what she fondly remembered. In a sense, she'd been looking for that town again all her life.

She parked her car in front of the courthouse. After the air conditioning of the auto, the outside heat was a slap of a hot hand. Even her summer blue jeans and red T-shirt seemed too warm on her skin. Grabbing her hair in one hand, she tied it into a ponytail with a Scrunchie she kept in her purse and meandered the sidewalks peering into the store windows, nodding her head to the people lounging on the porches. They nodded or smiled back.

She caught wisps of conversation: *Myrtle broke the wheel on her wagon this morning. She got so mad. I saw her dragging it, grumbling the whole way, down the street.* Laughter.

Someone's got to do something about that sister of hers. I swear she's got a hundred critters living in her house. It looks like a zoo. I delivered a package there the other day....

...they say that house needs a lot of work. The old lady had been sick a long time before she passed, and didn't keep the place up. Strange old reclusive woman. No, no relatives...not living that is. She had a younger sister once. What ever happened to her? She got up and just left, her and her kids. Off to greener pastures, I suppose. A long, long time past, I recollect. No one ever saw them again.

It's so hot today, ice cream sounds good. Let's go get a banana split.

But Abigail felt at home…in a strange town in the middle of nowhere with people she'd never met before. This was where she belonged. She continued exploring the shops and the streets. In the air there was a tantalizing perfume, a combination of cotton candy, summer flowers and hot dogs. In the distance she could hear the purr of a lawn mower. She could smell the aroma of cut grass. The sweet smells alone were enough for her to want to stay. Somewhere, phantom children were frolicking and laughing. There were the usual summer noises. She expected to glance up, any moment, and see kids playing with their hula hoops or skating down the sidewalks on old-fashioned roller skates. The kind of skates which used to have those tightening keys, like the one she used to wear on a shoestring around her neck so she wouldn't lose it.

Stella's Diner was tucked in a tight corner a few stores down from Mason's General Store. The diner was as good a place as any, she figured, to get a bite to eat and ask where the local real estate office was. She was hungry because wandering around had given her an appetite.

The café was cozy and packed with individual booths, and a bar with tall stools against one wall. Everything was old, worn, but clean. Homey in a thrift store way.

Frying sounds came from the rear of the diner and chicken smells filled the air. They made her mouth water.

Abigail claimed a stool at the bar and sat

down. "What's the special today?" she asked the older woman behind the counter.

"Chicken and dumplings."

"That sounds good. Can I have a plate, please? Oh, and do you make malts?"

"The best in the county. The old-fashioned kind made in the metal tumblers. Thick and creamy. What flavor you want?"

"Chocolate, with extra syrup in it." Abigail smiled, but the woman didn't return it.

"An order of chicken and D's for the lady out here," she said to a young man standing over a grill behind her. Then the waitress began scooping globs of ice cream into a tall shiny container and adding the other ingredients. The woman had snow-colored hair in a short bad haircut, weary blue eyes, no makeup, but bright crimson lipstick. She had to be seventy if she was a day. Her arms were skinny, her face a map of lines, and her back crooked from years of hard work. Abigail wondered how she could lift more than twenty pounds. But she had a feisty attitude and seemed to know what she was doing.

"Seems like a nice little town you have here," Abigail made casual conversation.

"Nice enough." The woman set the malt before her, then a plate of steaming dumplings and chicken. "If you like eccentric and nosy."

"I've been thinking of moving to a place like this." Abigail began eating, gazing around. There were two other customers in the restaurant, locals by the look of them, a middle-aged lady with large eyeglasses and an elderly gentleman with unruly gray hair. They were staring at her from behind their menus, pretending they weren't. Abigail raised her malt glass to them and grinned. They quickly averted their eyes and went back to whispering together as they had been doing before.

The waitress stopped and looked directly at her for the first time. "You want to move here?" There was a hint of a smile and Abigail couldn't tell if it was welcoming, or sarcastic.

"I think so. I've been looking the town over and I like it. So quaint and peaceful."

The old woman snickered. "Appearances can be deceiving," was all she said.

"Reminds me of the town I grew up in."

That got her a raised eyebrow and a begrudging smile. "Does it now?"

"Any houses for sale around here?"

"Maybe a couple. But you need to talk to Martha Sikeston, our real estate expert. She handles all the property in the area. She'd know if there were any houses available. Office is the third building down, on the other side of the street, next to the local newspaper."

"Thanks."

The waitress took care of her other customers, leaving Abigail to eat and eavesdrop. The diner had no air conditioning, but there were stand up fans in the back going full blast. They made it comfortable enough. Lush trees, which would help keep the electricity bills down, shaded the diner as they did most of the town's buildings and kept the heat at bay.

In the corner, a middle-aged lady, when she

ordered lemon pie, called the waitress *Stella.* She had the sort of voice which carried, made a person want to cover their ears, and she was complaining about her brother to the man sitting beside her–who couldn't get a word in edgewise–by what Abigail could glean from the conversation. Stella, having overheard what the two were discussing, had ambled over, and was talking to them hands on her bony hips.

Another customer walked in the door and Stella acknowledged him with a wave of her order book. "Be right with you," she hollered. She was busy.

Abigail let her mind wander. In small towns everybody knew everyone and their business. That was kind of nice. So different, Abigail thought, than the city. She turned her head and peered out the front window. People were walking by with packages going here and there. A child in pigtails skipped in the front door followed by an adult; the two found a booth, and waved at Stella, who went to take both their and the earlier arrival's orders.

Abigail finished, and took money out of her purse, by the time Stella returned.

"That was the best chicken and dumplings I've ever eaten," she complimented as she paid the bill, leaving a generous tip.

The old woman's attitude was suddenly friendlier and she smiled at Abigail for the first time. "Thank you. I can't take all the credit for it, though." She tossed her head in the direction of the kitchen. "The young man back there, my grandson, cooks nearly everything these days."

"You must be proud of him then. He's a good cook for as young as he is."

From the kitchen a boy's voice shouted, "I'm not that young!"

Stella rolled her eyes. "He'll be sixteen next week. A good boy. He lives with me upstairs." She pointed at the ceiling with her finger. "His folks died in an airplane crash two years ago."

"Well, delicious food," Abigail shouted back at the young man.

"Thanks," the boy's voice came again. "Come back sometime for breakfast. I make a mean pancake."

"I might just do that," Abigail replied loud enough for him to hear.

Stella continued, "I couldn't handle this place without his and my brother's help. The two of them take turns. Then I have a few friends who fill in for me and give me a day off once in a while. Running a restaurant, being a waitress, isn't as easy as people think."

"I know. I used to be a waitress in a burger joint when I was younger. I wasn't much good at it. I was always dropping things, and hated being groped by the men."

"Well, I don't have to worry about being groped any more, thank goodness. Not unless a man likes to pinch a bony old woman." Stella fixed her eyes on Abigail. "You gonna go to the real estate office now?"

"I think so. Will somebody be there? It being late Friday afternoon and all?"

"Should be. If not, check back here about

six. Martha usually has supper before she heads home, unless she's taking care of business, or has a date."

"I'll remember that, thanks." That was three hours away.

Abigail stood up and slung her purse over her shoulder. She'd absolutely made the decision to find a house to buy. The longer she was in Spookie the more she liked it, even if the inhabitants were a little…quirky.

The afternoon was cooling off, and with a gentle wind racing down Main Street, she thought it would be a lovely evening. She roamed through the mini park around the courthouse, observing any townspeople she encountered. A few ignored her, or stared, but most waved or smiled. She conversed with the merchants in the shops she entered and asked questions about this and that. Once they realized she was interested in them, and their town, they opened up and chatted with her as if they'd known her for years.

The grocery store, or general store, as the owner, John Mason, called it, was a pleasant surprise. It was old-fashioned and full of nostalgic stock and food stuff like there might have been in the last century, rows of glass jars filled with the kind of penny candy Abigail remembered fondly from her childhood; as well as hand-made crafts and artwork from local artists. The store had the strips of colored candy dots on paper, candied watermelon slices, tiny marshmallow ice cream cones, Mary Janes, Necco Wafers, and licorice whips, she also remembered. It was as if she'd stepped forty years back in time. The grocery also had an excellent, modest but adequate, selection of meat and produce. She could do her basic shopping there. Prices were fair. John Mason, a nice looking older man, never took his eyes off her the whole time she was browsing, but said little unless she asked him something directly. He watched her as she walked out into the sunlight. He must like younger women, she thought, amused.

Next to the grocery was a hardware store where besides the usual hardware stuff they sold paint and wallpaper.

There was an ice cream and candy parlor, Ice Cream & Sweets, which made its own candy and pastries. Abigail bought a vanilla ice cream cone and a cherry tart for later, and continued her exploration of the town.

There was a bookstore which not only sold new books, but had a selection of discounted used paperbacks on a card table near the front. On her limited budget recycled books would be about all she could afford. That and a library card. She was into science fiction and mysteries these days.

Eventually, she found herself at the real estate office and since there was no receptionist, she asked the only person there where she could find Martha Sikeston.

"You're looking at her," the woman retorted, coming over to meet her. A short brunette, with brown glasses framing brown eyes, she seemed sure of herself. She was dressed in casual black slacks and a T-shirt which had an American flag across the front. She must have had ten rings on her fingers. Abigail had a hard time not staring at the woman's hands. Beautiful rings.

"And yes, I'm a real estate agent. Here in Spookie we don't stand on ceremony much, don't dress in suits. Most of the time. Oh, I'll wear one when I'm showing a rich client something in a high price bracket. Otherwise, we're pretty informal. You aren't from around here, are you?"

"No. But I'm interested in looking at small fixer-upper houses for sale around town because there's just me. Name is Abigail Sutton." Abigail put out her hand and shook Martha's.

"There's a few houses available." Martha gestured her to a chair in front of a desk. The desk had a computer, papers, books and maps strewn all over it, and at least three days' worth of empty meal bags and containers.

Abigail sat down, dropping her bakery sack and purse to the floor at her feet. "I don't have a lot of money, either."

Martha eyed her intently through her thick glasses, as if she were thinking about something. "You sure you want to buy in this town that badly? Now, don't get me wrong, I've lived here all my life and it's a nice little place, though some people might say a bit strange. But we don't have many outsiders moving in. We're not big city."

"That isn't a problem, me being an outsider?" Abigail tried not to sound overly eager but she wanted the woman to know she was serious. "Spookie reminds me so much of this little town I grew up in. I'm kind of starting my life over, you see. I quit my job in the city last month. I was a graphic artist, I mean, I am an artist. I live in this cramped overpriced apartment which I've been renting since my husband disappeared two years ago–they found him dead last month–and…I want to start over. Someplace entirely new with new people, new experiences, new surroundings." She never blabbed this much to people she'd just met, but there was something empathetic about the real estate woman, which lowered her defenses and made her want to confide secrets. She reminded Abigail of her older sister, whom she hadn't seen for years. Last she heard her sis was living up in Washington State selling furniture, working her butt off, no free time and unable to get away for a visit. Abigail missed her.

Martha put her hand up and flashed her a smile. "It's okay. You don't have to explain to me why you want to move here. I can see you're sincere. And I wasn't trying to discourage you from buying a house. I merely wanted to make sure you understood most of the people in town have lived here all their lives and are pretty set in their ways and habits. They're secretive, simple people. And I have to warn you, gossip is a way of life here."

"Everyone I've met so far has been so helpful and kind."

Martha seemed pleased. "Have they?" She began paging through a notebook, every once in a while glancing up at Abigail, her expression one of restrained friendliness. "No, no…no," she muttered, turning pages, and shaking her head. "Too big, probably too expensive. No, too…not you. This one has a horse barn and pastures."

"I don't have horses," Abigail informed her. "Don't have any animals. Now, anyway."

When the real estate lady found a house which was a possible, she'd show it to Abigail and they'd talk about it, when they weren't talking about the town.

After a half-hour, during which the two women found they had a lot in common, Martha had compiled a list of three potential residences. All three were empty and ready to move in and inside Abigail's budget.

"All three houses are practically within walking distance and if we use my car it'll take no time at all," Martha said as Abigail followed her to a Ford Taurus. Outside the evening shadows were descending and the hot day was waning. Abigail had stopped wearing her wristwatch weeks before, but she guessed it was near six o'clock.

An hour later they were back. None of the three houses had appealed to Abigail. One had been in unlivable disrepair, the second was full of bugs, and the third had a wet basement.

"Martha, aren't there any others I could look at?" Abigail was discouraged. "I really have this feeling about this town. I want to live here, but preferably not in a cardboard box."

"That's funny." Martha stared at her, and after her smirk faded, a look of uncertainty crossed her face. "Well, there is one place left for sale hereabouts. I wouldn't normally mention it except you said you were handy with a hammer, wallpaper and paint, and really wanting to find something cheap. The house is isolated, yet still close enough to town, but…I'm not going to lie to you, it needs work. Cosmetic, mostly. It's the old Summers' house about a mile down the road. Cute little yellow frame house with a hundred flowers around it and a lovely bay window in the kitchen overlooking woods. It's been empty for over a year, needs fixing up–paint and elbow grease mostly. Old lady Summers was too sick the last couple of years to take care of it."

Abigail was grinning. "The house sounds perfect. What happened to the old lady?"

"The old lady, Edna Summers, died there. Right there in the living room. She had a reputation as being eccentric, to say the least. She had no friends, and fewer visitors, and kept to herself. Everyone thought she had these terrible secrets."

"No family to take the house?"

"None that we could find. Edna once had a younger sister who drove away one day with her two kids and never came back. That was thirty years ago. They've been living somewhere else or so some have always believed. But, they never returned, any of them, not even for Edna's funeral or to claim the house and property. Edna was totally alone the rest of her life. And she died alone. Some people say the house is haunted. I don't know why; it just has that reputation. Sad story, huh?"

"Very."

"That isn't the strangest part. Towards the end of her life, when she wasn't in her right mind, Edna hinted to a few people that her younger sister and her two children hadn't driven away all those years ago, but had *vanished*. No one believed her, but when Edna died and her sister never showed up for the funeral, then people began to remember what Edna had been saying. They remembered the other sister and her kids hadn't been seen, not once, since that summer thirty years ago. Kind of a mystery, hey?"

"The world's full of mysteries," Abigail muttered, but her interest was tingling, her face flushed. Only someone who'd had a loved one disappear, as Joel had disappeared on her, would know how she felt. That house. She knew even before she saw it, it would be the one. She just had a feeling. "Let's go have a look. I don't care who used to live, or died there, who vanished from it. It isn't the house's fault. I want to see it."

The moment Abigail walked up the sidewalk and onto the porch, she knew it was going to be her home. Gigantic elms shaded the structure, yellow and ivory rose bushes nestled along the front, and there was a wooden swing hanging from the porch roof. On the lower level were four rooms and there was one loft bedroom upstairs sparsely filled with left behind furniture, Martha said she could pitch or keep. The loft bedroom had three tall windows and the view was soothing, of trees, woods, and a sky fading into a summer evening of wispy pastels. Abigail couldn't believe how right it all felt.

"How much is it?" she asked Martha, unable to take her eyes off the house, after they'd locked the front door and were sitting in the car. She was thinking about Edna's sister and her two children. Had they disappeared the same as Joel, into death, or were they growing old somewhere in another town? She shivered.

"Real cheap. You can have it for back taxes and bank fees. The house belongs to no one, just got out of probate, because there was no will." She wrote down a figure, and showed it to Abigail.

It was ridiculously cheaper than Abigail could have imagined. "You got a deal."

"Well, then, welcome to the town. Maybe you'll even fit in. It takes a crazy person to live around here and you strike me as crazy as they come. Being an artist and all."

"Thank you, Martha." Abigail chuckled. "By the way, what was the younger sister's name? The one who may, or may not, have vanished all those years ago?"

"Her name was Emily Summers and her ten year old twins were Christopher and Jenny."

Then Martha drove them back to town, talking the whole way as Abigail daydreamed of her new house. She daydreamed about how it would feel to own it, the colors she was going to paint the walls, and how happy she'd be living there.

Chapter 2

Abigail didn't mind the packing. She moved all her belongings herself, except for the heavy stuff, for which she hired professional movers. Emptying the apartment and throwing unneeded objects away from her past was the most fun she'd had in years. It was therapeutic. In the end, she had so little. Her personal items only took two trips in her car.

The morning she moved into her house was a sultry Saturday. Martha showed up early with donuts from the town's bakery. Earlier meetings between the two unattached lonely women had begun a friendship. Martha didn't ask where Abigail's family and friends were, she just pitched in and helped.

When the mover's truck drove away and the big items were all in place, Martha made Abigail take a break. They sat in the kitchen in the rear of the house, drinking coffee, talking and looking out the bay window at the woods.

"Tell me more about Spookie, Martha," Abigail requested, as she stared out at the swaying trees and the turquoise sky.

"Most of the folks keep to themselves. We have our share of odd birds. And the weather's unpredictably bad, the mist gets so thick sometimes you can't see an inch before your nose. Wait until you have to drive through that blanket one morning. You get up and want to go into the village and can't for the fog. It's worse in the fall and winter. You can't see a thing."

"I don't care. I love this place already. I like to walk and the town's close."

Martha laughed and changed the subject. "I noticed those drawings and paintings you lugged in. You're really good. That watercolor of the house was beautiful. I know you designed computer ads at a newspaper, did computer art, but do you ever sell anything of your own, on commission?"

"I used to." Abigail was surprised, unsure how to answer. It'd been a long time since she'd thought of herself as a real artist and not just some hack typesetting newspaper ads, where quick, but speedy mediocrity was the desired result. "The truth is, I've been thinking about freelancing–to make money."

"Then, I'll be one of your first patrons. I've wanted a rendering of my home done for a long time. Think you could handle that?"

"I could try."

After Martha left, Abigail continued putting her house in order, her mind going often to what Martha had said about her drawings. The notion of making a living with her art no longer seemed so far-fetched. Living in Spookie was going to be inexpensive and in a small town where people loved their homes, their families and their pets…why couldn't she sell them drawings of those things?

That night she slept better than she had in years, her body tired and her mind untroubled. Outside, in the summer woods night creatures stirred and hunted, mysteries whispered and the mist crept in with curling fingers.

Abigail dreamed of her old life. She was at her job, and outside the windows it was raining. She caught a glimpse of her dead husband, Joel, running through the drizzle, and she bolted from the building to chase him, beg him to come home and love her again. Though his figure was in her eyesight the whole pursuit, she could never catch him. He'd glance back at her, smile, and then run on. She woke up crying. It wasn't the first time she'd dreamed that dream. She thought with his death they'd stop, but apparently not.

She got out of bed and made coffee. The light of day, and the reality of where she was, reclaimed her contentment. Most of the house was in order, and only a pile of boxes stashed in the basement were left to unpack. Taking her cup of coffee and a left over donut onto the front porch, she sat in the swing to admire her house and her yard. There wasn't much of a yard. It merged into woodland a short distance beyond the house. But where there was yard there were flowers and bushes. The elderly woman who'd lived there must have loved her home. She must have planted a lot before she got too sick. Abigail started smiling and couldn't stop.

Now this, Abigail gloated, *is all mine.*

Today she would go into town and buy groceries, wallpaper and paint. Then she'd paint one room after another in bright cheery colors and wallpaper the kitchen. She hadn't done that sort of thing in a while, but, she was sure, she could handle the job. She ached to give the neglected house a makeover so it would feel as good as she was feeling. So, she and Joel had never built their dream house out in the woods, it didn't mean she couldn't have that dream now. She was going to make her house beautiful, fill it with exquisite things, and she was going to be happy in it.

Dressed in blue jeans and a yellow flowered T-shirt, which brought out the green in her eyes, she tied her hair on top of her head, and put sandals on. Grabbing her purse, and her list, she drove the short distance into town. If she hadn't so many supplies to buy, she would have walked because it was a lovely day.

Martha had mentioned some of the stores were open half a day on Sundays, but the hardware store was practically empty. The owner, a short man with sharp eyes, and a bald spot surrounded in tufts of wild hair, came up to her. "I hear you've bought the old Summers' place?" being the first words out of his mouth. News spread fast in a small town. His tan apron clanked and clinked when he moved, his pockets bulging.

"I have. And, I need cans of paint, rolls of wallpaper, brushes, rollers, drop cloths and instruction pamphlets so I'll know what I'm doing."

As they gathered the materials she'd need for the job, he explained their uses and gave her shortcuts to make the work easier.

"This pre-pasted wallpaper is great. You

start at the top and smooth it down towards the bottom. Use masking tape to line out your painting, and add a few drops of vanilla extract to the paint. It'll help get rid of the paint smell," the owner advised her.

Between the instructions he threw in juicy tidbits about her new house's history or the town's. He'd owned the hardware store, Nails and Bolts, for fifteen years, had a wife named Alma and five kids. "That Edna was an awful recluse," he told her. "Even when she was healthy she rarely came into town."

"She was alone," Abigail reminded him, finding she was curious about the woman who'd lived in her house. "Maybe she missed her family more than people thought; her sister, and her sister's kids?"

"That was so long ago. Edna never spoke about them, or any of that, not even after the three left, from what I've been told. Me, I say Edna didn't care. Never did. She was a cold fish all right. I was a kid back then but I remember people talking. Some thought they just up and left. Simple as that. Some people believed they…disappeared. The sheriff at that time, for some reason, didn't follow up on their leaving. He said there was no reason. But, this one cop, don't remember who anymore, looked everywhere for weeks, though he never found where the three went."

"Edna didn't have any other family?"

"No, she was a spinster. She didn't have any education or money. All in all, she had a terribly hard life. She worked in a clothing factory somewhere over in Chalmers, which is two towns over, when she was younger, until she inherited that house. No one knew where she got her money after that. She never went back to work. She was a weird old thing. Kept to herself, except for some community service woman who'd come out to the house and clean, fix her meals, or sometimes go into town for her prescriptions. Edna hadn't driven for years; didn't have a car I ever knew of.

"You should ask John Mason next door about Edna. He's been around longer and knew her better. He knows more about the town, too. The General Store's been here forever. I think he took it over from the last owner about the time Edna settled into her house. Ask him."

Abigail thanked the man for his help and loaded her cans of paint, rolls of wallpaper, a pretty pattern with muted sunflowers sprinkled through it, into the trunk of her car. It'd transform her kitchen into a field of flowers if she could pull it off. Pre-pasted or not getting the wallpaper up wouldn't be easy.

She entered Mason's General Store and filled a plastic basket full of supplies. She needed all the basics. The man smiled again at her, as she shopped, not taking his eyes off her for a second. Martha had mentioned he was divorced and lonely.

If she hadn't known better she would have said Mason was flirting with her–at his age. He wasn't bad looking, she thought, tall and thin, with gray stylishly cut hair and icy blue eyes, his clothes neat, and every hair in place. An expensive watch and diamond rings, gleamed on his wrist and fingers. He had money and liked to show it. Must have been a real heartbreaker once. But, not her type. Too old. Too attentive. She hadn't taken the gold ring on her left hand off and she made sure it was visible. A month knowing her husband was dead, even after years missing, wasn't long enough. Abigail still felt married.

When she checked out, she tried to talk to Mr. Mason about the previous owners of her house. "The guy next door says you knew Edna Summers fairly well? I bought her house, you know, so I'm curious about her," she made conversation.

"Sure, I knew Edna Summers," he replied, his smile gone. "Poor old Edna. Batty, selfish, as they come; friendless, and alone to the end. I hope you're happier in that house than she was. It needs a lot of work. She never took care of it."

She got right to it. "I heard three people drove away from that house thirty years ago and never came back; you know anything about that? The hardware store owner said you might have been in town during those years."

He hesitated. "No, that was before my time, I'm afraid. Oh, I've heard the stories, but it's all ancient history. I didn't know them, sorry." John Mason's manner was brusque as he packed her purchases in bags. "Anyway, I barely remember what went on in this town last year, much less thirty years past." He gave her an apologetic smile. Maybe he didn't like dredging up old news, especially news that reflected badly on the town–or maybe old gossip just didn't interest him.

She pulled the bags into her arms. Mason

was staring at her again. A soft smile playing on his lips. *Oh boy,* she thought as she said goodbye and left the store. *Next thing I know he'll be asking me out.* He had that look in his eyes. *Run, Abby, run.*

Back at her house she unloaded the car, put the groceries away, made herself a sandwich, and slipped into her painting clothes, humming cheerfully all the while. She cranked up the volume of her kitchen radio, set at an oldie's station, and began working. Even the weather was cooperating, not as warm as the days before, in the eighties with a cool northern wind. She'd propped open all the windows with sticks because they were timeworn and wondered how she'd get them fixed. In time, she told herself.

Abigail worked until after eleven that night, and had to practically crawl upstairs to bed, she ached so. It'd been a long time since she'd done so much physical labor. Yet she was pleased with what she'd accomplished, having wallpapered the kitchen, and started painting one of the rooms. The following two days she painted the living room a delicate salmon color and the next day she did the bathroom in a bright white. She painted her loft bedroom a gorgeous shade of mint green on the fifth day and the day after she painted the hallway a pale yellow. Then she finished up odds and ends on the bottom floor; cleaned and straightened, hung pictures, and put out knick knacks.

On the morning of the seventh day, a Saturday, she limped through her home. There wasn't one muscle in her body which wasn't tired, and sore, but she didn't care. She was so happy with the results of her labor. The house looked so different and so pretty. The vanilla had done the trick and there was barely any paint smell. The sunflower wallpaper was perfect. She'd hung art on the walls in strategic places, but left spaces for the pictures she'd create herself. She wanted some of her own work in her home.

There was a rear hallway with an exit door connecting the kitchen and living room, which had two large windows facing the back yard; it gave the area a great deal of light. It wasn't a large space, but Abigail imagined it would be perfect as an art studio. An easel could go in front of the windows and shelves for her art supplies could go along the rear wall. No need to waste space. Because of all the different room colors, to pull them together and cover the worn wood, she'd paint the baseboards and doorframes a glossy white throughout the lower level. Then, add multicolored area rugs in the front room and bedroom, and the house would look almost done.

While cleaning the baseboard in the living room, she noticed it was loose, and had the hammer in her hand ready to nail it down again, when she spied a scrap of paper sticking out from behind the piece of wood.

Such a simple act, yanking at that slip of paper, but it would change everything. Pulling it carefully from its hiding place, she saw it was a tightly folded and yellowed, scrap of white paper laced in spider webs and dust. It was the sort of drawing paper she used to sketch on as a child. She unfolded it slowly. There was printing on it, bright red crayon scribbling, as a child might do. At first, Abigail wasn't sure what it was. Then, she looked closer and read:

ME AND CHRIS ARE SO SCARED. HE WAS MEAN TO MOMMY AGAIN, MADE HER CRY. HURT HER. WE HATE HIM!!! in a childish scrawl. There was a *J* at the bottom.

She stared at the scrap of paper and reread it. It was obviously old. No telling how long it'd been behind the baseboard. She refolded it and tucked it into a compartment of her purse. The two children's names who'd once lived there, if she recalled correctly, had been Christopher and…Jenny. Amazing, the note could have been from them. How strange, after all these years, for her to find it. But who was *HE*?

Abigail couldn't stop dwelling on the note as she resumed her work. She made it a point to search for other scraps of paper sticking out from hidden places. A treasure hunt. By the early evening, when she had to quit painting for the day because her body refused to move, she'd uncovered yet another scrawled note in red crayon, all caps, similar to the first one from under the baseboards.

It said: *WE WENT TO BED AGAIN WITHOUT SUPPER. SHE WAS MAD. I AM SO HUNGRY. C*

Was it from Christopher? She put the note in her purse with the other one. She was trying not to feel sorry for the mistreated children. After all, it had been so long ago. But she couldn't stop thinking about them and what those notes meant. Had they been abused and in danger? From whom?

And why should it bother her so?

She'd been working for days and needed a change, she needed people, wanted to hear human conversation, and eat someone else's cooking. Cleaning up, she walked into town to Stella's Diner. It was a warm June afternoon, the sun low in the sky, the crickets in melodious voice as she strolled down the road admiring the wildflowers and the loveliness of the woods. Walking helped ease the soreness in her body and fresh air cleared the dust, and paint fumes, from her lungs.

A tiny woman with silver permed hair, and a wrinkled body in a tattered dress, was shuffling down the town's sidewalk pulling a rickety wagon of junk. As she passed Abigail, she mumbled something, not looking up, and yanked her wagon along behind her on down the street. The woman had to be at least eighty years old, and she, probably, wasn't in her right mind. But, she made Abigail grin. Every town had their bag lady or in this case, wagon lady. The woman moved down the road and around a corner, singing an old Perry Como song, something about catching a falling star, loud enough to make an alley cat jealous.

Fifteen minutes from her front door, Abigail arrived at Stella's. Apparently, the diner was the social gathering water hole for the town. It was packed, she could tell from outside the windows. People inside were laughing, talking, and eating.

She took a deep breath, and strode in.

Chapter 3

Some of the people inside Stella's Diner gave her a fleeting look when she entered and one or two of them, the man from the hardware store and Stella herself, who was busy waiting on tables, smiled and waved. Martha in a back booth gestured furiously for Abigail to join her. She was wearing a black lace top and white slacks. Her short hair a halo of brunette curls.

Abigail headed for her new friend, a safe harbor in a squall, and plopped down in the seat beside her. Martha wasn't alone. Sitting across from her was a large man, not heavy, but strong looking. It was hard to tell what his age was, middle or late forties, perhaps, or younger, or older. He had a deep blue button down shirt on, blue jeans, and his hair was dark, longish, and streaked with gray. His face was sharp angled and clean-shaven, except for a neatly trimmed mustache.

"Abigail, this is Frank Lester, our resident Jack-of-all-trades retired lay about and a friend of mine. We grew up together here in town. He's the brother I never had. These days he's writing a mystery novel. Imagine, our town not only has an artist in its midst, it has a writer as well. Frank's been living in the big city of Chicago for years and only recently returned to the town of his birth. And we're thrilled to have him back."

Martha winked at Frank, then looked sideways at Abigail. "Single, good-looking, intelligent men are rare in these parts, let me tell you."

"Shucks, ma'am, you've made my ears turn red with embarrassment." Frank reached over and held out his hand. Abigail had no choice but to give him hers. His grip was strong and sure, his big hand warm.

"Nice to meet you," Abigail remarked. "So you've just come back to town?"

"Not exactly, I've been home for over a year. I grew up here, until I went off to the big city to seek my fortune." There was humor in his words, and amusement in his expression. His eyes had this way of taking in a person, as if he were aware of more than most people were, and little could be hidden from him. For some reason, something she couldn't put her finger on, he ruffled her. He had the same inquisitive gaze as that detective she'd hired two years ago to find Joel when she'd become exhausted with putting fliers all over town and calling everyone in the world Joel had ever known. But the detective, who'd charged her a bundle and had never uncovered any answers, hadn't found Joel. Some other cop had found Joel years later. Dead.

"Did you find your fortune?" Abigail shifted in her seat. Memories of Joel did nothing but unnerve her and Frank was watching her too closely.

He shrugged. "I did. But it wasn't what I thought it'd be. That's why I'm back."

"It never is." She sighed. "Life is never like you think it's going to be. We ought to be allowed to stop our lives at any point and relive over what we didn't like. Change it if we want. Maybe, then, we'd have a fighting chance to do it right."

"Ah, an introspective woman. So…how do you like our little village so far?"

"So far I like it," she managed to get out, lowering her eyes. Too many people were gawking at her and she was too tired to be going through this tonight. She should have stayed at the house and opened a can of ravioli. But that would have been the old Abigail and she'd pledged to be different. She needed to get out. To make friends. To have a real life. Now.

"And soon," Frank murmured, "you'll feel as if you've lived here all your life. This town grows on you. You'll see. Characters and all." There was a sureness, and compassion, in his voice which put Abigail at ease. Here was a man who said exactly what he thought. A man who was exactly what he appeared to be. She was sure of it.

Martha patted her hand and Abigail finally smiled. "What's the special? I'm starving. I've been cleaning, painting and wallpapering, all week and I've worked up an appetite."

"They have the best cheeseburgers in the state," Frank suggested.

Stella was hovering over her by then with her order tablet and Abigail asked for a cheeseburger, onion rings, and chocolate malt. An older man, Stella's brother, Abigail guessed, was cooking in the back kitchen.

"Martha informs me you've been redoing the old Summers' house," Frank stated, when Stella left. He was on his second cup of coffee since Abigail had sat down. There was a small notebook on the table beside him and every couple of minutes he'd scribble something in it.

"I have." She turned to Martha. "You wouldn't know the place. I've been cleaning, and painting, and I think it looks beautiful. You'll have to come over and see it."

"I'll do that." Martha popped another French fry into her mouth.

Frank had fallen quiet, listening, as Abigail raved about her house. Someone had turned on a radio and country music floated in the air along with the hamburger aromas.

"I met this elderly lady out on the street coming here," Abigail casually remarked. "Pulling a wagon behind her, and singing old songs. She looks poor and a little bizarre."

"Oh, that's Myrtle Schmitt," Frank cut in. "Our resident crazy rambling woman. Don't let her appearance fool you. She may dress and act peculiar, she wanders all over town salvaging junk out of people's trash cans, and she lives out in a ratty RV along Highway 21, but she's filthy rich. She has a broker, a financial portfolio, and probably millions of dollars in assets."

"If you think old Myrtle is weird you haven't met the cat and dog lady yet." Martha chuckled.

Frank laughed and satisfied Abigail's curiosity. "Evelyn Vogt. She lives behind you actually. A patch of woods is all that separates your two properties. Be grateful for that. She hoards animals, that's what they call it these days. Mostly cats and dogs, but she collects all kinds of creatures. She must have thirty or forty in and around her house. I imagine, on calm nights, you'll be able to hear the meowing and dog yapping even at your place."

"I can't wait." Abigail was studying the folks around her. The couple to her left had paid their tab in quarters, dimes and pennies; tip as well. Another couple hobbled out on walkers. Canes were propped against booths or hung from chairs. There seemed to be a lot of elderly in town.

Her food arrived and she sat eating, and listening, to Martha and Frank magpie about town stuff and gossip about the other townies. She learned a lot about Spookie and its people, during the meal. She learned a lot about Frank, too. He seemed like a sweet guy. A little nosy, maybe.

"By the way," she said to Martha between munching onion rings. "I'm looking for rugs for my living room and bedroom. Nice, but not too expensive. I'm on a tight house decorating budget. Know where I can find any?"

It was Frank who spoke up. "My sister, Louisa, sells carpets and flooring in a store in Chalmers, fifteen miles down the highway and two towns over." He tugged out his wallet and removed a white business card, which he gave to Abigail. "Tell her I sent you and she'll give you a discount on top of a fair price."

"Thanks. I couldn't ask for more, I guess." She accepted the card and put it in her purse. She'd finished her meal and exhaustion was claiming her.

The day outside was shifting into twilight. Soon it'd be dark. She stood up. "It's been nice meeting you, Frank. And, seeing you again Martha. But right now, with my stomach full and my body one big ache, my bed is calling me. I'm heading home. I think I have just enough energy to limp back there."

"If you walked, let me drive you." Martha stood up, grabbing her purse. "I've been here for hours. It's time I go home, too. Besides, if you don't mind, I'd love to take a quick peek at what you've done to your house. I'm dying to see it." There was a plea in her eyes which Abigail couldn't deny. Martha wanted to be her friend in the worst way.

"Okay, I'll take you up on that ride. It seems my legs have stiffened into two rock pillars anyway, since I sat down. They don't want to work."

She wasn't sure how it came about, but Frank spoke up about seeing them both home safely, and before she knew it, all three of them were heading to her house. The old Abigail would have squashed that quickly enough but the new Abigail let it happen. After paying their bills and saying goodnight to everyone, the three of them left the diner.

She and Frank rode with Martha because Frank had also walked to Stella's. "I'm obsessed with walking lately, since one of my friends had a stroke. Exercise, says my doc, is the key to living a long healthy life. I own a truck but I walk whenever I can. It saves gas, too."

Leading her visitors through the front door, Abigail announced, "I'm not done with the house yet. It's a work in progress. I've still got to paint the porch and hang my collection of birdhouses from the ceiling. Bird houses, that's my porch motif."

Martha made a beeline for the kitchen. "I love what you've done in here. Love the wallpaper," she hollered. "Ooh, I love sunflowers, too."

Abigail left Frank, who was standing in the middle of the living room seemingly lost in thought, and she hobbled into the kitchen. Now she could barely walk. Old age setting in early, she fretted, relieved the hardest work was behind her and a soft bed awaited her–as soon as she could get rid of her visitors.

Martha had settled at the kitchen table. She was admiring Abigail's handiwork. "You've been busy. It's astounding what you've done to the place in such a short time. I adore it. Looks like something you'd see in one of those house beautiful magazines. You sure have a flair for colors and such. Must be the artist in you."

"You want coffee, Martha? It'd only take a minute. I always leave the pot ready to plug in."

"Nah, I won't keep you. I know you're tired. I only wanted a quick peek at the house. I'll visit again soon, I promise, and stay longer. I'll bring you lunch one day next week and we'll have real girlfriend time together. Where's Frank?"

Frank walked into the kitchen.

"Lordy, Frank, you look like you've seen a ghost," exclaimed Martha. Her face had turned grim. "Oh, how stupid of me, you have been in this house before. I remember now."

"You have?" Abigail echoed, looking at

Frank, who stood in the kitchen doorway, his face shadowed. He was eyeing the room as if it stirred up some sad memory.

Martha explained for him. "I never told you, Abigail, Frank's a retired cop. Early retirement. He spent most of his time being a Chicago homicide detective but he began his career here in Spookie, as a deputy sheriff, in the early nineteen seventies; during the time when that woman and her two kids lived in this house. Frank was on the sheriff's department when the alleged disappearances took place, weren't you Frank?"

"I was," Frank admitted. "It was one of my first cases. I was twenty-one, and had only been on the job for a few months. I…knew Emily and her children," he spoke softly. "Sweet, sweet woman. She was a friend. Her children were good kids. Bright. So hungry for love."

"The three were never located, never seen again, were they?" Abigail's interest was captured entirely. There was something Frank wasn't revealing, she could sense it.

"No, they weren't. We didn't have the technology we have today. People got lost and stayed lost. I was about the only one who thought something fishy had happened." He sat down on the chair next to Abigail. "When they disappeared I worked here in town, but I'd applied earlier for the Chicago P.D. I'd been notified a week before I had the job. I stayed here as long as I could trying to find them but there weren't any clues, any leads, so when the time came to move to Chicago and begin my new job, my new life, I had to go. Either that or

I would have lost the position and the opportunity. I made senior detective over the years, had a good run, a good life, and my retirement benefits can't be beat. I don't regret leaving Spookie back then but I regret not finding Emily and the children. If I had been here I wouldn't have stopped looking as everyone else did. The sheriff, at the time, thought they didn't want to be found, so he just gave up."

Abigail was watching Frank. Ah, ha…a retired police detective experienced in digging up hidden clues who'd known the woman and her children, and here he was in this house again after so many years; right after she'd found notes from those missing children. The coincidence, of it all, didn't escape her.

"Well, it's late and I'm going home," Martha declared. "Frank, want a ride home?"

Martha had most likely seen the way Frank had looked at her, so she probably wasn't surprised when he excused himself with, "No, thanks, it's a lovely night and, with shortcuts, I don't live that far away. I'll hike it home. Walking helps me get my thoughts straight for my late night writing sessions."

"Okay. Abigail, I swear he's safe. I'd trust him with my life. I don't hesitate to leave you alone with him. Being an ex-cop you can be sure he won't steal anything or make improper advances towards you." It was a joke but no one laughed. Abigail's wedding ring glittered in the kitchen's light.

At the door, Martha reminded Abigail about the commission to paint her home. "The house is over one hundred and twenty years old. It's been in my family since it was built." She dug into her purse and handed over a couple of colored photographs. "Here it is. You think you can do it from these or does the house have to sit for you?"

Abigail examined the photos. "These aren't bad, but since it's summer, I'd prefer to draw or at least begin from the real thing. I'll call you next week and set up a day to start. I'm about done with my house's cleaning and painting, for now, and wouldn't mind working on a smaller canvas for a bit." And she wanted to see if she still had it in her, see if she could draw anything which wasn't in Photoshop or on a computer screen.

"Okay, you call and I'll show you where I live. Out in the woods, it's hard to find." Then Martha was gone.

"I realize you don't know me well and I've barged in on you," Frank told Abigail. "I wanted to talk to you. I also had to see this house again. Be inside. It's brought back so many memories of when I was a young cop just starting out. The past. Some of those times were good days."

"I understand. There are times in my youth, my past, that I reflect back on with great fondness too." She was thinking of Joel. "I understand."

"Can I look around? I won't disturb anything. I won't stay long."

"Go ahead, be my guest. I'll wait here for you. Resting. Making coffee."

Frank moseyed around the house, snooped upstairs, and returned to the kitchen. She was tired but she didn't mind. As Martha had said, she was safe with him and he seemed reluctant to leave. It was a spur of a moment decision to offer him coffee. He accepted.

Over cups of black liquid they began to discuss their lives and to form a bond. He was easy to talk to, an attentive listener, and was intrigued with the same thing she was: what had happened to Emily and her kids. In the end, she confided why she'd come to Spookie, about her last job, the old apartment, Joel's disappearance and his death.

Frank listened and said gently, "Unexpected and unexplained disappearances. You wouldn't believe how often that happens. For what it's worth, you can be at peace now, knowing your husband didn't just leave you. He was taken. Mugging gone wrong. At least you have closure." His eyes fell on her wedding ring. "People disappear every second of every day–someone's fault, or not anyone's fault. Merely moving on. Or foul play. I was a detective in a big city, I know. It can be heartbreaking."

Abigail was touched when he told her about his wife, Jolene, who'd died the year before in a car crash. "That's why I retired from the force early and returned home to Spookie. My son, Kyle, is away at college and I couldn't keep living that lonely life once Jolene was gone. There didn't seem any point to it. She was the one who loved living in the big city. She loved the concrete, the stores, and the hustle and bustle. Over the years I'd accepted I was, and always would be, a small town boy. I love the country, the trees, and everyone knowing everyone else's business.

"So, we're both starting over, hey?" he finished with a soft smile. "What a coincidence."

His eyes were scanning the solid black view

outside the kitchen window. No moon had risen yet. It was all darkness. "I sat here one night so many, many years ago, just like this, having coffee with Emily Summers. Her two kids were playing with firecrackers and sparklers out in the yard, giggling and yelling. It seems like another life. I'd only been a cop for a short time and had brought her boy, Christopher, home after a close call with a car. He was lucky. The car nearly hit him, but Christopher had sworn the driver was trying to run him over. The kid was really upset."

Abigail opened her purse and retrieved the two scraps of paper. "Strange you should mention those children. While I was working on the house I discovered these messages tucked under some baseboards. I think you might find them interesting."

She handed over the notes so he read them. His face was expressionless, but his hands shook slightly as he refolded them. He didn't say anything at first and then, "These are from the children, all right. They were always writing things in crayon and drawing pictures. Jenny was an artist, even at her young age. I can't believe you found these…after all these years."

"Maybe," she interjected, "there are more notes hidden in the house. I'll keep looking. Maybe these are clues to what happened to the three of them."

Frank only replied, "The trail would be so cold, you'd need snow boots. Now you sound like the mystery writer."

"You could help me." She ignored his lack

of enthusiasm. "You knew this town, these people, who their friends were and how they lived. You can fill in the gaps no one else could. Were the children often sent to bed hungry? By their mother? And who do you think the *HE* in the one note referred to?" she grilled, though Frank seemed uneasy with the subject.

He moaned. "The *HE* might have been Emily Summers' secret boyfriend. We never figured out who it was. No one knew, except the kids, and they weren't talking if you know what I mean. Emily Summers was divorced. She'd gone back to her maiden name. Being divorced in 1970 was scandal enough, but to be dating someone who was somehow unavailable, was worse. She was already the town pariah. All the married women in town disliked her anyway. They were afraid she was going to steal their husbands. You know how insecure some women can be.

"But, I believed then and now, the boyfriend was part of the reason for their…leaving. Him, and our illustrious sheriff, who wouldn't leave Emily alone, either. I never discovered who the boyfriend was, and Edna, who'd been living here with her sister that whole summer, swore she'd no idea who he was, either. Edna worked days in a factory in another town, slept like the dead at night from exhaustion, and didn't seem to know anything."

Abigail was disappointed.

"And no, Emily would never have mistreated those kids, or sent them to bed hungry. I don't understand that at all. She was a good mother."

Frank gave her a thoughtful look. "Tell me. Are you so intrigued by this because of your husband's vanishing act two years ago?"

"This has nothing to do with that," Abigail snapped back too quickly.

"Doesn't it?" Frank's voice was sympathetic. "Listen, it's late, and I've stayed too long. My advice is let the past be the past. There's no one left anymore that remembers the Summers' family, except a few old town people and me. We don't know if there even was a crime. Edna said her sister ran off in the middle of the night with the children because she was a flighty woman. The sheriff claimed Emily left because she was hiding, or running, from someone and she didn't want to be found. We should leave things be.

"To complicate matters, Emily had an abusive ex-husband she was afraid of. I looked for him but that was when the world was larger before a central based criminal computer system like Regis, NCIC, computers, Facebook, and emails. People could get lost easily in those days. And some did."

"But from what Martha told me, Edna, Emily's own sister, never heard from them again. Never in all those years. That's not normal, is it?"

"If you knew those two back then you'd understand. Edna and Emily weren't close. They were continuously feuding. Everyone knew that, including me, though I didn't know them well. Edna hated her younger sister for some reason or other. Maybe, because their parents loved Emily and her children best. No one knew why for sure, only that it was so."

The more Abigail learned about the four people who had once lived in her house, the more fascinated with them she became. They were becoming real to her.

"Well, I'm going home now, Miss Marple," Frank concluded sarcastically as he stood up to leave. The carefree smile returned. "It's been nice meeting you, Abigail. Having coffee and talking. Welcome to our town. As small as this burg is, I'm sure I'll be seeing you again soon.

"Don't drive yourself crazy over this old mystery. They were four people who used to live here; one's dead, probably three of them are all a lot older; living somewhere else right now. They didn't just evaporate into thin air, they moved away, and started a new life somewhere else. It happens all the time. Not all suspicious circumstances point to a crime."

"Okay, I hear you, Mr. Ex-cop. I won't make this into something it isn't."

Frank left, and Abigail, as tired as she was, still went to sit on the porch swing. The swing and the night had called to her one last time. A cat's weak meows haunted the night air. Abigail thought she heard children's voices out in the woods somewhere and contemplated that thirty years past two children had sat on her porch and romped in the yard before her. The same two children who'd written those notes. She imagined they were dancing in the moonlight, their bodies skinny and coltish, and their laughter hauntingly sad as they pranced across the grass and faded into the night. If they weren't dead…what had happened to those two children? Where did all the missing people go anyway?

In a strange mood, she pushed the swing. She couldn't stop thinking about those kids. Above her the stars sparkled in a velvet sky and it felt sweet to be alive. Meeting Frank made her want to wear more make-up and buy new clothes. Yet her sad heart wouldn't let her dwell on anything further with him than friendship, for now. After all, she was a recent widow. Or, at least, that's the way it felt. To her, Joel had died a month ago, because before that he'd only been missing.

Chapter 4

Outside, the air smelled of coming rain. Didn't mean it would rain soon, maybe it'd hold off long enough for Abigail to begin her drawing. Art supplies in a duffel bag, a sketch pad under her arm, she was dressed in shorts, her hair gathered up on top of her head. Ready to go. She'd sketch the house first, then do a watercolor, take her time and do it right. A perfectionist, she had an eye for details. Now if she could just remember how to draw.

The rugs had come the day before. Frank's sister had given her a good deal on them and now the house felt like a home. Tomorrow she was going to paint the front porch, hang the birdhouses she'd had packed away for years waiting for her house. She hadn't found any more messages from the kids but she was still searching.

"Martha, your home is gorgeous." And it was. It was a huge stately dwelling, covered in ivy vines with a beautifully landscaped yard, statuary, shrubs and rock gardens which glittered in the sun. An elaborate marble water fountain, with unicorns sprouting water streams, was in the back. "I'm impressed. If I didn't need money, I'd draw it for free."

"Thanks. I spent the last five years restoring, redecorating it. The house, and lands, are worth a fortune. But I'll never sell them. I've lived in this house all my life. When I'm lonely or sad all I have to do is sit in the garden, sip a cup of tea, and I'm happy again. It restores my soul." Martha gave Abigail the grand tour. The house was as lovely inside as out.

"The house has an interesting history. My great grandfather had it built for my great grandmother, when they were first married, as a wedding present. She brought a lot of the woodwork and sculptures with her from England as part of her dowry. They had quite a love story. They were married for sixty years, had eight children, though three died in infancy, and the other five gave them twenty grandchildren. I have about a thousand cousins spread out across the globe. My great grandfather really loved my great grandmother. They were never apart, not even one night, their whole lives. My grandmother said when her mother died her father buried her in the garden, so they'd always be close."

"So sweet. I'm a sucker for a good love story." Abigail was looking out the window at the garden.

Martha smiled amiably. "My great grandfather is rumored to be buried out there, as well."

They were at the front door, tour finished. "Oh, great, graves under the flowers. Don't expect me to ever stay overnight here with a graveyard right outside the door."

Martha laughed and offered, "Anything you need, bathroom or snack, help yourself. I have to get back to work but I'll leave the door open. Just lock it up from the inside when you go." Martha was exiting out the door. "You sure you can find your way back to town?"

"Sure. I drew a map in my head coming here. I can get back. Go, let me get to work before I lose the daylight or the rain comes." Abigail was already sketching the house when Martha drove away. She sketched for hours, out of practice, though it was slow going. She redrew the house over and over and almost gave up. She didn't. If she couldn't complete this first commission she couldn't make money freelancing. Then, it'd be back to a tedious nine to five job. She didn't want that.

When the picture didn't make her grimace, she packed up, and drove into town. She'd work further on the drawing at home. The rain had held off but angry clouds blanketed the sky and lightning streaked along their fringes. A storm was coming. The infamous fog rolled in, snuck up behind her car, and closed off the world. She could barely see five feet ahead of her, it was so thick. Coming out of the fog when she hit Main Street she pulled up before the bank, parked the car, and went in to get some cash.

Then she made a quick stop at Mason's General Store for candy and milk. She could live without milk, but not chocolate.

"You've been sketching Martha's house?" John Mason had been helpful to Abigail from the moment she stepped in the store. Every time she turned around; there he was. At Abigail's quizzical glance he explained, "Small town, remember? And Martha was in here earlier, boasting about it, and how great an artist you are.

"Abigail, I can call you Abigail, can't I?" His eyes were on her as she put the milk and the chocolate bars on the counter. He'd nudged closer to her.

"Sure, that's my name." She scooted away from him.

"As you can see, I let the area artists and crafts people sell their creations in my store. I like giving local talent a chance. If you want to place any of your work here, Abigail, feel free to do so. I charge a fifteen-percent commission, the rest is yours. We'll sell a lot to townspeople, and visitors passing through, during our Fourth of July celebration this weekend."

Abigail studied the art on display, thinking her watercolors old and new, could compete with what was on the walls. It was a good idea, another venue to sell her artwork from, and she was excited over it.

"All right, I'll bring in some stuff in the next week or so. Thank you."

They spent a little conversation on what she'd been doing to her house, though their exchange was short, because she told him she was tired and had to be getting home.

As she left the store, bag in her arms, she was hopeful for the future. Spookie was fast becoming her home in so many ways. Everything was falling into place. In the spirit of belonging, when she spied Myrtle and her wagon bouncing up Main Street, and the old woman stopped to glare at her, Abigail waved. Then Myrtle gestured her to come over.

Abigail put the bag in her car and walked across the street. The old woman had on the same print dress, but somewhat dirtier and more wrinkled, as the previous time Abigail had seen her. Her hair, a silver crown wired out from her skull, looked as if a comb had never touched it. She barely came up to Abigail's shoulder, as she clasped Abigail's hand and shook it with a grip stronger than Abigail would have thought she'd have. Up close, Myrtle seemed older than her years, her scrutiny of Abigail a fever in her eyes. But a smile spread across the old lady's face, and Abigail knew she was making a new friend.

"Why, I thought it was you, dearie. So good to see you again. Where have you been? You've been gone so long, haven't you?"

Abigail was confused. Myrtle acted as if she knew her. "No, I've just moved here. Thought I'd introduce myself."

"Ah, you don't need to do that, I know who you are…Emily. You changed your hair color again, it's brown now, and you've aged some, but you don't look half bad for all the years that have passed. What's your secret? My memory may be bad, but not that bad. Oh, Emily, you're a sight for sore eyes. We all wondered where you went. Some of us looked so long for you." She patted Abigail's hand affectionately. "How's little Jenny and Christopher doing?"

Myrtle mistakenly thought she was Emily Summers. How odd. "Oh, no, I'm not Emily. My name's Abigail Sutton. I bought Emily's old house,

I live there now, but I'm not Emily."

"Not Emily?" The old woman inhaled and her frail body shivered. Abigail felt uncomfortable. It was bad enough to grow old, but it must be awful to have your mind go as well.

Abigail smiled at her. "I stopped to say hi, just being neighborly, you know?"

Myrtle's eyes refocused and her expression changed to one of embarrassment. "Oh, yes, now I see, you're right; you're not Emily after all, are you? You're–"

"Abigail Sutton?" she supplied again. "Recently moved into town?"

"Ah, yes, what was I thinking? You're Abigail, yes. New resident to our fine village. People have been talking about you. Welcome. Emily and me were friends, you know? It's just that you do look so like her. Anyone tell you that yet? But older, of course."

That she resembled Emily came as a shock. Oh, boy. This was getting creepy.

"Speaking about Emily Summers," Abigail forged on. "Perhaps one day you and I can talk about her. Living in her house, I'm curious to what she was like. And the twins."

"As well you should be. Terrible thing happened. Nobody else hereabouts believes me, but I know what I know. Something evil befell them, that's what I say. Cause I know things–"

The skies opened and the rain began to fall, not a light drizzle but a deluge. Myrtle obviously didn't like rain, for she shrieked and flailed her arms about as if she were melting. She didn't bother saying goodbye, but scurried away through the downpour, yanking her wagon behind her.

"My treasures don't like getting wet," she yelped back at Abigail.

The items in her wagon looked more like junk, but who could say. "Bye, it was nice meeting you!"

"Come by and visit me sometime!" Abigail yelled through the raindrops. "Anytime! You know where I live."

Darn it, Abigail thought, *and I'd wanted to hear what else she had to say about the Summers.*

Myrtle reminded Abigail, in temperament and looks, of her grandmother, Ethel, and the similarities brought out a fondness for Myrtle she wouldn't otherwise have had.

Making a dash for the dryness of her car, Abigail drove home in a fierce summer storm, where the sky was vivid shades of purplish blue, the trees wailed and shook their leaves like angry clenched fists to the sky. With the low-lying fog in the woods she couldn't see anything but a bit of the road, and a sea of mist, between the drops of rain. In time, no doubt, she'd get used to driving in it but for now she was eager to get home and out of it.

Entering her front door, her home warm and dry around her, brought her the truest joy she'd felt in years. Not since being with Joel had she felt so safe and welcomed. With any luck, she thought, the roof wouldn't leak.

As the storm raged beyond her walls, Abigail ate a sandwich, a bowl of tomato soup, and examined the drawing of Martha's house as she sat at the kitchen table. Until she had time to furnish her hallway art studio the table was where she worked. Her morning's creation wasn't as feeble as she'd feared and she worked a little longer, from memory and photos, on the drawing. The coffeepot was perking cheerily and the 13" television on the counter was saying the electrical thunderstorm would get worse as the night wore on.

Needing another pencil she went to the mahogany chifforobe up in her bedroom, which was one of the vintage pieces of furniture Edna had left behind, to get one. The chifforobe was massive, had so many drawers and hidey-holes, and with a whole open top section once used for hanging clothes, it was perfect for her art tablets, canvases and supplies. Rummaging around in the top drawer, a pencil slipped from her fingers and fell behind the drawers towards the bottom. She had to get down on her knees and dig for it. Pulling out the bottom drawer, she stuck her hand into the abyss and came out with a sheaf of yellowed, web-encrusted papers bound by a dirty rubber band. They were legal papers of some sort. She fished out the pencil and took it, along with the papers, to the kitchen table.

Leafing through the document, she was puzzled. It was a 1969 house title…to her house…in *Emily* Summers name, *not Edna*'s. The house had belonged to Emily? According to some of the other papers in the bundle, the parents had willed the house to Emily when they'd passed away, apparently within a couple weeks of each other, sometime in 1969. Now, that was strange. Martha had specifically said Edna, being the oldest daughter, had owned the house.

On the back of the title there were some words written, but so faint Abigail had to tilt them in the light to read them. *The house is mine, I told you so, Emily, and it will always be mine. You got what you deserved–and so did I.* Had Edna written them? If so, she'd had the queerest handwriting, the E in Emily was pointy and the edges were like antlers; her y's had shelves on the bottom, and her c's were almost script they were so fancy.

Her house was a house of secrets, Abigail pondered, putting the papers away in a safe place. She hadn't stopped hunting for more messages from the kids and every time she moved something in the house, she looked. What kind of woman had Edna been? She must have loved this house as much as Abigail was beginning to. Abigail was becoming as obsessed with Edna as she was with Emily and the children. These people had lived here once, paced these floors, and gazed out these windows; cried, laughed, and dreamed in this same space. Now, it was like all of them were ghosts living with her, trying to tell her something. But what?

It was later that night outside in the storm when Abigail again heard the phantom meows. She opened the door and her eyes searched the yard through the flashing lights and rain. Nothing was there. She checked the front porch. Nothing. She returned to her sketching.

So she jumped when the knocking came at the front entrance. She put her artwork away, it was too soon for anyone to see it, and answered the door.

"Frank! What are you doing out in this storm?" was what came out of her mouth, though she was happy to see a real human face hovering in front of her, and not some ghost.

"Visiting you. I know, I should have called first but the storm messed up the phones. Is it a bad time?"

"No, other than there's a hurricane out there. I was ready for a break. I've been working on Martha's watercolor of her mansion, er, house."

Standing in the doorway, rain was dripping down Frank's face, his hair was soaked and in his hands was a tiny bit of white fur which moved. He held it out to her and she took it. "What's this?" she asked, when the ball of fur peered up at her with huge frightened eyes. It meowed and attempted to hide in her hands.

"A kitten I found on your porch. It came right to me. I thought it was yours, so I caught it. I think it's hungry."

"No doubt." Abigail could feel its tiny heart beating. Wet and dirty, the creature was quivering. "But it isn't mine. I don't have a cat." Not anymore, she thought. Joel and she had had a cat, Shadow, who'd disappeared after Joel had. She'd loved that cat and had hunted everywhere for it. Losing Shadow, too, had made the pain of losing her husband even worse. Yet Shadow had been eighteen years old and Abigail had concluded that, pining for Joel, the cat had gone off to die somewhere. Something, at the time, Abigail had wished she could have done, as well.

"Oh, my mistake. I felt sorry for the poor

thing. It's all bones and fur."

Abigail tried to give it back to him. "Oh, no." He pushed it away. "I have two monster German Shepherds at home. They'd eat this kitten as an appetizer."

The kitten was purring, probably from the warmth of her hands, and Abigail wasn't sure what to do with it. It was licking her fingers, its tiny tongue rough and eager.

"The kitten most likely came from the cat lady's house." Frank let her off the hook. "She lives behind you about a half mile through the trees. Evelyn Vogt. Remember we told you about her–the village's animal hoarder? Every town has one. Evelyn's ours. Nice enough old biddy, but a little off in the attic. She has a full zoo living in that house with her."

"Then someone," Abigail exclaimed. "Ought to do something about her. Hoarding animals is a criminal offense. I saw a special on it on television last week. Animals crammed and locked in cages, neglected and starved. Terribly mistreated. Sometimes not on purpose, but suffering all the same. Ugh!"

Frank's shock was genuine. "Not in Evelyn's case. Her animals are not abused but treated like little kings and queens. She's well-off and adores them. She merely has a lot of them."

"Through the woods a half a mile behind me?"

"Yep. Straight back. Head for the barnyard sounds and you can't miss it."

"How did it get a half mile from home in

this weather?" She lifted the creature high and looked at it. It swatted a paw at her and began to purr. "It's no bigger than a fly."

"It sensed a potentially soft touch; a home where it didn't have so many siblings hogging up all the food.

"Abigail, you going to invite me in or what? It's pouring out here."

"Oh, sorry, come on in. Make yourself at home, Frank. Can I get you some coffee, or soda, to drink?" She led him into the kitchen.

"Coffee would be nice. Black. Please. After battling the squall out there, a hot cup of anything would be welcome."

Abigail poured the coffee, handed the cup to Frank, and against her better judgment, warmed up a saucer of milk for the cat. "There must have been a reason you came by and I'm guessing it wasn't the cat."

"And you'd be right. I wanted–needed–to tell you something." He hesitated, unsure.

She looked at him over her shoulder. "Then do."

"The other night, when you and I were discussing the history of this house and Emily and her kids, I'm sorry, I wasn't as forthcoming as I should have been. The truth is, Emily was more than an acquaintance, she was a good friend. I cared for her…a lot."

"You mean you dated her?"

"Not exactly. I wanted to. I asked her out enough. Maybe I even thought I loved her. Puppy love, you know. She was vibrant, pretty, smart, and artistic like you, but she was much older than me. She didn't take me seriously. I was only a small town sheriff's deputy. I was a child in her eyes, I'm sure.

"Besides, she had a past, this other life…this secret boyfriend. The whole town knew she was seeing someone she was crazy about and who was ferociously jealous of her. No one knew who he was. As sweet as Emily Summers was, being divorced with kids in 1970 was still frowned upon. A town scandal. I was more forgiving than others because I was young and she was nice to me. She had kids, was alone, and yet she wanted more out of life; wanted to be someone. She had dreams. I admired her for that and for never giving up. Truth is, until I moved back to town, I hadn't thought of Emily and her kids in years. They were a faded, distant memory from my past.

"Then, around the time of Edna's death, I discovered by accident, they hadn't returned to town, for any reason, in all those years. Living in Chicago, I'd never known that. No one here had seen them again, not even at Edna's funeral, or to claim the house. But, what really made me think, was when I was here the other night–which revived so many memories anyway–and you showed me those notes you'd found. I thought, something's not right. My cop nose was itching. I haven't been able to get Emily, or the children, off my mind since.

"Now I have unanswered questions I never had before. Back then, most people saw nothing suspicious about their sudden absence. Emily packed up, people thought, and left, looking for a fresh start. A better, new life. That's what Edna told everyone. I was only one of a handful of people who believed something didn't fit. Emily wouldn't have left town without saying goodbye to me or her friends, or leaving a note. I spent time asking questions, and looking for a crime, which no one else saw as being there. It made me look foolish, but I was leaving town anyway and didn't care. But I never found out anything.

"I've been thinking of looking into it again. Oh, I know," he put up his hand, "it was a very long time ago, but I owe Emily and those kids, that. At least that."

Abigail sighed. "Well, I think you should. I want to know about the people who used to live in my house. Even if the three are safe somewhere in Florida, eating potato chips and watching television, I'd like to know. Yet…those notes are suspicious.

"And, speaking of Emily and the children, I found some interesting papers upstairs this morning in Edna's old chifforobe. I'll go get them."

As Abigail was coming back into the kitchen, the kitten, with a belly full of milk, launched herself into Frank's lap. He awkwardly petted the cat until the creature jumped to the carpet and climbed up Abigail's leg.

"She thinks you're her mistress already," he said.

Picking the cat off her thigh, Abigail hugged her, and handed over the papers to Frank. "They're Edna's, I think. Did you know this house legally belonged to Emily and her children? Not Edna? Obviously, by what someone wrote on the back there, there was bitterness over it."

Frank began rifling through the papers. "No, I had no idea. Edna always acted as if it were hers, called it hers, even when Emily was living here with her." He returned the documents.

"*Who* do you think got what they deserved?" Abigail referred to the words on the papers.

"Not a clue. You haven't found any more cryptic messages from the children, have you?"

"No. I'm still looking. The next sunny day, when I can see the spiders and bugs coming, I'll tackle the basement. When I was a child I used to play and hide things in ours. Maybe, the kids hid some messages down there."

"Yell, if you need help. I've had experience searching for hidden evidence and I'm good at killing spiders."

"I may do that."

Frank stood up as the rain slammed against the house walls and the thunder rocked the foundation. "I ought to go. My dogs are probably throwing themselves at the doors, by now, in fits of fear. They're terrified of storms."

Half way out the door, he said, "Saturday is the Fourth of July and here in Spookie we have a yearly tradition. There's a picnic at the town park, a sort of outdoor festival along Main Street, with game and craft booths. There are fireworks in the evening. Everyone goes. All the businesses close early. The food, barbequed chicken, hamburgers and hot dogs on the picnic grounds, is the best in the county, and there are honest-to-goodness grown up carnival rides I can guarantee are safe. Want to go with me?"

His request took her off guard. She didn't know what to say.

"It's okay if you don't want to, I'll understand. I meant, as a friend? No pressure. I could show you everything and let you know who is who. It's hard being the new person in town."

She was relieved. "As friends, sure. It sounds like fun. When does this shindig start?"

"The picnic begins at ten in the morning, the food and craft booths open then as well, and the fireworks commence the moment it's dark. Is ten too early?"

"No, it's fine. I'm an early riser."

"Great. We can walk from here, if you don't mind? Parking in town is tough on a holiday."

"Good, you know I like to walk. See you then." Through the open door, she watched Frank run out to his truck, dodging raindrops, and drive off into the fog. So, she and Frank were to be friends. Friends were nice. She looked at her gold wedding band and experienced the old sadness. How long would she feel married and continue to mourn for Joel? *Till death do us part*…she'd made that promise so long ago. But now that Joel was dead, why did she still feel this way? As if by going out she was cheating on him? She wished she knew.

She prepared a box lined with a soft towel for the kitten to sleep in; thinking tomorrow she'd return the little feline to its real home. Then she went to bed. Sometime in the middle of the night she woke up to a soft purring and a fluffy body, curled up beside her neck, tiny paws patting her skin. The kitten smelled of dirt and urine, and she gently shoved it away from her face, but it was back in moments. Not having the heart to push it away again, she realized the cat was lonely like her, so she let it stay.

Chapter 5

The kitten woke her up, licking her face. It was hungry again. Abigail found a can of tuna in the cabinet, refilled the milk saucer, and the creature gobbled every morsel and drank every drop. "Hungry little mite, aren't you?" she spoke to the kitten as it ate. Yet, the cat did look half-starved and Abigail felt sorry for it.

Outside, the rain had ended and the sun was shining. Abigail got dressed and tugged on boots. The woods would be muddy, but at least, there'd be no more water coming from the sky.

The Fourth of July picnic was only two days away and she was looking forward to it. Barbeque chicken was one of her favorite foods. She loved picnics, especially the ones with the carnival rides. She used to love holidays, any holiday, with Halloween her favorite and Christmas, second. The Fourth of July brought back poignant memories of being a child, of hot nights, cold watermelon and multi-hued sparklers lighting up the dark with whiffs of fireworks burning in the air. Her family had never had much money, yet every holiday her parents scraped together every penny they could to give them those happy times. They'd had a lot of love.

She ate a bowl of cereal and picking up the kitten, headed out the door. Frank had said to go straight behind the house, through the woods, to get to Evelyn's, so she began walking in that direction.

The whole way, two phantom children skipped around her among the trees, laughing and whispering secrets. Since Frank had mentioned sitting so long ago at Emily's kitchen table, with the kids outside playing, she'd had this image of them out there, twirling sparklers, laughing and running through the mist. She'd go to the window, peek out, and be surprised they weren't there.

Abigail was beginning to wonder if there was something wrong with her. This morbid fascination with a past she had nothing to do with and could never change was nagging her. Why were these children haunting her? And, when Myrtle had mistaken her for Emily in the street, and Frank had compared her, as an artist, to Emily, why had it bothered her?

Evelyn Vogt's house was a sprawling estate with a dilapidated structure, which passed for a house, on it. Abigail noted the peeling paint and the grimy windowpanes, each one filled with some animal or other, making faces at her. Cats and barking dogs romped all over the grounds. She had to be careful of where she stepped. What a portrait it all would make. Crazy Animal House.

She marched up to the front door, and *knock-knock-knock*, the kitten asleep in her arms. She was glad to be getting rid of it before its tiny claws got hooked into her heart. A woman most likely in her late seventies or early eighties, stringy, and as tall as Abigail, answered the door, dressed in a bright ruby dress. She had jewelry at her throat, ears, on every finger; red lipstick smeared awry on thin lips, eyeliner on her eyes, as if she were about to go to a party. She looked like a surprised squirrel. In her arms was the smallest, fattest, bulldog Abigail had ever seen. The dog growled at her.

"Now, now, sweetie, be nice," party lady cajoled the dog, caressing its ugly head.

"Mrs. Vogt? Hello, I'm your new neighbor, Abigail Sutton."

"Well, well, I know all about you child. You bought that haunted Summers' house. Poor thing. Come on in for tea and we'll talk. I'll tell you all about it."

"Mrs. Vogt, I have found one of your kittens and I'm returning her."

"Keep her if you wish. I could do without her, I have others."

"No, thank you. I don't need a cat."

"Who ever really needs a cat, dearie? They need us. Come inside."

Abigail moved into the house. Before her eyes grew accustomed to the gloom she nearly tripped over a huge sheepdog. Once the house must have been beautiful but now it was shabby and dirty, over run by animals, and apathy. Streams of dried water stained the walls and there were missing tiles in the ceilings. The smell of mold and animal was heavy. Urine. Bugs.

Abigail put the kitten down; it scampered off. Her eyes followed its path and she felt a twinge of regret. "You have an awful lot of animals living here with you. How do you feed them all?"

"Last count? Over fifty something. You spend what you have to, for your children. They love me, so I take care of them. Animals live in another reality than ours, you know. There's a network where they tell each other which humans can be trusted to care for, love, and feed them. That's how a cat, or dog, knows which house to go to for shelter."

"Oh," was all Abigail could think to say. She hoped she wasn't in that network now.

Tea was a grand affair, with sandwiches, cookies, and gossip. Evelyn's body might have been old but her mind was sharp. She was very entertaining and eager for company.

"That house you're living in is full of ghosts," Evelyn confided as they were sipping tea. "It's probably Emily and those kids. Not Edna, though, she was too ornery to be a ghost."

"So you knew Emily and her children, then?"

"I surely did. You know," she squinted her eyes at her, "you look like Emily. My, my. She was so special. Nothing like that sister of hers. Now, that Edna was a hateful woman. She hated people. She hated animals. I can't prove it but I think she poisoned some of my poor little pets over the years. When Edna was alive, I found dead carcasses everywhere. That kitten, which wandered over to your house, must have known it was under new ownership. Well, anyway, back to Emily. Edna despised her younger sister–and Edna wanted that house."

"But, it belonged to Emily, didn't it?"

"Yes. It did. Now that wasn't widely known. Edna kept it secret. How did you know?"

Abigail explained about finding the legal

papers.

"Well, I'm glad Edna's dead, but she took all the rest of her secrets to the grave I'm afraid, and she had secrets. Heaven knows." She shook her head. "Jenny and Christopher used to come over here that last summer, it seems like yesterday not thirty years ago, and have meals with us. They'd do odd jobs for me for extra money because they never had any. They never had anything. And they came over here to get away from Edna while their mom was at work. They were always hungry, and needing this or that, like two little orphans. Their lives were dismal. My husband, Abner, was alive then and, oh yes, Myrtle Schmitt, my big sister, was living with us that summer, too. She knew them. She loved Emily and the kids; despised Edna."

Wagon Myrtle was Evelyn's older sister? It figured. Both were sweet old ladies, but neither woman's wick went to the bottom of their candle; no surprise they were related. "I've met your sister."

"You should talk to her about the Summers family. She was closer to them that summer than I was. She'd go over there and tell Edna off, when she thought the woman was neglecting or frightening those kids. Which was all the time. The two had a few heated go-rounds, I'll tell you that. Myrtle can be formidable when she wants to be."

"Was there anyone else the kids were afraid of?"

"One of Emily's boyfriends, I think. She had a few unwanted admirers, like the old Sheriff Cal. Emily seemed to attract the wrong sort of men. I tried to get the kids to tell me who was bullying them but they were too afraid, of whoever it was, to squeal. One boyfriend drank too much, as I recall, and Myrtle was sure he was married or something. It explained the secrecy."

The lost kitten which Abigail had brought back had returned with friends and all of them were tumbling crazily through the rooms, meowing, swatting at each other, and playing.

"Ah, it was all so long ago." The woman gave Abigail a wistful smile, staring out the window. Then she said, "I heard a fight over there one night. I heard a man shouting. Sometimes, the woods carry sound in the queerest fashion. If there's no wind and no other outside noises, you can hear for miles. I told the sheriff at the time, Cal Brewster, the present sheriff's daddy, but he never put much store to it. He said it was probably cats fighting and never checked it out. Which was unusual, because he was always looking for an excuse to go and pester poor Emily. He had a thing for her, married as he was."

"Sheriff Cal didn't sound like much of a sheriff." Abigail huffed.

"Enough of ancient news," Evelyn said. "Not very neighborly yakking only about the past with a brand new neighbor. Tell me, what have you done to your house so far?"

Abigail told her, and they ended up discussing wallpapering, birdhouses, and Abigail's wish to be a freelance artist. By the time she left Evelyn's house she had another commission, to draw Evelyn's long dead childhood cat, when it was still alive of course, posed next to a vase of lilacs.

The old lady even gave her a photograph of the feline next to a vase. Abigail took the photo, said goodbye, and went home.

She wanted to paint the porch before the daylight was gone, so she gathered yellow paint and the painting materials, slipped into her old clothes and got to work. Within hours, the porch was done and so was the swing. It looked good. Later, the swing would be dry enough to rehang, and then she could decorate the porch with the birdhouses.

She sat in the grass of her front yard, leaned back, and proudly regarded her work. Then her eye was caught by some stray trash. She peered under the porch. The shiny object glinted from a corner deep beneath the foundation. Fetching a broom, she used the handle end of it to dig the glass Mason jar out. There was a rim of wax, which looked as if someone had melted a candle and let it drip around the opening, sealing the lid, to keep out water and air. The jar, partially caked with mud and dust, had something in it. She took it inside through the rear door, scraped off the wax with a knife, and pried off the lid.

Her heart was racing. The finding of the notes had become an intriguing game. With each new message another part of the past slid into place. Emily's fate was becoming a mystery Abigail ached to solve. In the jar were pieces of paper, one was a child's drawing of a galloping horse done in crayons, and the other was a scribbled note similar to the two she'd found.

The horse was well drawn, the proportions perfect, the colors intense. The artist had had talent.

It was signed: Jenny. No telling how good she would have been when she'd grown up.

The letter was composed in blue crayon, lower and upper case letters, this time. Some of the words were misspelled and it was easy to guess a ten-year-old had written it.

Last nite Mom and HIM had a bad fight. Then Aunt Edna and Mom screamed at each other. Aunt Edna don't want to sell the house. Christopher spent the night hiding under the porch he was so afraid. I hate HIM. But Mom says Dad is coming to see us next month. I cain't wait. I want him to take me and Chris away from here, but I know he wont. Dad gets so mean when he drinks too. I said a prayer to GOD to help us. We're leaving this note for posterity. Christopher's idea. Like leaving a time capsule. My brother sure is nutty. Maybe when we grow up, he says, well dig them up for laughs. Ha, ha. Were going to the picnic tomorrow and I can't wait to ride the ferris wheel. Mrs. Vogt gave us money for cotton candy and cherry bombs. I told Chris he's gonna blow his fingers off, he don't care, though.

Abigail tucked the papers back in the jar and almost called Frank. But she'd see him in the morning, so it could wait. What she felt like was crying. Those poor kids.

She spent the next hour searching for more letters in the nooks and crannies beneath the porch but, weary, finally gave it up. Enough is enough for today, she told herself.

I told Chris he's gonna blow his fingers off, he don't care, though.

Kids never changed, did they? She'd said about the same thing to her younger brother, Jimmy, on a long ago Independence Day. Jimmy lived in California now with his family and she rarely saw him. How she missed him and her two sisters, Carol and Mary, sometimes. Missed her brother, Michael, who'd been dead for years. She'd have to call her siblings. Find some way for the four of them to get together and catch up on their lives.

She put off hanging the swing, and putting up her birdhouses, until the following day. In the morning, bringing the birdhouses out one at a time and unwrapping them, it was like rediscovering old friends she hadn't seen for a long time. She remembered where she and Joel had bought, or found, each one as she hung them along the rim of the porch. There weren't so many that it looked gaudy. She was appreciating her birdhouses, from the swing, when she glanced down and saw the white kitten bounding up onto the porch.

"Oh, no, you again!"

The kitten leapt into her lap and clawed its way up to cuddle at her neck, purring the whole time. She laughed and hugged it. "I can see you've adopted me and I'm not going to be able to get rid of you, am I?"

She took the cat into the house. "First thing for you, if you're going to stay with me, is a bath. You stink and, if you're going to live here, you have to be clean. Only clean kittens allowed in my house." The cat didn't protest and seemed to enjoy playing in the water.

Abigail had to go into town for cat stuff. The

tuna had run out. If the kitten was going to live with her, she had to have a litter box and, of course, cat toys. When in town, buying cat necessities at the General Store, John Mason inquired on how her artwork was progressing.

"I have another commission, which comes first, and then I hope to get the time to gather some of my older drawings and paintings together. I'll bring them in soon, I promise," she told him. "Hopefully by Saturday."

That seemed to make him happy.

On her way home, she came up with a name for the kitten. Snowball. Well, so much for getting rid of the little pest. Once you named an animal, it had you.

Chapter 6

"I see you collect birdhouses." Frank was on the porch examining one with a miniature fake-feathered tenant in the opening. "Nice. Wait until you see the craft booths today at the picnic. Some will have really unique birdhouses. Me, I collect ancient weapons and guns."

"Hmm, an ex-cop who collects guns and such. Imagine that?" Abigail closed the door, not bothering to lock it. No need to in Spookie because according to Frank, there wasn't much, if any, crime in their little town.

"Everyone meets at Stella's for breakfast first. It's a tradition," Frank said, as they walked to town. It was a perfect summer day, hot with clear skies and enough of a breeze that the heat wouldn't be bad. The sound of fireworks exploded in the sky above them and a pungent smoke scent hung in the air. The celebration had begun early.

"We can't buck tradition, can we?" Abigail felt like a young girl again in her pink short-sleeved blouse, her white shorts; her hair tied back with a red, white, and blue ribbon. She hoped she looked pretty. The physical activity of moving and refurbishing the house had helped her shed a couple of pounds. She was happier than she'd been in a long time, which also made a difference. For the first time in a long time, she *felt* pretty.

She'd shown Frank the Mason jar the minute he'd arrived at her house that morning.

"Have you told anyone else about these messages?" he'd asked.

"Just Martha and you. She called this morning and it slipped out."

"Martha? Then, the whole town knows. That woman can't keep her mouth shut even on pain of death. I know. Maybe it doesn't matter. It was all so long ago, if there'd been a crime involved, the culprit is probably dead or long gone. But then again…maybe not. So be careful."

"You think like a cop."

He tilted his head to the side and breathed in the summer air. "Do you see that baby rabbit there in that bush?" He pointed. "It thinks we can't see it. It thinks it's safe. Like you. That'll be its downfall. Better if it lays low and stays quiet. Safer that way."

"You trying to tell me something? That I'm putting myself in danger by publicizing my interest in these people's disappearance and I should keep my mouth shut?"

"Something like that."

She ignored his warning. "Smells like summer out here…wild strawberries, and clover. When I was a child, Michael, my brother, and I used to run around barefoot in the dirt on a road like this. The sun so hot, the air so thick with these same smells. We were looking for something to eat, like wild strawberries or grapes. We were always hungry. My dad was a salesman and not a real good one. We didn't have much money, or food, most times. We did without. But, I had brothers, sisters, parents, and a home I loved; woods to play in, trees to climb, and dusty paths to follow. I have many fond memories of my childhood and this place reminds me of where I grew up."

"You had a hard time of it, didn't you? Like the Summers' kids?"

Never wanting any pity, she downplayed things. "A lot of kids did. I'm not complaining." She met his gaze. "But, I was loved, protected, that's all the difference. No one neglected, browbeat, or demoralized me. My father would have punched out anyone who hurt any of us kids, in any way. In that respect, we were better off than most."

"Then you were one of the lucky ones," Frank remarked, looking handsome in jeans and a green shirt, his hair freshly washed, and his eyes a movie star blue. The man had this confident way about him. He made her feel safe and comfortable, at the same time. From observing him, she'd learned he could read people and he had an eye for anything out of the ordinary. He must have been a heck of a detective.

Childishly giddy with the anticipation of a picnic and fireworks, Abigail couldn't wait to get to town. It'd be nice to be among other artists, and to spend the day looking at what they'd created. She'd meet more of the townsfolk. Perhaps, some of the older residents would recall Emily, and her children. Which reminded her.

"Frank, do you remember what the Summers' kids looked like? The artist in me wants faces with the names."

"You really want to torture yourself, don't you? Oh, all right. They were tow-headed with hazel eyes. Shy smiles. You could tell they were twins, alike in appearance, a little too thin to be healthy, with Jenny having more delicate features and longer blond hair. They were constantly hungry, their hand me down clothes were shabby. Jenny had this scar in the middle of her forehead, from accidently walking into a brick wall, she said, when she was five. Artistic. Dreamers. Too smart. Different from the other kids. Didn't have many other friends, so they usually played together. I thought they were good kids. I used to bring them hamburgers from the town diner. I remember one time Christopher got beat up and I gave him advice on how to defend himself.

"They had a swing set in the back yard that they played on, singing songs in the dark as they'd swing. Let's see, what else? They loved to play in the woods. Come to think of it…they had a tree house out there somewhere, don't know where precisely. They spoke of it but I never saw it. Oh, yes, Jenny had a white cat, but I can't remember its name."

"I have a white kitten now."

He sent her a humorous look. "So the storm kitty returned, huh? Couldn't get rid of it?"

"No. The funny little thing. She hides and then pounces out at me like a great tiger. She doesn't know she's as tiny as a gnat." They both chuckled.

They were at Stella's by then and, as usual, the diner was packed. "Does this place ever empty out?" she wanted to know as they squeezed in and claimed a booth.

"Sure, but I told you breakfast here on a holiday was a tradition. Everyone shows up."

As they ate bacon and eggs, Frank introduced her to more of her neighbors. Children ran in and out, setting off firecrackers and cherry bombs in the street. Abigail had never seen a place go so crazy over a holiday. The town was decorated with flags, balloons, and red, white and blue streamers everywhere. Everyone was celebrating. Everyone seemed happy.

Martha came in with a young woman and headed for them. The woman looked about twenty-something, wore thick glasses and carried a notepad. Abigail smelled reporter.

"Abigail," Martha spoke first, "this is Samantha Westerly, Senior Editor of our town newspaper, *The Weekly Journal*."

Samantha zeroed in on Abigail, "So you're our new townie? Moved here from the big city, I hear. Martha tells me you are an artist and you're doing a watercolor of her house. How about letting me do a story on you? Our readers would enjoy knowing more about their new neighbor and that you do house portraits. The personal touch, you know."

Abigail had had enough of newspapers, having worked at one for years, but it would be free publicity, and it could get her commissions. "Let me think about it?" Samantha nodded.

Then Abigail had a thought. If she got Samantha interested in a story about the Summers' disappearance as an unsolved old mystery piece like: *What happened to the Summers?* She might get some answers. Heck, it could even tie in as a personal look back at the times and people of Spookie thirty years ago. Bring the whole town into it. It was worth a pitch, but Abigail didn't feel comfortable talking about it in the middle of a crowd. She'd visit the newspaper one day next week and talk to Samantha then. With that in mind, she was friendlier to the editor than she would normally have been, which was easy because Samantha turned out to be an interesting, amiable woman and Abigail liked her.

The picnic was fun. Main Street was crowded with craft booths covered from the sun and decked out in American flags. She went from booth to booth chatting with the artists. There were potters, painters, watercolorists, glassblowers, and a woman who made tiny button people. Food booths served fried chicken to Baklava, and everyone was friendly.

The birdhouses in a few of the booths were exquisite, yet inexpensive. Abigail bought one with elaborate trim and a shiny tin roof for her collection.

Frank remained nearby most of the day, though he left for a while in the late afternoon to take care of his dogs. He wasn't gone long.

Frank hadn't returned yet when Martha asked, "How's my house portrait coming along?"

"Nearly done. It's ready for you to see. Come by tomorrow, if you want."

"I'm dying to. I have three other people, if they like what you do for me, in line to have their houses painted, as well. I should demand a share of the profit."

"You should." Abigail was encouraged at the prospect of more work. Between the freelancing, owning her house, having no debt and having savings, she would make it fine for about another year. Then, if her artwork hasn't caught on, she'd have to find at least a part time job somewhere. But she'd been stashing money away like crazy the two years before she moved to Spookie, and if she lived simply, she could make it last for a long time.

When Frank reappeared, they rode the Ferris wheel and the roller coaster. Martha got Abigail to throw darts at balloons, and hoops at bottles, and she won a stuffed bear with an American flag for a shirt. She enjoyed the day, the picnic, the people, and ate barbequed chicken, on a blanket in the park with the lake behind her. The blanket had been stashed at Stella's the day before by Frank, along with a cooler of soda and beer.

People strolled by and stopped to visit.

Myrtle came by with her wagon, crooning another Perry Como song, "*Dream along with me, I'm on the way to a star–*"

The old lady stopped in front of Abigail. "I've been thinking about our conversation from the other day…about Emily Summers?" The old woman totally seized Abigail's attention.

"Sit down, Myrtle, have barbeque with us." She smoothed the blanket beside her. The elderly woman was sweaty, and tired looking, dabbing away at her face with a wash cloth. "We have soda." Abigail held up a can of Pepsi from Frank's cooler.

"Okay." Myrtle crumpled down beside them. She devoured chicken and potato salad, washed down with the Pepsi, as if she hadn't eaten in days. Her dress, still a garish print, was different, but as worn and tattered as the last one. She had a flag barrette in her thinning hair. "So you're trying to find out, my sister says, what happened to Emily and her kids?"

"Yes, I am." Abigail shielded her eyes from the sun and noticed John Mason had ambled over to see Frank. Mason was smiling, but he kept staring at her. She gave him a smile and a half-hearted wave. It made her nervous, he had such an interest in her, but no one else seemed to notice because the man was charming with everyone. But she could tell the difference.

Frank offered Mason a beer. "No thanks. I don't drink alcohol, but I'll take a soda."

Meanwhile, Martha was watching Myrtle, her condescending smirk barely detectable.

Myrtle's grin was crimson from the barbequed chicken. One moment she was alert, and the next, she was confused. She wiped sticky hands on her dress as Abigail handed her a napkin. She'd stopped talking for a moment and then suddenly said, "Ah yes, Emily. At my age, the memory comes and goes. Emily had a spiteful ex-husband, and a couple of jealous wives tormenting her. She wouldn't talk much about it," she mumbled. "She was too nice a lady to have all those problems. I do recall she was really scared of someone so much that last summer she was going to leave town, in the middle of the night, with those kids. She told me.

Said she'd say goodbye first. She promised she would. She never did. That's why I know she didn't just leave. Emily never lied. Something bad happened to her, to them."

"Because they never said goodbye to you, you think something bad happened to them?" Abigail was surprised at the old lady's reasoning.

"Possibly. No one ever heard from them again. But hey, on the other hand, they could be lost in the ghost dimension somewhere. Because Emily wouldn't have just run off the way everyone says she did. And…she had the death shadow in her eyes, I seen it clear, I did, many times that summer. She was marked for death. Already a walking, talking ghost. Poor kids, too. I tried to tell Sheriff Cal, but that old Billy goat never listened."

Myrtle snorted. "Sheriff Cal had a thing for Emily himself. Maybe she rejected him and he got rid of her. Who knows? The sheriff sure acted funny when I wanted him to look for the three of them…couldn't get him to search the woods around their house or nothing. He said they'd run off, plain and simple, and why look? He was paid off, if you ask me."

It didn't make any sense. But, Abigail had to admit the old woman wasn't completely in her right mind, so how could she believe anything the woman said. "Paid off by whom?"

"I don't know. There's something else. My memory's kind of fuzzy, but Jenny might have had a diary. I think her mother mentioned it one day. I bet it's somewhere in that house, if Edna didn't find and burn it." The old lady cocked her head, and winked. "That Jenny was always doodling words on paper, or drawing pictures."

Around them twilight was creeping in and a short while later the booths began to close, as the townspeople got ready for the fireworks.

Myrtle got up. She grabbed the handle of her wagon. "I got to go now. The ghosts come out after dark, so I need to be home. I can't let them get me. Or I'll disappear as well…into the ghost dimension. Thanks for the supper, dearie. I do so love barbeque." She hurried off, singing Perry Como's "Goodbye Sue" at the top of her lungs, the wagon's wheels bumping along the street in rhythm to the song.

A teenage boy with a Walkman on his hip, and earphones on his head, threw a lit firecracker at Myrtle's wagon and when it exploded, Myrtle jumped, grabbed something from her wagon and threw it at the kid, narrowly missing him. Then, muttering to herself, she and her wagon trundled off.

Frank and Martha laughed, shaking their heads.

"Both she and her sister are as goofy as they come," Frank said. "But, Myrtle is around eighty years old, and Evelyn is not far behind. I hope I'm as spry as them when I'm that old."

"I hope I'm alive when I'm that old," Martha joked.

"Where is Evelyn today anyway?"

"She never leaves that house of hers." Frank shrugged. "She won't leave her animals."

"What a pair, one sister won't stay in one

spot and the other won't leave one spot," Martha quipped. "Anyone for ice cream?" A minute later, she was up and heading for the ice cream booth with everyone's order.

They'd lost John Mason to another huddle of people. Stella's grandson stopped by to say hi. "The fireworks are supposed to the biggest, and best, we've ever had," he told them. "We closed early at Stella's because we can't compete with the picnic food. And I'm glad. Now I can enjoy the festivities with everyone else." Then, a pretty girl came along and trotted him away as a county band began playing on the other side of the park. Abigail stood up and saw him, and the girl, in a line dance with a group of others.

Frank rose and held out his hand. "Abigail, you want to dance?"

She said no, twice, but on the third time gave in. The dancers seemed to be having fun, and most of them were learning as they went. "Okay. I'm rusty, though, and I'll probably stomp all over your feet."

"Just don't stomp too hard."

She danced with Frank. The faces around her were becoming familiar; the town was becoming familiar. She tried to keep up with the steps. People smiled, or nodded, she smiled back, and she had the feeling everyone knew everything about her.

When it grew dark and cool, Abigail sat on the blanket with her friends and watched fireworks, thinking how different her life had been just a year ago, when she'd spent the day alone in her apartment listening to faraway celebrations; sipping wine until she fell asleep.

After the last rocket faded into the smoky night sky, Frank walked her home.

"Your front door's wide open," he whispered, as they came up on the porch. "Stay here. I'll go in first." He stalked into the house.

"It's an old door. I probably didn't slam it shut all the way when I left and it popped open. That's all," she called out. "Frank?" Frank didn't answer and Abigail experienced unease. The murkiness around her was silent. Eerie. She'd thought she'd left a light on in the house, yet inside there was nothing but blackness.

Lights came on inside her home.

She was ready to barge in, when Frank reemerged. "Unless you're a very sloppy housekeeper, and I know you're not, it's been ransacked. I called the sheriff. He's on his way."

"Oh, no," she moaned and went into the house. Inside it was a disaster.

"Where's Snowball?" she cried, but then the kitten loped into the room and scrambled up her leg. "Thank goodness you're okay. If only you could talk, kitty. You could tell me who did this." She put the cat down, it jumped onto a chair, and promptly fell asleep.

Abigail went from one room to another, straightening up. It wasn't as bad as she'd first thought. There'd been no real vandalism, mainly objects moved around, or thrown on the floor. Cabinet doors, drawers, had been opened, and clothes were in piles on the floor in her bedroom.

"Nothing seems to be missing. Nothing big, that is. The televisions, and the microwave, are still here. I wonder what they wanted?"

"Someone was looking for something, I'd say, or it was a powerful poltergeist."

Abigail didn't laugh. "Yeah, looks like that. But why? I don't have much money or diamond rings lying around."

"Do an inventory tomorrow, and maybe, you'll find something missing." Frank's tone was sympathetic. He looked as if he would put his arm around her at any moment.

Abigail moved away from his sympathy, and sat on the couch. "It could have been worse, but I feel awful. I thought I was so safe here."

"I think basically you are. Someone was scavenging for something specific. Whether they found it, or not, is another matter. My guess is whoever did this won't be coming back tonight." His optimistic expression was meant to comfort her but it didn't. "If you want, if you're scared I could stay, or I could leave you a gun for protection?"

She was tempted, but shook her head. "No. You're probably right. I'm safe now. Besides, I don't like guns. Thanks for the offer though." She went to the closet and pulled out a two by four piece of wood she'd had for years. "I have this." She waved the wood at him.

"My husband used to say that a good whack on the head with this would stop anybody. I dare anyone to try to break into my home when I'm here. I'd knock the stuffing out of him."

"I bet you would."

Sheriff Mearl Brewster arrived and filled out the report. He was polite, too attentive to her apparently for Frank's liking, because she could tell Frank wasn't happy with the cop asking her so many personal questions. The sheriff was a heavyset man, with thinning hair, in a wrinkled uniform; he talked too much, and smelled of beer. Abigail had met him earlier that day at the picnic. She imagined he somewhat like his father, a womanizer, which meant it'd be best to stay away from him.

"It's not bad, Mrs. Sutton. And if you can't account for anything big missing, then you're lucky. It might simply have been a teenager, or a drifter, looking for cash or jewelry. Someone who knew everyone would be at the picnic. I wouldn't be too worried," Sheriff Brewster told her. "These things happen. Just be sure to lock your doors when you leave next time. Spookie's a quiet town generally, we don't have much crime, but even a small town has its share of break-ins and petty vandalisms. Most places do."

Abigail hadn't locked the front door, so perhaps it was partly her fault. She thanked the sheriff for coming, and offered him a cup of coffee. He accepted with a smile, too friendly for just business, and complemented her endlessly on how lovely her house looked.

Frank was sticking his finger in his mouth behind the sheriff's back, making a face, when Abigail glanced at him. She almost laughed, but yawned to cover it up.

"I hear you've been asking questions about

old lady Edna's sister, the one who left town and never came back?" the sheriff stated over his coffee. "As I told Frank here when he came by the office last week, there isn't even a case file on it. Everything before 1980 got burned up in the warehouse fire last summer. My pa, Cal Brewster, was sheriff in those days. I was a kid. The only thing I recollect about the incident was overhearing that Edna's sister, a wild thing, probably met a man and ran off with him. Edna swore she saw her sister, with the children, drive away that night. No crime committed. That was that."

Abigail was irked at his lack of interest. No wonder the police hadn't solved the case. They'd never investigated. The old sheriff had left office soon after.

"I think he's got a crush on you," Frank said after the officer drove off.

Abigail snickered. "Not my type. I like my men leaner…and smarter."

Frank insisted on helping her clean up, and was as puzzled as she, when later, she confirmed nothing important was missing.

"I was a cop for a long time, Abby." He'd sometimes begun to call her that and she hadn't stopped him. Joel had called her that.

"And I don't think it was an innocent break-in. I'd bet it has something to do with these questions you've been asking around town, about Emily Summers, and her children. Call it a hunch. Someone was looking for something, they suspect is hidden here somewhere; something they don't want you to find. Or they're trying to scare you off."

"This was a warning? Well, it could have been a little clearer, don't you think? Like a letter or something?"

"Maybe. Give me a piece of paper and a pen." She did. It was after twelve, she was tired, and wanted to go to bed, wanted to forget the break-in had ever happened.

He wrote something on the paper and handed it back to her. "That's my home, and cell, phone numbers. Call me anytime, if you need anything."

When Frank was gone, and she'd cleaned up most of the mess, she couldn't stop fretting. She ended up sitting on the porch swing, her eyes peering into the hushed darkness. The large wooden piece of wood, her club, was in her lap. The remnants of firework smoke, a steamy haze, hung high in the air and raced across the crescent moon. The day had been so happy, everything had been going so well…until someone had violated her home.

Myrtle had said something about Jenny having had a diary. Perhaps, the diary was what the intruder had been hunting for? Tomorrow, she'd explore the basement, spiders and bugs be darned, what the heck. Perhaps, she might find more notes, even that mysterious diary, or anything that might clarify why her home had been broken into.

Again, she thought she heard children romping out in the woods somewhere, and the full-throated call of a mature cat. At the edge of the trees, she thought she saw two misty figures running, their pale hair floating about their heads.

Abigail blinked, and the mirage was gone. The woods were silent and empty, once more. She went to bed, the wooden club, and phone, nearby; and the kitten on the pillow snuggled up beside her.

Chapter 7

The following morning, Abigail awoke and finished straightening the house, then she covered herself in old clothes and gloves, for protection. She grabbed a broom, and trash bags, and descended into the basement. Aside from looking for more messages, or the diary, the dungeon had to be cleaned because it was time.

Her bottom floor was a partial basement, low in height and stacked to the ceiling with unwanted furniture and dusty boxes. The smoky, glass block windows didn't let in much sun so the whole area was bathed in shadows. One thick metal pole stood in the middle of the room, for support, and rusted beams in a grill design laced the upper ceiling. One bare hanging light bulb was the only source of illumination. The basement's gray concrete floors were as smooth as eggshells and its walls were a dirty lumpy white.

The kitten had descended a few steps and was watching her, as it cleaned its paws. "Don't come down here, Snowball," she chided. "Or, I've have to change your name to dirtball." She chuckled softly.

With the first object she picked up to move, an army of tiny eight legged critters scampered away into the dark. She must have disturbed their spider home. "Yeck!" It was nearly enough to make her run back upstairs, but she didn't. She began cleaning in one corner, and kept going; throwing away everything, after she'd poked through it, which Edna Summers had left behind. Mostly boxes of old crinkled papers and bills. The woman had been a hoarder. Martha had apologized for leaving all the junk, but Abigail hadn't grasped how much there really was, until she began filling trash bags. It took twenty of the extra big ones.

At the end of the day, she was rewarded with a clean basement and the discovery of a grimy locked box she'd found by accident stuffed deep underneath a wad of old newspapers in a tall metal cabinet. Someone had hidden it so well, even the burglar hadn't found it. Abigail hadn't been able to open the box, though. It'd resisted everything she'd tried. She'd used a hammer, but even that wouldn't break the strong lock.

But she hadn't found any more scribbled notes from the kids, and hadn't found a diary either.

Upstairs, she took a shower, put on clothes and a little make-up, and made a call to Frank asking for his help to open the metal box. He said he'd do it, if she'd come and stay for supper. He had some things he wanted to discuss with her, anyway, and would take an extra steak out of the fridge and put it on the grill for her. He said it'd give her a chance to see the log cabin he'd built with his own hands, and was proud of, and that he showed to everybody every time he got the chance. "No strings, Abby. We'd be just two friends having dinner together." She couldn't resist and said yes. She'd found it a strange coincidence, Joel and she, had planned to also build a log cabin, so she'd been curious about Frank's since Martha had mentioned he lived in one.

Frank gave her directions to his house, she grabbed her purse and the box, and headed to the door, Snowball bouncing along behind her. She scooped the kitten up, nuzzled her furry face, and gently placed her back inside. "Sorry, you can't come with me. There be dogs there. Big dogs with big teeth."

All her windows and doors were shut, locked, and before she stepped out of the house she'd scanned the yard. No one lurking about, that she could see. Jumpy since the break in, she was afraid the intruder would return for whatever he, or she, hadn't found the first time–if he, or she, hadn't found it. For all she knew, the intruder had taken something she wasn't aware of from her house.

Frank's home was beautiful, and much larger, than Abigail had imagined. It was a true log cabin with a wraparound porch and a multitude of windows. Wooden rocking chairs with plush cushions waited on the porch, for people to sit in, and he'd hung plants from the roofline. She lugged the metal box to the front door, which was framed in oak with an oval of stained glass in the center. Frank opened it before she had a chance to ring the bell. He must have been listening for her car.

Somewhere, she could hear dogs barking.

"Come on in." His eyes went to her face first, he seemed glad to see her, and then to the box in her arms. "Looks heavy." Dressed in faded jeans, a blue shirt, and barefooted, he took it from her. "Can I get you something to drink…coffee, soda or wine?"

"Maybe later. I'm okay for now." She trailed behind him, gawking at the inside of his home. It was done in southwestern themes with Indian blankets and feathered mandalas, Indian rugs on the floors, and a huge stuffed brown couch with a coffee table in front of it. There was an impressive collection of weapons, in a glass case, displayed along one wall adjacent to a massive fireplace. "I love your front door, Frank. I love your house."

"Thank you. My friends and I did most of it ourselves. I learned carpentry as I went; learned to do stained glass so I could make the door's windows myself. It wasn't as hard as I'd thought it would be, but I cut my hands up something awful on the glass, before I got the knack of it." He set the box down on the rug by the sofa, as she ran her hands over the fireplace's cool stones.

"I collected the stones from the creek, in the woods, behind us," he told her. "And built the fireplace piece by piece and carved out the mantle, by hand."

"Oh my, you are a man of many talents. Your home is lovely. Did your son help build it?"

"Kyle helped as often as he could. Chicago's four hours away. He spent a month here end of last summer, when the walls went up. But, he's pre-med, second year, and on scholarship. He has to keep his grades up. I imagine that will come in handy someday for me when I'm old, and sick, having my own doctor in the family."

"You must be proud. Do you get to see him often?"

"I am proud. And, I see him about once a

month, when he drives down for the weekend, or I drive up. I miss him, but he's doing what he wants, and that's why we have kids…to send them off into the world to live their own lives. He loves this place. Like me, at heart, he's a country boy. One day, all this will be his. My secret hope is that someday, after he becomes a doctor, he'll be a small town country doctor. Here. Old Doc Andy isn't getting any younger."

"Does Kyle know you have these designs for his future?"

"We've never talked about it, no. I wouldn't put that on him. But, I can dream, can't I?"

Getting up, she went to the gun case. "How many guns *do* you have?"

"A lot. I collect them. Some of the weapons, in that case, are antiques; very valuable. When I get old, and need money, I can sell them off. I figure they're better than stocks and municipal bonds. Their value only keeps going up, never down."

"If you say so."

"For now, I'll get the tools and we'll open this box. My curiosity is killing me. Then, we'll have supper." He left the room and returned with a hammer. In a few whacks, he had the box open.

They looked at what was inside. The box was stuffed with papers. Frank lifted the contents out and laid them on the coffee table. At the bottom was a smaller cardboard container marked personal.

Frank, sitting down beside her, skimmed through the loose papers. "Mainly, receipts for everything from china to blankets. Edna loved to spend money. But, from what I'd heard, she was only on Social Security. So, I wonder where she got it all?"

"And, she wasn't always. Social Security doesn't kick in until you're sixty-two. How was she living before that?"

"I don't know. I wasn't living here, in town, during most of that time, remember?"

Abigail checked out the cardboard container. Inside was a red record book of some kind. There was nothing written on the front. She opened the first page, and the next and the next, her face baffled. "Appears to be a record of payments for something. Look." She handed the book to Frank, and looked over his shoulder, as he flipped the pages.

"Numbers," he said. "Looks like money amounts with dates behind them. Earliest figures, a hundred a month in September 1970–around the time Emily and the kids left town–and steadily larger every month. It doesn't mention who the payments are from, or what they're for. No names, nothing. Just amounts and dates. Add it all up, that's a great deal of money." He turned the pages. "Over years and years. Last payment being the month before Edna died."

Abigail stared at the entries. "I'm pretty sure that's Edna's handwriting. Anyway, it's got the same distinctive y's, and c's, like the writing I found on the back of the house deed. But, was she paying out, or receiving it?"

Frank shook his head. "One or the other. My cop instincts say it looks like blackmail. Old Edna was either blackmailing someone or she was being blackmailed. That's my guess."

"My money's on Edna being the blackmailer. It'd explain where she got her money all those years. From what I've heard, she was spending a lot…and if all she had was Social Security, she had to be getting it from somewhere, or someone else."

"That makes sense."

"I wonder if this–" she took the book from Frank and held it up "–was what my intruder was looking for?"

"It could have been. How did you find it anyway?"

"As I said, I was cleaning the basement, looking for more notes from the children or the diary Myrtle claimed Jenny might have had, or might have hidden in the house somewhere. But, if it exists, I haven't found it."

"It exists. Jenny *did* have a diary. It was a little pink thing with flowers on it. I remember, because one night I was there, and she and Christopher were fighting over it. He'd been reading it or so she'd thought."

"Then, I'll keep looking for it."

They put the papers, and book, away and ate supper out on a deck shaded by lush trees. The day had been hot, but there was a breeze as Abigail looked out across the rolling hills and valleys. The sun was setting, the air was golden, and filled with the sounds of summer insects. Far in the distance, she could see woods and tiny houses. The steaks were delicious, the company was pleasant, and the scenery was captivating.

"That view was the reason I bought this piece of property and built here." Frank noticed where her attention was. "I'd spent too many years staring at concrete, steel, alleyways, and people in their cardboard boxes. Jolene really loved the city. But when she was gone, I wanted my final years spent enjoying trees and sky."

She could understand that, she felt the same way, and told him so as they lounged on the deck. They watched the sun set and night creep into its place. In the soft glow of Tiki lamps, they ate ice cream for dessert and talked. They played with Frank's German Shepherds, which he'd finally let out, as they romped around on the deck with them.

"You really miss your wife, don't you?" She couldn't help but ask.

"Every second of every day, but it's better than it was. I don't bawl as often. Coming back home, and building this house, was my way of healing. Like the writing."

She was unable to imagine this man beside her, crying. Not many men would admit to such a weakness. "By the way, how's the book coming, and what made you want to write one?"

"It's nearly finished and, believe it or not, I've always wanted to be a writer. Being a cop paid better, and had retirement benefits. I'd been writing on this book for years, a little at a time, long before I retired. Being a detective, I've seen so many crimes go unsolved that solving one of them, in a book, gives me great satisfaction. Even if I don't get it perfectly right, it makes a good story."

"And me," Abigail murmured, "I've spent

so many years clocking in for a paycheck, now I just want to do my art, because it makes me happy."

"You remind me of Emily when you talk like that. The memories of her are coming back more often now. She had to make a living, but she dreamed of taking college art classes, going to art school someday and of being a real artist. She was good. I saw some of her drawings."

"You think of Emily often, huh?"

"Only lately. You started it with all your questions." Frank cleared his throat. "I didn't say anything earlier, because I didn't want to spoil our dinner, but I've been doing a little investigating on my own. I have a police buddy back in Chicago, my old partner, Sam Cato, and I had him do a computer search on Emily and her kids. See if they were ever spotted, or heard from again, after 1970. If there were any paper trails at all."

"And?"

"Not a trace. Sam also contacted the DMV, and there's been no license renewal for Emily Summers since 1968–in any state. She could have remarried, I know, changed her name, but Sam did a credit search, too…no credit card receipts, not even a credit application, is on the record. And, here's the clincher. There are no school records for the kids, nothing. Ever. Not under Summers, or Brown, which is their biological father's last name. Sam did a worldwide missing person's search and there's no paper trail, for any of them."

Abigail wondered what that meant.

"Unless they went underground, and changed their names," Frank went on, "it seems more likely, now, that something happened to them. They didn't run away, Abby, they really disappeared.

"After Sam did the computer search and came up cold, he did one on Todd Brown, the kids' father, and located him. Sam made a telephone call and discovered that Brown never saw Emily or his kids alive again, after that summer, either. Brown didn't make a police report, though, which is strange, and he didn't come back here and beat the bushes for them. He talked to Edna, Brown told Sam, who told him the three of them drove away in Emily's car, wanting to start a new life, and he had no reason to not believe her.

"The truth is, the Summers' official existence ended here in that summer of 1970. Yet Emily wasn't the sort of woman to keep her kids from their father, as much as she disliked him. She wasn't like that."

A dark suspicion was growing in Abigail's mind. Before, it'd only been a normal curiosity about the former occupants of her house, now it was becoming an enigma that cried out to be solved. *What had happened to Emily and her two children?*

Frank leaned forward in his chair, brought his glass of wine slowly to his lips, his eyes on Abigail's face, but she suspected his thoughts were probably in the past. In the night woods, katydids croaked, and the wind was a sigh through the leaves. The heat had left the earth, and on the deck, Abigail was chilly. She should have brought a sweater.

"And," Frank added, "I walked our friend

Sheriff Mearl to his car last night and he let it slip, I believe by accident, that there was some question about old Edna's death, after all. That it wasn't completely natural. The coroner found a trace too much of prescription drugs in her system. He thought, as most would, her being feeble minded at the end, she'd forgotten, and taken too many pills. According to many people, Edna had been frail most of her life. She'd been sickly since her early thirties, which kept her from working. People wondered, as we did earlier, how she made it, alone in that house, no job, and no income that could be accounted for."

"So she took too much of her medication and died from it?"

"If it was only that. The coroner found medication in Edna's stomach which wasn't hers. It could have killed her. But, because she was elderly, chronically ill and unloved, there was no inquest and she was simply buried. No one cared."

"It's funny, how a person's death is only as important as that person was in life," Abigail made the observation, cynically.

Frank groaned, stretching out his long legs. "Oh, and there's something else you'll find interesting. The sheriff confided that after Edna died last year, her house, your house now, was rummaged through during the funeral service. He thought it was one of those obit burglars. You know, a thief reading in the newspaper someone has died and breaking in because the house is empty. So the sheriff didn't think much of it. As far as he knew, the old woman hadn't anything to steal."

"What a coincidence. Well, either the house I live in is a burglar magnet, or Edna must have had something somebody wanted badly enough to break in for. Twice."

"Could be it's that record book you found in the metal box, Abby. If Edna had been blackmailing someone, for something, there'd be someone out there who'd want the evidence disposed of. I'd put it in a safe place, if I were you."

"I intend to."

They talked a bit longer, of unrelated things, and then Abigail said goodnight. "The supper was fantastic and the company was, too. I should get home. I worry about Snowball. All that cleaning I did today, and a full belly, has made me want to sleep."

Frank escorted her to the door. "We have to do this again, Abby. It was nice cooking for someone else besides myself. Nice having someone to talk to."

"My turn, next time. I make a tasty pot roast and the best apple turnovers you've ever had."

"I'll take you up on that, one night. Give me a time, and a day, and I'll be there."

Abigail picked up the box, her purse, and left. Driving into the lightless woods, and navigating through the night fog, her mind was churning over what Frank had told her.

It was possible someone had murdered Edna. Now why would anyone want to do that? An old lady? Abigail thought of the metal box, on the seat beside her, and the record book with the figures in it. There had to be a connection there somewhere to Edna's death, if she could find it. She had to find Jenny's diary, if there was one. She bet that would answer some questions. Kids put secrets in diaries.

Where else could Jenny have hidden her diary? That question filled her mind the rest of the way home.

Chapter 8

When Abigail got up the next morning, she finished Martha's watercolor, called her, and informed her she could pick it up. It was as good as she was going to get it. Propping it against the front room wall, she sat on the couch and studied it. Her smile came slowly. *It looks pretty good for the artist being so out of practice. I hope Martha likes it.*

As she waited for her new friend, she roamed the house poking into the nooks and crannies of cabinets, closets and drawers, looking for notes or that elusive diary. The children's room had been upstairs, according to Frank, and they shared it with their mother. Edna had slept downstairs on a sofa couch. With a flashlight, on hands and knees, Abigail explored the loft bedroom along the baseboards and in the walk-in closet. Sixty watts wasn't enough light, so hundred-watt bulbs were on her grocery list.

About to give up, she noticed the heater vents on the floor, found a screwdriver, and pried them open. Being summer, she hadn't cleaned them out yet, so they were thick with webs and years accumulation of vent dust. Using a cloth to wipe away the covering of matted grime, in the second vent she hit treasure: a piece of twine attached to the side of the vent. She tugged it up through her fingers, and at the end, was a small brown paper lunch sack. Inside were drawings, and another crayon message, from Jenny. All in caps, again.

SOMEONE TRIED TO RUN CHRISTOPHER OVER WITH A CAR. SOMEONE BROKE OUT MOM'S CAR WINDOWS. I KNOW ITS HIM. MOM SAYS IT WAS BECAUSE HE WAS SO MAD. CAIN'T HELP HIMSELF. I SAY BALONEY. HE IS BAD. EVIL AS CHRIS SAYS. I HATE HIM. I KNOW GOD SAYS YOU SHOULN'T HATE NOBODY SO I'M SORRY GOD BUT I DO. I SENT A LETTER TO DAD TO COME GET US. HE NEVER CALLED OR WROTE BACK.

The drawings were of the house and a kitten. Christopher's house picture wasn't half bad. Abigail's house circa 1970 looked about the same as it did today, except the trees were smaller, there were two bicycles against the porch, two hula hoops laying in the front yard, and a swing hanging from one of the elms. The other picture, signed by Jenny, was of a white cat sitting on the house's front porch, eyes wide and blue, one paw stretched out. Snowball grownup.

A shiver began in Abigail's fingers and rippled through her body. Strange how the past and the present kept merging. Abigail believed she'd been destined to find this town, this house, and these clues. It was her fate to solve the mystery of what happened to the Summers. And, as much as she disliked newspapers, it was time to visit Samantha Westerly at the *Journal*.

Scooping up the children's messages and drawings into a large envelope, she drove into town. A breezeless July day, it was too hot to walk. Someone out there knew what had happened thirty years ago, and if there was a newspaper story that someone might read it and step forward.

"You decided to let me do that story on you, after all?" exclaimed Samantha, when Abigail walked in.

"Sort of." Being there with people bent over computers, slaving away on stories and ads, or on the phone selling classifieds, revived unpleasant memories. She had to remind herself she was only a visitor. She could leave whenever she wanted to. "I have an intriguing feature concept for you, Samantha."

"Come into my private cubicle and tell me about it, Abigail. I'm a sucker for a good story idea. Some weeks I can't think of a darn thing to write about."

Abigail did. She explained about Emily, and the children's, disappearances; showed Samantha the scribbled messages, the drawings, and exposed what she and Frank had uncovered, even about the ledger. Samantha was sold.

"You're right. People love a good mystery. And it's a hometown conundrum! We could lay it out as something we–the whole town–might want to solve…what happened to Emily and her two kids? Let's play Sherlock Holmes and unlock the secret. We could frame their story with the trappings of the times. The seventies…what were they like in Spookie? What did the town look like back then? The stores and businesses. The clothes we wore, and the movies we were watching. The politics of the day. What we did for fun. It was pre-computer, and the Internet, of course. Who was mayor, who was sheriff? I could interview store owners, and citizens, who remember the town and what it was like in the summer of 1970, to get new perspectives. The human touch." Samantha was so excited; she couldn't stop talking.

"Heck, we could make it a series of stories. Print, and follow the clues each week, and get feedback from the readers. The individual material on people's memories of those days, alone, could be a gold mine. Imagine it! *What were you doing in the summer of 1970? What was it like? And, did you know Emily or her kids?*" Samantha clapped her hands. "I can tie you, and your drawings, into the first story. Give you free publicity and generate some commissions for you. You being the owner of the house now, and the originator of the quest, so to speak." It was easy to see this woman loved her job.

Abigail suddenly felt anticipation. At last, she was doing something. "Good idea. I won't refuse free publicity. So how do we start this?"

Samantha's eyebrows arched, and her eyes behind the glasses were thoughtful. Even without makeup she was pretty. Her face had classic lines and good bone structure. Age wouldn't harm her too quickly. "We'll start by taking pictures, of your house, and you in it, Abigail. I'll send a photographer over tomorrow, if that's okay with you? Deadline is in three days if we want to get this in the next issue. If we could get photos, of the missing persons, that would be splendid. I could ask around, do some digging, and maybe come up with pictures of them from our archives. The newspaper's been around for over fifty years. Or, for the kids, school records, from wherever they went to school before they came here. Since they were here in the summer."

Samantha set up a new file on her computer. Glancing at Abigail, she said, "No time like now…so begin at the very beginning, and this time I'll write it down."

Now there was no going back.

***

When the front page full color story came out the following Wednesday, Abigail bought extra copies. Samantha had done an amazing job. Under the pictures of Emily, Christopher and Jenny, the headline said:

What happened to these people? A mother, and her two children, mysteriously vanished from Spookie thirty years ago this August…help us solve the mystery.

Samantha had gotten the facts straight and had woven the threads into an intriguing tapestry. The story made the Summers' family as real as if they'd been alive yesterday. She'd located photos of them, though they were only black and white. Emily had been a pretty woman, with light colored hair and large eyes, and her children had looked like her. Abigail cut their photos out of one of the copies and taped them on her refrigerator. Their haunted eyes watched her whenever she opened the fridge.

From the moment the newspaper story came out, the reaction was phenomenal. Everyone wanted to help solve the old mystery. Everyone had stories from that summer and wanted to be heard.

***

“The phone’s been ringing nonstop,” Samantha breathed, sitting in her cubicle, hands flying over her keyboard. “I’ve never had this kind of feedback to a story. It’s amazing!”

She stopped and rustled through a stack of papers. “Look at these letters from townspeople of what they were doing that summer. Get a load of these photos of Main Street, the police department. Here’s some of the July Fourth Celebration picnic that summer. Those clothes! Leisure suits and mini-skirts. Puka beads. All the guys had such long hair. Sideburns. The women with those teased up hairstyles or the younger ones with those tiny braids in their straight hair.

“And as coincidence would have it, there, in the crowd–see in the far right–is Emily and her two kids. It’s fantastic. Stella sent us a picture of her diner dated 1970. Look at that decor. All chrome, and Formica. Look at the way the customers looked…dresses for the women, and pastel colored shirts for the men.

“We have information, too. Memories of Emily, and her kids, and what people overheard, and saw, of the trouble they were having that summer. Some of the accidents that befell them.”

She handed a couple of letters to Abigail. “Here. Start reading the first batch. Take them home. There are some really interesting things in them. Emily had quite a few people who didn’t like her. Some woman–who said she’d heard it from another woman who’d heard it from a guard at the jail–wrote to tell us Sheriff Cal Brewster, Mearl’s father, was obsessed with Emily. He once had her falsely arrested, and put in jail for a night, because Emily wouldn't go out with him. Imagine that? Emily claimed he tried to rape her that night and suddenly all charges were dropped, on both sides. That Cal Brewster was no credit to the police department, I'd say. Later, from what I've learned, he was involved in other scandals, and was practically forced to resign early. He's dead now, or I'd go have a little talk with him. He might have had something to do with Emily's disappearance.

"You know," Samantha stopped, looking directly at her, her voice going soft, "Emily had some enemies in this town. I hope none of them resent you for bringing her up again. Hmm, I hadn't thought of that before." Samantha shook her head, and then seemed to let her concerns go. "But wow, this is going to be some series of stories."

Abigail read a few letters before she left. Some were cranks. A few were advice to let the past lie undisturbed. Some wanted their houses drawn, yet many wanted to contribute a snippet of the past and see their name in print.

Outside the skies were cloudy, the smell of rain heavy, but the heat was relentless. She stopped in at Stella's for something cold and creamy. When she walked in, half the people waved, acknowledging her. They gave her big smiles and okay signs. They'd read the story.

Frank was glaring at her from a booth. "You went and did it, didn't you…painted a target on your forehead? You shouldn't have run that story. You've put yourself in danger."

"How can running a story, about something

which happened so long ago, hurt me?" She slid in across from him. She was bluffing. For the first time, after hearing what Samantha had said, and now Frank, she was a little worried. What if Emily, and the kids, had disappeared because something awful had happened to them? What if murder was involved and the killer was still living in town? Frank seemed to read her mind.

"Worse scenario? Those three met foul play. Murder. What about that break-in at your house? A killer could be out there, and if he or she is…you dredging it up again might piss him or her off."

"It was *thirty years* ago, Frank."

"Time doesn't matter, when it comes to murder. There's no time limit. Guilty thirty years ago is the same as guilty last week. When I was a rookie homicide detective, I was partnered with an officer, Henry McRaney, who was retiring in six months. He had this old case, from early in his career, he'd been unable to crack, and unable to let go of. It was the killing of a young girl twenty-seven years before, committed with a jewel-handled knife found on the scene. McRaney was obsessed with finding the girl's murderer before he retired. We gave it one last shot. We revisited the earlier suspects. The ones still alive anyway. We retraced all the leads. Everything we could think of. After all that time.

"I was a weapon collector, even back then, and from the photos, I'd noticed the murder knife was a rare variety usually sold in sets of two. McRaney and I stumbled upon the other knife in a knife collection, which belonged to the dead girl's cousin, during our follow up. Turns out, as a teenager, he'd killed her with one of the two knives and kept the other knife as a sort of trophy. After so many years, sure he was safe from the law, he put it on display in a glass case in his house. Big mistake.

"We surprised him with our visit, and he didn't have time to hide the knife. McRaney made a mistake in judgment, asked to see the knife, and that was the end of it. The killer knew he was caught. He was married, with three kids, and he wanted to protect the new life he'd created. He found out McRaney was going to accuse him of the old murder, he came after him, and killed him.

"The guy was later caught and executed for his crimes. But McRaney was still dead. So don't tell me the passage of time makes a difference. Twenty or thirty years after their crimes, murderers are still as dangerous as poisonous snakes. You kick at them; they'll bite you." There was genuine concern in his voice.

"Sorry about McRaney." Abigail touched his arm. "And, it didn't occur to me I would be endangering myself when I started this. The story can't be taken back. I'll be careful from now on, that's all. Though I don't believe–*if* they were murdered–that the killer stayed in town. If he were smart, it makes sense he'd be long gone."

"He might be gone. He might not. He could be anybody, even a woman. I've known women murderers who'd make your eyes change color. Women can have motives, too, you know, same as men. Jealousy is a prime one. A lot of women were jealous of Emily. And, who ever said murderers were smart? That's not always the case. They sometimes make mistakes, small ones, and that is how they're caught. As I said before, you better be careful."

Abigail nodded. "Always."

The police, and the private investigator she'd hired, had never found Joel's murderer, and she wondered if they ever would. Only if the killer made a mistake? That dismayed her.

Stella bustled over and asked her, "What can I get you, sweetie?"

"Tuna fish sandwich and a chocolate malt, thank you."

Stella nodded. She wrote the order down. "I saw that story in the newspaper. You looked real good in front of your house." She grinned, plunking down beside her. "I sent some old stuff in on the diner myself."

"I know, I saw them. Great photos. So this place was called the Main Street Diner in those days, huh?"

"Yep. My husband, Ernest, owned it then. I was a waitress. He was a great cook, and could gab with the best of them, but he was a lousy husband. We were married for twenty-five years before he kicked the bucket. By the way, about Emily Summers? I knew her, she even worked here for a while, to make money after her divorce, so she could go to art school in the fall."

"That's right, someone else mentioned she wanted to go to art school." Abigail shot a look at Frank, as he played with the sugar container.

"Anyway," Stella continued, "I remember a

strange incident which might be of interest, but thought I'd give it straight to you, instead of the newspaper. It was that awful summer of 1970. It was August. Steamy and humid.

"Her parents had left Emily the house so she'd come back to town. I was surprised because she was the younger child. Both her parents, Mary and Robert, had died within a few weeks of each other the year before. Edna had been living with the parents for a while, before that, to take care of them. Ha, it seemed to me to be the other way around. Edna had trouble holding a job. She was always getting sick. Sick in the head, is what I said. That Edna was a misfit, a parasite, from the word go.

"Well, Emily, and her kids, had been in town all summer. One day they were in here having ice cream and this man comes busting in. Big burly brut, with a foul mouth. He and Emily have this horrendous fight, in front of all of us, him screaming and yelling, and he yanks her from her chair, as if he's going to drag her off. The kids are wailing and crying. A couple of the locals, being nice fellows, and eager to get on Emily's good side, hauled the guy out the door, and tossed him in the street. Most excitement we'd had around here all year. Next day, Emily tells me the guy was her ex-husband."

"Wait a minute," Frank interrupted. "My friend, Sam, said that when he talked to Emily's ex-husband, the guy stated that he hadn't seen his wife, or kids, at all that summer. Stella, are you sure it was that particular summer? 1970?"

"Pretty sure. It was a long time ago. But, it

was one of those things you don't forget. Sticks in my mind because Emily, and her kids, vamoosed–or disappeared–two weeks later. I thought it was partly because of what happened that day. Emily was scared of her ex. When they'd been married, he'd regularly beaten her up, put her in the hospital a few times with broken bones, she'd confessed to me once. She came home to escape from him."

"Then her ex-husband, Todd Brown, lied," Frank said. "Why is the question."

"He was afraid of being a suspect, if Emily turned up a victim of a crime." Abigail gave him the answer.

"Yep, Todd Brown was Emily's ex-husband's name. I remember, now." Stella got up. "I'll go put your order in, Abigail."

Hanging his head mockingly, Frank muttered, "The fun's only beginning. You'll have every crackpot, and lonely old person, banging on your door with an Emily Summers' story. Wait and see. You're going to be a very busy lady. Your anonymity is gone forever."

An elderly man, in a straw hat, and with hearing aids in his ears, hobbled over and gave them another story about the two Summers' children. He also provided a recollection about how the children used to roller skate down the sidewalks of Main Street, singing Beatle songs, like two wild banshees.

Frank grinned widely at her behind the guy's back the whole time. "You're a celebrity. Don't let it go to your head," he teased her afterwards.

She promised it wouldn't.

Frank followed her to her house to take a look at Evelyn Vogt's cat picture, and go through the newspaper's letters. Not finding anything he thought was important in them, he was disappointed, but he liked the drawing she was working on. "Cute cat. Looks real. And those lilacs. Very pretty. The old lady's going to go daffy over it.

"How about you do a portrait of my dogs, on my porch, with the cabin behind them?"

"Sure, as soon as I finish Evelyn's picture."

After Frank drove away, Abigail read through the remainder of the letters. Then she spent time on Evelyn's cat picture.

In the evening, she sat on her porch swing and played with Snowball, reflecting over what she'd read. The letters had made her cry. Those poor kids had had such a measly existence. Earlier, she'd had a string of phone calls about the article. Some of the information was helpful, but none of it, like the letters, had been pertinent to solving the riddle of where the three had gone. No one seemed to know that.

The pounding, at her door, came after two in the morning. She climbed out of bed, slipped on a robe, and on the way, grabbed the wooden club. Her visitor could be an enemy as well as a friend.

It was Myrtle.

"What are you doing out here in the middle of the night, Myrtle?" Abigail pulled her inside.

The old woman was in a tizzy, her hair going every which way, and her face dirt smeared, her clothes disheveled. She was dressed more for winter than summer. She had a raggedy heavy coat on, a black sock cap, and mittens. It had to be at least eighty degrees outside. "I remembered something really important about Emily for you. I saw the story in the paper," she exhaled breathlessly.

"I thought you never went out after dark because of the ghosts?" Abigail reminded her, sleepily.

"Ghosts can't travel when there's a full moon. Moonlight scares them. Too bright."

"And there's a full moon tonight?"

Myrtle rolled her eyes, moaning. "Behind the clouds, yes. I ran the whole way. I'm pooped."

"Then, come in and sit down. How about taking that coat off? It's warm inside." With Abigail's help Myrtle shed her winter clothes, and flopped onto the sofa. Abigail waited for her to talk.

"I know where that diary of Jenny's could be hidden. I was checking my financial portfolio on the Internet tonight and–whoa." She lightly slapped her forehead. "It came to me. I had to tell you. Show you. When you get my age, dearie, you can't count on tomorrow coming, if you know what I mean."

"Where's the diary?"

"The tree house. I should have remembered that before. I think, I know where it is." She stood up. "Give me something to eat, then grab a flashlight, and I'll take you there."

Something to eat? "You'll take me to the tree house…now? In the middle of the night?"

"Sure. I can't come back tomorrow. I got a

bus trip, to the casinos in Las Vegas, with my ladies' group, and won't be back for a week. Two weeks, if I'm on a winning streak." She grinned. Her teeth were as dirty as her face.

The woman's habits were odd. Yet, if she knew where that tree house was, it was worth the night journey. "What do you want to eat?"

"Cheese sandwich. Chocolate milk."

After the snack, they took off into the night woods with two flashlights. Abigail felt as if she were in some weird dream. Was she actually doing this? She was as nuts as Myrtle, running around with flashlights, chasing ghosts in the dark, looking for some lost children's tree house. They tramped through the trees and brush, Myrtle chattering the entire trip; and Abigail, behind her, tripping over her own feet. Myrtle was a tiny thing with short legs, a short stride, or Abigail would never have been able to keep up. The old lady was a rocket with legs.

"I got this theory, dearie," Myrtle yapped back at her. "I can't prove it, but I'd stake my mutual funds on it. Edna murdered her parents."

Abigail nearly walked into a tree. "She did what?"

"I was around, I should know. She poisoned Mary and Robert, like she used to poison my sister's animals. That's what happened, I'd bet. She wanted them out of the way, wanted their money, and she wanted the house. Plain and simple. They were sick of her free loading, and were ready to kick her butt out. She frightened them. Mary called me one night to ask my advice. She'd been sick all week, throwing up, and her husband was sick, too. She'd seen Edna putting something in her tea. I told her to call the police. She didn't. She died two days later. I tried to tell people what was going on, but no one wanted to believe me. That stupid Sheriff Cal again. Mary had been sick a long time, with one ailment or another, so her dying didn't raise eyebrows. No one cares when an old person dies. Robert lived a little longer. Edna was clever not to kill him off too quickly after Mary's death. Edna was a lot of things, but she wasn't as stupid as most people believed.

"Edna thought she was home free. Then, the will was read, and Emily and her kids came back to claim what was theirs. Mary and Robert left the house and the money to their younger daughter. After all she'd done to get her inheritance, what a laugh on old Edna. Then, to put salt on the wound, Emily decided to sell the house, take the money, and start a new life somewhere far away. Edna would have gotten zip. Boy, was she upset.

"I never pushed it with the police, because I had no proof, and Sheriff Cal wouldn't have believed me no way. He was as dumb as a rock; had about as much insight as a carrot."

"Did Emily suspect her sister had poisoned their parents?"

"I don't know about that. Emily was wary of her older sister, that's for sure. One of the reasons she was selling out and moving away. Along with her men problems, there were some other bad things going on that summer for her. Emily had more than enough reasons to skedaddle. But, I bet the money was the reason Emily's ex-husband wanted his wife and kids back so bad."

"He did?"

"Yep, he was sneaking in town here all the time trying to get Emily to go back with him." Myrtle was more talkative than Abigail could stand for that time of night. She attempted to keep track of the direction they were traveling. They'd left the house from the rear door and had gone left. She paused, looked over her shoulder, through the trees, for the second time. The first time, she'd been able to see the lights from her kitchen. This time all was blackness. She was lost.

"How much farther, Myrtle?"

"Almost there. I can navigate these woods in the dark because I've walked through them my whole life. I know every inch of them. I sleep out here sometimes."

"Aren't you afraid of wild animals? The ghosts?" Was all Abigail could think of to say, and she couldn't keep from smiling.

"There are coyotes out here mostly, or sometimes wild dogs. A fire keeps them, and sometimes the ghosts, away–or a big stick." Myrtle chuckled. "Here we are." Myrtle halted and Abigail practically bowled the woman over.

They were under a monstrous tree with a car-sized trunk. The moon had freed itself from the clouds and the woods were bathed in light. Abigail looked up. "I don't see anything."

"It's up there all right. Covered in leaves and branches. After thirty years, there's not much left. A platform on the lower branch about seven feet off the ground." The old woman was huffing and puffing. "I got you here…what you do now is up to you."

It'd be useless to search before daylight. Yet, she'd never find her way out here again in the morning. She should have left breadcrumbs. "It's going to be hard to find the diary in the dark, Myrtle, even with a flashlight. Any idea where we should start? Myrtle?" No answer.

Abigail moved her flashlight around, seeing only trees. She was alone. Now where had that woman gone to now? Martha was right, she was unreliable. Nuts. Just wait until she saw that old so-and-so again. She sighed. It wasn't as if Myrtle had left her in a blizzard or anything. She was safe enough. If a wild animal attacked her, well, she had the flashlight. She'd clobber it. Morning would come soon; in two or three hours, by her guess.

Sliding down against the trunk of the tree, Abigail switched off the flashlight. No choice but to wait. The clouds were moving, her eyes slowly adjusting to the pale light, when the moon peeked through. It was peaceful sitting there, a light breeze stroking her skin. The moon a thoughtful face above her. The twins had skipped across this ground, climbed this tree, and dreamed their dreams so long ago; beneath a moon like the one above. Decades ago. Just yesterday.

Closing her eyes, a moment later, she was opening them to morning. After stretching to get the kinks out of her stiff body, she climbed up into the tree. It'd been a long time since she'd done that. She was out of practice, and her muscles let her know it.

The platform, as Myrtle had said, was there, though the planks were worn and splintered, with gaps missing. She hunted everywhere. She found no diary, no secret stash of notes, or left behind bag of cat's eye marbles. She found nothing. The police would have searched all this, she reasoned, squatting in the middle of the tree house ready to give up. Or would they? If they'd even known about it. If they'd even cared.

Where would a child have hid a diary? One of the boards seemed higher than the others. She got a stick and pried at it until it lifted.

There, squeezed into the narrow space, wrapped in a plastic bag, bound by rubber bands, was a tiny pink flowered book. She couldn't believe she'd found the diary. It'd been too easy. Climbing down, she retrieved the flashlight, looked around, and headed in the direction she thought home would be, yet a few feet later her face was in the grass.

A wooden grave marker had tripped her. Sticking straight out of the dirt, it was small, a sliver of wood with a name scratched on it. *Emily.*

"Oh, no," she moaned, staring at the name. The E looked like it had antlers on it and the y had a shelf on the bottom. Beside the first grave marker, covered in weeds and bramble, were others. The name Jenny carved on one and Christopher on the other.

She'd found Emily and her two children. No more speculating over what had happened to them. No more hoping they were safe living somewhere else. They'd been here all along, for over thirty years, beneath the dirt. That is, if there were bodies in those graves beneath her feet. She was filled with a dull sorrow. Poor Emily. She'd never gotten to go to college, or to be an artist. She'd never seen her children age, and have children of their own. Jenny and Christopher had never grown up, fallen in love; had lives of their own. None of them had had lives. They'd been here all the time, long dead and gone.

Abigail found her way home. It wasn't far. She got lost only once. She called Frank. He said he notify the sheriff.

And, within a half-hour, she had a house full of people.

Chapter 9

Abigail had a kitchen full of noisy people drinking coffee, and a yard full of the curious tracking back and forth from the tree house, debating over the graves she'd discovered.

The newspaper story, on the Summers family, had opened her life and everything in it, to the townspeople. Whatever new developments, she discovered in their disappearance, were the town's business now, too. She didn't know how the news had spread so quickly, but it had. She'd called Frank, and then Samantha, so she could get photos of the graves. She'd also called the police to ask a few questions of her own, but had no idea how the other people, Martha included, who'd showed up at her house, had learned of the graves.

The sheriff was at the gravesite doing what he was good at, scratching his head, looking for clues, taking notes, and trying to figure out how he could get out of doing anything that smelled like work.

Abigail had snuck off to take a quick shower, put on clean clothes, before she'd led Frank to the gravesite.

"This feels like a wake," she said, staring at the people milling around, and feeling a heavy sense of loss. She hadn't actually known the people buried beneath the ground, but she'd come to feel a strange sort of bond with them. She mourned their senseless deaths.

"It is," Frank replied, his expression sad. "I can't believe they've been dead all these years. I didn't even know. I was too busy getting on with my new life in Chicago to bother. I didn't try hard enough, didn't look hard enough. What happened to them?" He seemed angry with himself. "And, why didn't I *know*?"

"How would you? Frank, it's not your fault. You didn't look hard enough because you weren't absolutely sure a crime had been committed. Thirty years ago, *no one* looked hard enough for them. The sheriff at the time had a vendetta against Emily because she wouldn't date him. So he pretended to look for them, but sabotaged the effort. It might explain why the tree house, or the graves so deep in the woods, weren't discovered."

Frank stood above the graves for a long time. "All these years, no one knew they were here." She wasn't sure, but she thought she saw tears in his eyes. It was hard to tell, because a misty drizzle had begun falling. A rain which had come in suddenly with the people.

"Edna knew," Abigail mumbled. "She put those names on those grave markers, I'm sure of it. How could she have buried her own sister, niece, and nephew…hid it all those years…and not known who'd killed them? Unless, she'd killed them or been part of someone else killing them. How can a sister, an aunt, do that and live with herself?"

"People do awful things for money. Land. Security. Perhaps, Edna wanted the inheritance and the house more than she feared carrying the guilt–or maybe she was mentally unstable as some people believed. Murderers don't follow our rules. Are you so sure she was a willing participant in their deaths? She might have been scared into it, or found them dead, and buried them after the fact. Someone else may have done it, and Edna never knew who or why."

"Then why didn't she report it to the police?" Abigail wanted to know.

"Good point. She must have had her reasons. Maybe, she was afraid of Cal Brewster, or something else to do with what's in the red ledger book. The blackmail might figure into it somehow. I just don't know."

She'd told Frank about Myrtle's theory that Edna might have poisoned her parents, and he'd told Sheriff Mearl. "He should have the parents' bodies, as well as the three out there, exhumed. I don't know if he will, though. The crime, the remains, are decades old. DNA testing might be able to yet detect poison, if it'd been administered long term. If there are truly bodies in those graves, there could have been three murders…even five. Someone had to kill them. Edna's now a suspect."

"Or Cal Brewster…or the ex-husband, or the mysterious boyfriend, or…a couple of others." She hadn't told Frank, or anyone, she'd found Jenny's diary. She said Myrtle, and she, had been searching for the tree house and had found the graves by accident. Abigail had stashed the diary away, determined to read it first. Only then would she reveal she had it and hand it over to the sheriff.

Samantha had left with her grave and tree house photos. She was going to use them in the next article installment. Abigail had been surprised she was continuing the stories.

"Of course. It's an even bigger story now. We have three graves. If there are really bodies under them–who killed them? I can't stop the series now. The publisher wants more. People want more."

"Don't they always." Frank hadn't been happy. He still believed Abigail was in danger.

After the crowds had thinned out, the sheriff remained behind with Martha and Frank to ask more questions. Abigail wondered if he knew his father had also had a thing for Emily.

"Sheriff," Frank demanded, "are you going to exhume the bodies and have the state forensic guys run some tests on them? Edna's parents too?"

"Guess I'm going to have to. With all this publicity. It wouldn't look like I was doing my job if I didn't, now would it? We'll dig 'em up, let the forensics crew have a go at them–not that I can see much sense in it. The bodies been in the ground thirty years. No one's missed them. If Edna killed them, she's not around to stand trial, is she? So what's the sense?" The sheriff's eyes barely concealed his scorn. If he'd had his way, the graves would have been left untouched. Finding them all these years later made the department look bad. A terrible crime had been committed, and the local police hadn't had a clue it had. Now, it would be all over the newspapers.

"Justice," Frank snapped, "that's what."

"I can't promise how quickly we can get the results. Could take weeks. It won't be a top priority.

Not a crime this old." Then, the sheriff turned to Abigail. "Myrtle said she'd be gone how long?"

"A week or two." She'd given him the other details of Myrtle's trip earlier.

"I'll make a couple of calls. See if I can track her down. I have some questions for her."

Abigail expected he did.

When the sheriff departed, Martha, Frank and Abigail wandered out on the front porch. The rain was heavier and the day had become a gray shroud for the morning. They watched the rain fall.

"Girl, ever since you came to town, you've sure stirred things up." Martha was gently pushing the swing with her feet, a piece of toast Abigail had fixed her going into her mouth, a mug of coffee balanced in her other hand. "You just can't let sleeping ghosts sleep, or lost graves stay lost, can you?"

"No one could, if those ghosts kept slipping a person notes."

Frank was sitting on the step below them; getting wet, though he didn't seem to care. Since they'd come out on the porch, he'd been unusually quiet.

Martha sipped her coffee. "Do you two think Edna killed those three back there in the woods? I mean, I knew the old woman and she was…weird. Like half the people in this town. But I never would have guessed she was a murderess. She didn't look, or act, like one."

"Not many murderers do." Frank broke his silence, his arms crossed and resting on his knees. "About ten years ago, in Chicago, there was this man, couldn't have weighed more than ninety pounds, bald with glasses, and as ancient as a rock. He lived by himself in a mausoleum of a house with a baby grand piano he could play like nobody's business. There were dead plants everywhere. It was downright creepy. You couldn't walk through the house, there were so many dried up ivies and potted trees. I asked him why they were dead. He simply replied he liked them like that. To him, they were beautiful. That should have been a big tip off." Frank chuckled softly.

"A neighbor turned the man in because he'd seen him killing dogs, and cats, and burying them in his garden in the middle of the day. Anyway, my partner and I called on him, and had a chat about it. At first, he appeared sweet and harmless. He sprouted poetry from memory, and played us Mozart on the piano. He mentioned a son, a couple of grandkids. He served us tea, and cupcakes.

"But, the old guy reacted so violently to our animal inquiries, I knew there was more to it. We got permission to dig up his garden, and, low and behold, turned out he hadn't only butchered, and buried, animals in his garden, but people, too. Seven of them."

"You're kidding!" Martha was glued to the conversation. "Who were the victims?"

"Salesmen. I should say salespeople. Men and women. Anyone who'd knocked on his front door over the years, trying to sell him something, or anyone whose looks, or attitude, he didn't care for. He'd invite them in and–boom–hit them over the head, with a baseball bat, from behind. As many times as it took to kill them. Then, because he was a frail slip of a man, he'd cut them up into moveable pieces, with his chainsaw, and bury them out in the garden."

"Why did he do such horrible things?" Abigail shuddered, eyes on the rain a few feet away.

"We never got the answer. First night, after he was arrested, he died in his cell of a heart attack. We never found out anything, other than what he'd said when we'd taken him into custody."

"Which was?"

"He didn't appreciate pesky people banging at his door, trying to sell him crap he didn't need. He was on a fixed income." Those were his words. So he killed them. It'd been going on for ten years or more."

"Good thing you and your partner were cops, or you might have also ended up in that garden," Abigail threw in. "And, how was it no one ever caught on all those years…until the dead animals?"

"Because, he was smart enough to bury the people he killed at night. He only buried the animals during the day. People don't see what's in front of their eyes sometimes. That's how criminals get away with what they do."

"Okay," Martha conceded. "So, what you're saying is Edna could have killed her own sister, and the kids. Who knows anyone really, is that what you're telling us?"

"You got it." Snowball had jumped into Frank's lap. He petted the cat, then she scampered off into the rain. "Kitten's grown like crazy," he remarked. “Doesn’t look anything like that mud ball I brought to your door that stormy night.”

“Yeah, I can’t get rid of her. I tried. She loves water, and sneaks in the bathroom when I’m taking a bath, jumps right in with me. I have to fish her out quickly, because I like hot baths, and she starts yowling right away. When I wash dishes, she plops into the dishwater, soap suds and all. I’m always rescuing her. If I don’t feed her by a certain time, she bites me on the ankle until I do.”

Frank laughed. “No worse than my dogs. They’ll grab their dog food bag, and drag it–all twenty-five pounds–right to my feet. Hint. Feed us now.”

“Abigail?” Martha reached over and tapped Abigail’s knee. “I wanted to tell you, again, how much I love your watercolor of my house. The picture’s hanging in my downstairs living room. I kept it in my office a few days, before it was framed, and everyone who saw it complimented it, and wanted your telephone number. You did a great job. Hopefully, you’ll get more business from it.”

“I hope so, too,” Abigail said. “My savings will only stretch so far, as frugal as I am, and if I can’t make money freelancing, eventually I’ll have to look for a real job. The very thought of going back to advertising depresses me. I’d scream if I had to do one more newspaper ad.”

“Right now, you won’t have to. My picture’s next,” Frank reminded her. “I’ll pay cash.”

“Well, being a person on the clock, as you two aren’t, I’d better get in to work, rain or no.” Martha left the swing. “I need to sell a house today, or a garage. Something. I'll see you both later." Then she was driving away in her car, waving through the window.

Abigail waited for Frank to leave, but he continued to sit on her porch steps. She wanted to read the diary, didn't want to be inhospitable, but he didn't act as if he wanted to leave.

"I was thinking, Abby," he muttered after a few minutes. "If you really want to find out who killed Emily, and her kids, why don't you take a trip with me to Chicago? We'll talk to someone who might shed some light on what happened thirty summers ago. One of the only ones left who can. Todd Brown, Emily's ex-husband. He lives four hours away and we can do it in a day, if we leave early."

She didn't have to think about it long. "When do you want to go? We'll split the gas."

"Tomorrow? And, my treat. It'll be a field trip. Get me out of the house cause I'm growing roots. It'll be like old times, investigating something again. Besides, I'd like to know the truth as much as you do. I also know all the good truck stops along the way, with the best food, and souvenirs."

"You got a deal. After this last week, I'm ready for a road trip. I can't think of anything better than traveling the highway looking for adventure, with a friend, and getting answers to our riddles to boot."

"We'll leave about nine a.m.? Being the weekend, there's a better chance of catching Brown at home."

"I'll be ready."

Frank came to his feet, and looked at her. "I've been dying to see this new movie with Tom Hanks. Stanley, the next town over, has a theater with eight screens, and mouth-watering popcorn. I hate to go alone. Would you go with me tonight, Abby? We could get a pizza afterwards. We'd be just friends going to a movie together."

She thought of saying no, then changed her mind. She was lonely and tired of it. Frank was lonely. She, of all people, knew what it was like being one left over from a pair. And, he was helping her to solve her mystery.

"Sounds fun, Frank. I'd love to. You're right, it's no fun going alone. There's no one to share the buttered popcorn with. You pick up weirdos. They never want to discuss the film. Safer to go with an ex-police officer. Weirdos never bother a woman with a cop beside her."

"There should be a showing around seven or so," Frank said. "So I'll see you around six?"

She nodded. Frank left whistling. Abigail went straight to where she'd hidden Jenny's diary. She read it sitting on the sofa. It didn't take long. The entries began on June 18, and ended, months later, on August 13, 1970. It was in cursive, with the handwriting neater, as if the child had been trying hard to make it pretty. Most of the pages were filled with little girl fluff. What she was thinking, or feeling, about things. Who, and what, she liked, what she and her brother did on their bike rides, and thoughts on being a kid enjoying summer vacation. In the beginning, the entries were carefree and happy, but as the summer went on, and the adult world intruded, they became darker. Some of them, misspellings and all, made Abigail smile, while others made her sad.

June 18

Today was Chris and mine's 10th birthday! Had a party, ice cream and cake. I got this neat diary, a box of chalk pastels, colored pencils, sketch pads and a huge bag of cashews (my favorite) and a Polaroid camera. Chris got the same. Except he got a put-together airplane instead of a camera. Dad sent us bicycles but couldn't come because he had to work. I miss him. I hate divorces.

June 23

Mom has a new boyfriend. Saw him today while looking out my window. Don't like HIM. He drinks too much and he pushes Mom around like Dad used to and she takes it. He is a bad man. I told Mom but she won't listen. Mom says we can't tell nobody who he is. It is a secret. Why? She won't say. Chris doesn't like HIM either. Once Chris saw HIM hit her and Chris kicked him and ran home. HE was so mad.

June 29

Aunt Edna is a wicked witch. She locked Chris in the dark basement all nite (without supper) because he sassed her. I snuck food down to him after she went to bed and she caught me, shook me and I ran away to Mrs. Vogt's house. Mom was out all nite with that man again. I am another writing a letter to Dad to come get us. Aunt Edna is mean and she and Mom fight all the time over this money they keep talking about. What money? Mom, Chris and me are so broke.

July 4

the picnic and fireworks were great. Ate tons of cotton candy. Chris and I rode the Ferris Wheel and the Whip and spent all our allowance, empty soda bottle money and money we found along the road on the way to Tinker's General Store whenever we bought penny candy. Mr. Mason asked me about Mom, but I wouldn't answer his questions.

The sheriff followed us home that night pestering Mom again. But she wouldn't even talk to him. Mom told me that his wife would break her face if she did. I don't trust the sheriff. I don't tell Mom this, but lots of nights he watches our house in his squad car. Creepy. Good thing not all police are as crooked as he is. There is one that is real nice. He brings us food. Plays with Chris and me. Talks nice to Mom.

July 14

Someone tried to run over Chris when he was on his bike. With a car. Chris had to go to the emergency room to have stitches. Mom cried and said it was because of her. I don't know what she means. Mom let us call Dad and he said he was really coming this time. He promised.

August 3

Dad came and had a terrible fight with Mom in the diner, and Dad left town right away, didn't even say goodbye to us. Chris hid in the tree house all nite and never came home. Next day Mom had a black eye and a chipped tooth. Bruises. I think her boyfriend did it, but Chris said it was the sheriff. Mom said Dad did it. Don't believe that. I think Mom was fibbing.

August 9

Mom says we're going to sell the house and move far away from here and start all over where no one will find us. Mom and Aunt Edna screamed at each other all nite. Chris threw up. He's sick.

August 10

Mom didn't come home last night and Aunt Edna is acting very strange. I snuck on the phone and called Dad, but he wasn't there. Chris is still sick.

August 13

I am sick, too, now. My stomach hurts. I'm scared. Mom has been gone four days. I asked Aunt Edna where she was. Aunt Edna said she don't know. I think she does. The phone doesn't work. Maybe Aunt Edna didn't pay the bill. Now I cant call Dad or anybody. Chris hasn't left our room in three days and Aunt Edna won't get a doctor for him or me. Says we'll be fine sooner or later.

August 13 had been the final entry. Pages had been torn out after that date, and the rest were blank.

Who had been Emily's secret abusive boyfriend? What had happened with Emily and the sheriff? Where were those missing pages? And, was the Mr. Mason mentioned at the General Store, the same John Mason who owned the store now? Mason had told her to her face, that day in the store, he'd never known Emily, or her kids. Had he lied…and why?

Yet, it was what Abigail found, tucked in the last pages of the diary, which touched her most. They were faded black and white Polaroids of Emily, Chris, and Jenny, at the twin's birthday party, and at the Fourth of July picnic. They were blurry photos of smiling children on bikes, playing with their hula-hoops, and swinging on swings. There were pictures of their mom, smiling, and, someone who must have been Aunt Edna, scowling. She'd been a plain woman, and that was being kind. She'd looked like an old crone, even back then. Emily had been so pretty, with her long light hair, and her Cleopatra black-outlined eyes. Abigail didn't think she looked like her in the least.

Abigail reread the diary and laid it on the coffee table. Her mind churning over the glimpses of Jenny's life, and what they'd meant. The pictures were burned into her subconscious. She couldn't stop thinking about Emily, Jenny, and Christopher…these dead people who had taken over her life.

That night, at six, she was ready to go when Frank arrived. Dressed in jeans, a cotton top, and carrying a sweater because air-conditioned theaters were too cold for her, she met him on the porch, and the two climbed into his truck. She'd show the diary to Frank, later, after the movie.

She wanted to keep its contents, a piece of

the living past, secret, to herself, for a little bit longer.

The theater was fifteen minutes away. It'd been years since she'd been in one, without Joel. After buying their tickets, they were in line for popcorn, and soda, when Abigail glanced past her shoulder, and spied John Mason. He was dressed in tan slacks and shirt, and his silver hair was tucked under a blue baseball cap. Of all the people in the world to have to run into, she had to bump into him. Now of all times, after having just read his name in Jenny's diary–in an entry which made him a liar, if it was true. No one could say fate didn't have a sense of humor.

She glanced away, but he'd seen her, and bee-lined it over to her. Her skin flushed, as they made eye contact, and they exchanged the usual civilities. Frank gave her an amused look, because he could tell she didn't want to talk to the man. She'd told him how Mason flirted with her every time she saw him at the store, and how uncomfortable it made her.

"Imagine meeting you two here," John Mason exclaimed. His eyes on Abigail. "I'd thought you'd be home digging up the back yard, or something, looking for more messages from people long dead, or helping Ms. Westerly invent more nonsense about a woman who's probably living in retirement in Florida somewhere. Her kids both middle aged with kids of their own."

Abigail said nothing about the graves–not to Mason. He'd find out soon enough, but not from her. She felt uneasy being so close to him. Maybe, because he'd known Emily, and the kids, and had lied…maybe he'd been Emily's secret boyfriend, who knew. Now, there was a strange thought.

"I hardly think so, John," Frank spoke up. "This morning Abigail found all three of them."

Any pretense of casualness drained from Mason's expression. "Where?"

"Beneath their graves, in the woods, behind her house. Read all about it, and about the notes and stuff, Abby's discovered hidden in her home, in the next episode of the Weekly Journal's Emily Summers' saga on Wednesday."

Mason looked at Abigail, his face unreadable. Some people didn't appreciate digging up anything which might make their town look bad. Mason was one of those. Something unpleasant flickered behind the man's eyes. Abigail wondered what he was thinking. He brusquely excused himself, with an ingratiating smile, pleading he had to find a good seat, and practically sprinted into the darkened auditorium.

"Well, that was rude." Frank handed her a soda and a carton of popcorn.

"Frank, how well do you know Mason?" she probed.

"I've known him most of my life, but I don't know him at all. He's that kind of an odd fellow. More so since his divorce, which was way messy. No surprise, his marriage was even messier, and his divorce left him bitter. He's alienated from his kids. I think he has two of them. They moved far away; probably just to get away from him. The store is, and has always been, his life. Profit is his god. He smiled at you, Abigail. Mason smiling. That's unusual."

She would have asked more questions, but the movie had started, and they could talk afterwards. So they went in search of seats.

***

"That was a good movie, wasn't it?" Frank made conversation later in a restaurant as they shared a pizza and soda. They'd almost run into Mason again on the way out of the theater. Abigail saw his blue cap bobbing out ahead of them in the crowd, and purposely made Frank slow down until she was sure the man was gone. She didn't want to run into him again. Not that night.

"Very good. That scene on the ocean with the whale was amazing. That deflated volleyball, Wilson, was a cute touch. Yuck, but that tooth pulling part was gross," she summed the movie up.

"How do you know? You hid your eyes. I tried to imagine what I'd have done if I'd been him stranded on that island. Alone. I believe, I'd do about the same. Just thinking about it gives me the willies. It makes you appreciate the life you have, a movie like that, and how important your family and friends are."

They finished raving about the film, and Abigail confessed to finding Jenny's diary. She revealed some of what she'd read in it. "Pages had been torn out and the entries ended in mid-August of the summer of 1970."

"And you've known about this diary since this morning and are just telling me about it now?"

Abigail nodded.

"I knew Sheriff Cal had a thing for her. I worked for the guy. It was easy to see. A lot of men had designs on Emily. She was a beautiful, available woman," Frank spoke softly, but she had the impression he was holding something back. "I just didn't know someone was abusing her. I never saw that black eye or the broken tooth. But, in my defense, I was gone a lot that last part of the summer, trying to get the job in Chicago, and then making arrangements for the move. I was very busy." She could almost feel his guilt. "I never had a clue someone was intentionally hurting her and the kids, or I would have stopped it. I never saw any of it, though, so what kind of cop was I?"

"You were a young one, just learning human nature and your job," Abigail said, pushing away from the table. The pizza had been delicious, the movie diverting, and her company for the evening stimulating. It was hard to dwell on sadder things. Maybe, as Martha had said that morning, she was too involved in this Summers' mystery. It had nothing to do with her or her life. It really was none of her business. Why was she so involved with something which had happened so long ago? She wished she knew.

Frank checked his watch. "You ready to go? Early start tomorrow, if we're going to catch Brown. Also, I can't wait to have a look at that diary."

"I'm ready." She watched Frank leave a generous tip on the table, and afterwards he ushered her out the door.

***

The truck's headlights shone on the front porch as they pulled into her driveway. The front door of her house was ajar. The lights she'd left on in the house spilled through the opening and out into the yard.

"Oh, no, not again. I know I shut, and locked, that door before we left." Abigail sighed. She'd put regular locks on her doors after the first break-in. "I guess I'm going to have to put super sturdy dead bolts on, or get a whole house alarm system." She knew the drill and let Frank enter the house first.

"It's safe," he yelled from inside. "There's no one in here. Again." But, unlike the previous time, nothing appeared touched or out of place. The house was as she'd left it. Snowball, a puddle of white, was sleeping on the couch.

"False alarm," Frank announced, openly relieved. "You *must* have forgotten to lock the door and it just slipped open. Old doors do that sometimes. I'll have a look at it before I head home."

"No, it's not exactly a false alarm." Abigail was standing in front of the coffee table. "The diary's gone. I left it right here on the table. It's not here now."

"Damn," Frank said. "I really wanted to read it, even though earlier you summarized everything in it. How about the ledger, is it missing as well?"

She went out of the room and returned with the ledger. "No. I hid it somewhere safe days ago. They didn't find it. But it's all I have left. Besides the diary, the messages from the children are gone as well. I had them on my dresser in a large envelope. Nothing else is missing or disturbed."

"Damn," Frank whispered again.

"You're right. There's someone who doesn't want us to learn anything more about the Summers, or what happened to them. And, unless a ghost floated in here and took those items, it was someone very much alive. What I'd like to know is, how were they aware the house was empty?"

"They might have had it staked out. They saw us leave." Their eyes met and Frank's misgivings didn't have to be put into words. He squeezed her hand for a moment, as reassurance, then released it.

"I really will have to be more careful." She gave him the ledger. "Here take this with you. It'll be safer at your place. Hide it well."

"I will." Frank produced a faint smile. "You still want to go tomorrow?"

"Of course," her voice firm. "No one's going to scare me off that easily. How about you?"

"Me, neither. I'll see you tomorrow morning. We'll get breakfast on the way."

"Tomorrow at nine." Abigail walked Frank to the door, closed and locked it behind him. Then, she sat down at the kitchen table and wrote down every word, from memory, she could recall from Jenny's diary and the crayon notes, while they were fresh in her mind. If not the originals, at least, she'd have something to refer back to.

Chapter 10

"Oh, goodie, been a long time since I've been on a road trip." Frank was cheerful the next morning, lounging behind the wheel of his truck, as they moved down the highway. His baseball cap had the word POLICE on the front in small white letters. His long hair brushed his collar and he had a diamond stud in his ear. The earring was an unexpected touch, but it made him look more like a hippie than an ex-police officer, she'd teased. He'd laughed, saying she was showing her age talking about hippies.

A breeze fanned their faces from the open windows as summer fields and houses sped by. They'd stopped earlier at a pancake house and were two hours into their trip, worrying about the progress of their mystery as they'd begun to call it; reviewing what they'd discovered and what had occurred so far.

The graves. They'd been exhumed the afternoon before. They hadn't been empty. Three bodies, a woman and two children, wrapped and buried in blankets, had been in them. Until the forensic experts could examine them, the remains had been taken to the morgue. The medical examiner told Frank over the phone it definitely looked like there'd been foul play. They hadn't died of natural causes, that was for sure. It had to have been an accident–or murder. The medical examiner promised someone would get back to them as soon as they knew more.

They'd also been trying to figure out who might have broken into her house and taken the diary and the kids' notes.

"Someone who'd read the newspaper article and knew about the messages. They got the diary as a surprise bonus," Abigail groused.

"How would they have known to take it? That it was Jenny's?"

"Now that's a puzzle. It could have been someone who'd known Emily and her children, from the past, knew the diary existed and lucked out by coming across it on the coffee table." Frank threw Abigail a sharp look.

Her reflection in the windshield was distorted. She'd been relieved her house hadn't been trashed a second time, but the fact the diary had been taken bothered her. "How did Brown sound when you phoned and asked if we could speak to him about Emily and the kids?"

"Initially he refused, saying it was ancient history. He sounded cold. I broke the news we found their graves. He said he didn't care if they were dead. That they'd been dead for years to him anyway. I told him, if he didn't talk to us, he'd be talking to the police. We had evidence he'd been in Spookie the last month of their lives and he'd made a scene at the diner. He'd lied to Sam Cato. Lied to a police officer. It made Brown change his mind quick enough."

"I hope he's there when we arrive."

"If he runs, it'll tell us something, though fear often triggers the same response. Flight."

"Fear of being caught?" Abigail placed her fingers against the cool window glass.

"Or fear of being innocent but being accused of the crime anyway. Lots of innocent people run for it, and lots who didn't run are now behind bars. The system doesn't work for everyone, and sometimes if you're innocent or guilty doesn't make as much difference as how much influence or money you have for competent representation. I've seen that first hand. Being a cop gave me some immunity, but I've had nightmares of being an innocent arrested and locked up in prison for years for a crime I didn't commit. I've seen it happen. I can empathize.

"Brown did sound stunned when I said we'd found their remains, though murderers are good at fooling people. I've dealt with enough of them to know how well they can lie. He was surprised, but not upset, as if they'd been strangers to him and not family."

"Well, it has been thirty years. But for Brown not to have heard from, or been contacted by, the kids in all this time–and we know they used to call him–and not wonder what happened to them, does seem strange. Unless he was part of their deaths. Then the discovery of their graves would be an unpleasant shock," Abigail put her opinion in. "He'd be running scared."

"You got a good point there."

She was content to admire the passing scenery and listen to Frank rattle on about what the medical examiner might be able to determine from thirty year old bones. Murder, missing evidence, and dead bodies aside, she was otherwise in a good mood. Martha, and Mrs. Vogt, had paid generous amounts for their watercolor pictures. Tomorrow she would begin Frank's picture. She'd collected her old paintings to put in the general store and had ideas for new ones. Now she had hope she'd make it as a freelance artist, if she worked hard and lived simply. She didn't like the idea of dealing with Mason and his constant fawning. Oh, the things she did for her art…and for money.

At three o'clock they pulled up before a modest subdivision home with the name Brown on the mailbox. The grass needed cutting and one of the front windows was cracked. In the driveway was a twelve-year-old Buick, in need of a paint job and new tires. Apparently, Todd Brown hadn't gotten very far in life.

A man, bent with age and years, answered the door when Frank knocked. He could have been tall, it was hard to tell the way he was hunched over, but his puffy face and red-rimmed eyes gave away he was ill. His thin hair didn't look as if it'd been washed recently and the same for his clothes. There was the stink of cheap booze around him. She couldn't tell how old he was, but guessed he had to be over sixty. He looked eighty.

"Hello, I'm Frank Lester and this is my associate, Abigail Sutton." Frank put out a hand and the other man avoided taking it, retreating into the house so they could come inside. Frank had left his police cap on. Brown didn't know Frank was retired, and unless he asked, Frank had maintained, there was no need to tell him.

Brown hobbled past them and dropped his body into a worn chair. There was a television, with a blurry picture, and he turned down the volume with a remote. "Sit where you want." The sofa was stained and swayed-backed in the middle, but it was the only place to sit. So they sat.

Abigail couldn't help but feel sorry for the man in the chair across from her. He didn't look like a wife-beater, or a murderer, only a man who'd come to the end of his life and was living hand to mouth as many old people had to do. The inside of the house, drab and lightless, was as dismal as the outside. It needed a healthy cleaning. It was as if the person living there no longer cared.

"Do you live here alone?" Frank inquired of Brown once they were settled on the lumpy sofa.

"I do. Janet, my third wife, died two years ago of cancer. I've lived by myself since. I like it that way. Less hassle. If Janet wouldn't have died we'd most likely be divorced. All women are nags." He smiled, showing rotten teeth. "I have some charity broad who comes in a couple times a week, does shopping for me, picks up prescriptions, and dusts the house some. She's not much to look at, dumb as a cow, but she can drive and fetch. And I don't have to put up with any nagging. I have, er, ailments which make it hard for me to get out."

"Sorry to hear about your health, Mr. Brown." Frank was surveying the room, taking in everything, and trying to be as cordial as he could possibly stand to be. Brown wasn't very likable.

"Thanks. But that's life. Not much good, mostly bad." Brown's shoulders slumped. The man might have been handsome once, but ravages of time and booze had changed him into a face-sagging, speech-slurred man with his time running out. He didn't seem particularly happy they were there and Abigail began to feel uncomfortable. The house smelled. Brown smelled. She wanted to get their questions answered and get out. The sooner the better.

Brown didn't offer them anything to drink, or any pleasant conversation either. Sitting there glaring at them, he repositioned his legs, as if they ached. Abigail noticed an empty whiskey bottle on the floor beside the chair.

"You still drink the hard stuff?" Frank casually asked, as if he didn't already know the answer.

Brown's rheumy eyes mirrored a flash of animosity. "I was forced to be sober for a long time cause one day, drunk, I plowed into a family in another car and killed four of them." He didn't seem remorseful, just stated what he'd done. "To get and stay out of jail, hold on to that lousy job the state helped me find, I had to do what the court told me to. I had to go to AA. Stop drinking. For a while. But now, since I don't drive, don't have a job–I'm on disability–and don't got any harpy woman telling me not to drink…sure," he grinned, "I take a sip now, and again."

Abigail wondered if a whole bottle was his idea of a sip.

"Anyway, you came here to tell me you found Emily and the kids' bodies, right? I won't lie to you. I'm past caring. Emily left me a long time ago, a lifetime ago–her idea, not mine…I wasn't good enough for her. In the end, she wanted nothing to do with me. Those kids?" And, here for the first time, Brown seemed to soften a little. "They weren't bad kids, but I never helped raise them, and never saw them much after the divorce. I'm sorry they're dead, but what's it got to do with me? I didn't kill them. I even tried searching for them after that summer. I did." His face fell into a stubborn defensive look and a sarcastic smile twisted his mouth. "Never found 'em, though."

He shrugged. "And life went on. I went on. I thought they didn't want me to find them. You know, Emily hated me. She always was an uppity sort of woman." A past resentment in his eyes, he stared around the room, as if he were seeing things they couldn't. Ghosts, perhaps.

"I didn't kill them," he blurted the words out in a gruff voice. "If that's what you're thinking. I. Did. Not."

Frank pacified him. "We're not accusing you of killing them." Yet. "We're just asking questions, just trying to unravel what happened to them if we can."

Brown stared at Abigail. "Why is it so important to you?" He'd guessed she wasn't a cop. Ah, he wasn't as dull, and sick, as he acted.

The truth seemed to be her best route. So she explained about buying the house, finding the scraps of paper, the diary, and the photos. She told him about instigating the newspaper story, its repercussions; including the break-ins and finding the graves.

Brown sat there and listened, and Abigail thought she saw his hands shake, thought she glimpsed a glimmer of sadness in his hard eyes. For a brief moment. "I wouldn't have minded having one or two of those pictures you found. Pictures of kids make women feel sorry for ya. I got a couple of churchwomen who stop by once in a while and bring me things. They take me places I can't go to anymore on my own. I don't have any pictures of the brats. I lost them along the way. I've moved a lot." He repositioned his body in the chair and released a painful sigh. "Ah, I guess it doesn't matter no how. They're all dead anyway. They're no good to me. I could have used some help in my old age. A kid, or two, might have been nice…to take care of me, you know?"

Abigail stared. She'd rarely met someone as unsympathetic. She didn't need to know what Frank, sitting stiffly besides her, was thinking at that moment. He was probably ready to deck the guy.

"Yet, you visited them in August 1970, didn't you?" Frank pressed, not showing any emotion.

"Okay, I did. Sorry, I lied to your cop partner," Brown confessed. "I was afraid I'd be accused of something. Old reflex. And, yeah, I had a fight with Emily in the diner. I'd been drinking. I drank a lot in those days. I wanted her to get out of that town and come back to me. She was going to get that house. Money. I wanted my share. She wouldn't think of it." A snort. "She always was a selfish woman.

"What I could never understand was…she had this new boyfriend, and from what I heard, he was worse to her than I'd ever been. He was a drinker, too. I never met him, but I hated him.

"There he was getting what was mine. He was mean to my kids. I didn't go for that. He'd get drunk and push Emily, and them, around. Now Emily probably deserved it, with that mouth of hers, but he had no right to yell at my kids. I went down there to put him in his place, but Emily wouldn't tell me who he was, or where he lived; wouldn't leave and wouldn't let me take the kids with me. I guess, I got a little angry. I guess, I made a scene. Bad me.

"I didn't hurt her. The whole thing was blown way out of proportion. That nosy waitress and those nosy townspeople. Ha, Emily was probably dating half of those men who jumped up to get me off her." His hand plucked at his pant leg in a repetitive gesture. "Emily was wild as they come. Nah, I was never good enough for her. Never."

Abigail suspected Frank was boiling by then and probably wanted to hit Brown smack in the face, but he was behaving himself. She didn't think Brown remembered he was one of those men who'd known the real Emily. He probably didn't remember him at all. Good thing.

"Any idea who might have meant them harm then, Mr. Brown?" Frank asked. "Did Emily have any real enemies? She ever say anything to you about being stalked or threatened?"

"I don't know. It was so long ago," Brown

muttered as his empty eyes looked beyond them, maybe into the past. "Her sister, Edna, despised her and was jealous as all get out of her. I do remember that. Edna was mentally ill, if you ask me. The woman had tantrums, or episodes, or whatever you'd want to call them, where she'd see and talk to people who weren't there." He twirled his finger near his ear. "Edna was as nutty as a bed bug.

"It was Edna who swore Emily, and my kids, drove away in their car. Edna, who told me they were living somewhere else, that she'd been in touch with them, but Emily didn't want me to know where they were. Edna, who said Emily hated my guts, and wanted nothing more to do with me. I never liked that stupid woman. Edna would do anything to get what she wanted. She wanted the house, and inheritance money, Emily's parents had left. Jenny told me that over the telephone. Silly kid, yakked as much as her mother. Emily was going to sell everything. The house, too. She was going to move. Edna was the oldest and should have inherited, not Emily. I bet that made Edna furious."

"Anything else you can recall?" Frank's voice was firm, his eyes were flat. "Anything?"

There was a squinting of eyes and Brown spent a little time thinking. Then, "Ah, there was Emily's so-called stalker."

Abigail slid a sideward glance at Frank, who said, "I asked earlier if you knew of anyone stalking her and you said you didn't know."

"I forgot. I just remembered."

"The stalker?" She gently reminded Brown.

"Yeah. Someone was harassing Emily and

the kids. Now it's coming back to me. Chris was a victim of a hit and run, and he had to have stitches. I remember because I had to pay the hospital bill. Jenny said she was being followed, someone was scaring her, and there was vandalism. Rocks were thrown at windows; threats against them were left in the mailbox. The shed behind the house was burnt down. Their cat was found hanging dead from a tree in the backyard, and Emily's car brakes were tampered with. She had an accident with the kids. It really shook her up. She was really frightened."

No wonder she wanted to sell the house and leave, Abigail thought.

"She had no idea who this stalker was? No idea who was that mad at her, or for what?" Frank was fidgeting, as if he wanted to get the visit over with, and leave. Maybe the filth around them was making him sick, too.

"No, none at all. I don't have a clue, either, even now looking back. So long ago, it's all kind of fuzzy."

They didn't stay much longer. A few more questions, and when Brown pulled out a whiskey bottle and started pouring a drink, they wrapped the visit up and got out.

***

As they drove away, Frank mumbled, "He hasn't changed much. What a poor excuse for a human being. I don't blame Emily for leaving him. What I can't see is her ever being married to him and having two kids with him. Jenny and Christopher were sweet, smart, creative children. They were nothing like their father. Emily, no matter what he said, was a good woman. Another ten minutes in there, and I would have had him by the throat, sick old man or not." He pounded the steering wheel with the palm of his hand, his anger obvious.

"So," Abigail said. "We didn't learn much, did we?"

"Not so. We learned Edna was, along with being spitefully jealous, possibly mentally unbalanced…though I'd already suspected that, as young and green as I was in those days, just from knowing her. And…Emily definitely did have a serious stalker."

"You think Brown killed them?"

"Not sure. He had reasons and I sensed he was hiding something. He knows more than he was saying. He could just be clever, pretending to be sickly; pretending not to care. But, on the other hand, it's rare when a father kills his own children. But who knows? Men do awful things when they're drinking. We'll have to look into it. Murderers can be great actors.

"He might have lied about his not driving. I checked his car as we left and it has been driven lately, by someone. It might have been him. Then again, he lives four hours away, so it'd have been difficult breaking into your house either time, but someone did. Could have been someone else, for some other reason. It's another mystery, I don't have an answer to."

Abigail leaned against the seat, stretched her legs out, and closed her eyes. As they drove, Frank turned the radio on low and Bonnie Raitt's husky voice filled the truck's cab. When Abigail reopened her eyes again, it was dark outside. They were almost home.

"Let's get something to eat," Frank suggested. "There's a truck stop up ahead that's good."

"Sure. I could use a cheeseburger." Abigail smiled, still stretching.

At the restaurant over dessert, Frank asked, "How would you like to come over Saturday for a barbeque? Kyle's going to be home. You can meet him. Hey, we'll make a party of it. We'll invite Martha, Samantha, my sister and her husband. We'll sit around playing cards afterwards, and when we get tired of that, us old folks will migrate to the porch rockers. At night, the stars are beautiful from my front porch."

"Sounds like fun, Frank. Give me a time and I'll be there."

They were back on the road heading home when Frank asked, "Did you and Joel ever want kids, Abby?"

"We did, especially Joel. He loved kids. We tried for years. We just never got lucky."

"You still miss him, don't you?"

She hadn't wanted to talk about Joel, but at that moment, darkness at the windows and an understanding ear to listen, it spilled out. "Every day. For a long time I used to pretend aliens abducted him. That when he'd been out getting cigarettes, somewhere on the road he'd come across a spaceship and they'd taken him, car and all; and that someday they'd bring him back to me. I just had to wait. Be patient. It kept me from going crazy. Until I'd see one of those X-Files episodes which showed all the experiments aliens did on humans. Then, I'd freak out, and actually pray he'd merely vanished or ran off with a loose woman.

"Having him found dead the way he was, made it worse in a way. It made it all so final. At least, before, I could pretend he was still alive. Somewhere. Safe. On the other hand, finding him helped me accept things, remember the love we'd had for each other and the good times."

She let her voice go soft as she continued, "Because in the beginning, people told me, perhaps, I hadn't really known him. That he'd had a girlfriend and had run away with her. Maybe he had a gambling problem, or a drinking problem…on and on. They were trying to make me feel I was better off without him. Truth is, I did know Joel. We'd been sweethearts since high school. He was a carpenter. That's what he did for a living. He smoked too many cigarettes, talked too much, but he was a decent man; a dreamer and a loving husband. He didn't cheat, didn't believe in it, didn't drink much, and didn't gamble. I know he loved me and wouldn't have put me through that misery of his disappearance, if he could have helped it.

"Finding him dead cleared up all that uncertainty. I know, now, he didn't leave me willingly." She reclined against the seat, rubbed her eyes, and looked out the window at the night so she didn't have to look at Frank.

"The week Joel went missing, we were getting ready to break ground to build our dream house. I kept the land for years and only sold it after Joel was…found. I used the money to buy the Summers' house. Joel wouldn't get his dream but the money helped me get mine."

"Sorry, Abby. I shouldn't have brought Joel up. I know it's still too painful."

"It is. But, I don't mind talking about him to you, Frank. It's a relief. You understand because of Jolene. You know what it's like to lose someone you really loved. I think about him, dream about him. If I talked about him more, maybe I wouldn't be plagued by the nightmares. Thanks."

"Ah, you have nightmares, too, then?"

She turned her head and met his gaze for a moment. She nodded. "Sometimes. I'm always chasing him, but never catching him. He runs away from me. It's heartbreaking. I miss him in real life and in my dreams."

Frank didn't say anything to that, yet she got the feeling his dreams were pretty much like hers. It made her feel sorry for him, too.

She switched subjects. "Are your parents alive, Frank? I've never heard you mention them."

"No. My dad died about five years ago and my mom followed pretty soon after. They'd been married forever and neither one was any good without the other. They were simple, loving people. I had security and tenderness growing up. Along with missing Jolene, I miss them."

"Any other sisters or brothers besides, Louisa, the carpet selling lady?"

"A younger brother, Warren, who moved off to California after high school. He's one of those people who have a knack with computers and he's happily making the big bucks in the land of the sun. I don't see him much since our parents died."

Frank wanted to know about her family. "I have one live brother–one died years ago–and two sisters spread over the country. They're busy with their lives but we keep in touch by phone and e-mail. I see them a few times a year." They talked families for a while longer, comfortable, as if they'd known each other for years.

"Oh, by the way," Frank finally said, "I took more snapshots of my dogs on the porch. Shows the front of the cabin clearer than the last batch I gave you. They're in the glove compartment."

Abigail opened it and retrieved them as Frank turned off the highway and onto her two-lane road. They were getting close to her house and she was glad. It'd been a long day; her home and cat were calling to her…and so were the ghosts who lived in the graves beneath the tree house. They were like her family now.

Emily and her children were becoming more real each day. Abigail wondered if they were becoming too real. She could see their faces, hear their voices; almost feel their pain. Too real. And more than ever she wanted to know what had happened to them.

"Almost home, Abby," Frank's tired voice announced.

Yes, almost home, she thought, as she smiled at him in the dim light. *Home.*

Chapter 11

It was a hot day and Abigail craved ice cream. She'd come into town for her weekly shopping, but the prospect of facing Mason with that puppy dog smile of his, had sent her into Ice Cream & Sweets first. She was a coward.

"Banana split," Abigail ordered at the counter. "With lots of whipped cream and nuts."

The girl waiting on her was a typical teenager working a summer job. Her heart wasn't in her job, but she was courteous. Pretty, with bored blue eyes, she'd opted to go for the porcupine look, her head a ball of spiky blond tips. Abigail couldn't keep her eyes off the girl's head. Call her crazy, but by the time she got her ice cream, she'd begun to like the look.

Going over to a round table before the front window, Abigail watched the people pass by outside, musing over where they were going, what they were doing, and what they were thinking. Another newspaper episode of the Summers' murder mystery had hit the streets that morning. She was hiding. A copy was on the table next to her beside an empty sundae dish. Photos of the graves, and the tree house, center front page in glorious color stared back at her. *Who killed the Summers Family?* She didn't need to read the story again. She'd devoured the article three times. Readers were probably crying over their coffee, or lunch, even now.

Abigail looked up and spied Martha outside the window, waving at her, and heading her way. She came in and flopped down in the chair across from her. “That banana split looks scrumptious.” She cocked her head and hollered at the porcupine girl, “Another banana split over here, please. With everything and don’t scrimp on the chocolate syrup. Thank you.”

There was a grunt from behind them to acknowledge the order.

“It’s hot enough to melt a penny out there.” Martha was dressed up today in a suit, nylons, and low heels. She set her brief case on the floor at her feet, and using a handkerchief, dabbed at her face.

“How are things, Martha?” Abigail kept eating. Her ice cream was overflowing the dish, so she had to spoon quickly.

“Fine and dandy. Showing the old Fern house to a prospective buyer in fifteen minutes. When I saw you, thought I’d stop in and chat for a sec. Get something cold and creamy. I was dissolving out there. And I wanted to talk about the story. Samantha says the newspapers are flying off the shelves. Everyone’s talking about the murder mystery. That’s all they’re talking about. Such a tragedy, but so…absorbing.”

Great, Abigail thought, *I won’t be able to go anywhere now without people pestering me about it.*

“Read in the newspaper you found Jenny’s diary in the tree house that day we were all out there. You didn’t tell me, hey? And I thought we were friends. Was there anything juicy in it?”

Martha already had her banana split and was digging into it.

"The usual stuff a little girl would put in a diary." Abigail hadn't told anyone, but Frank, much about what she'd discovered in those pages, not even to Samantha for the newspaper article. "As the story reported, I don't have the diary anymore. Someone waltzed into my house–again–and snatched it, along with the crayon messages from the kids." She hadn't divulged the ledger's existence to the newspaper, either. Frank's idea. And, she positively wasn't going to mention the ledger to blabbermouth Martha.

"At least you got to read the diary before that happened," her friend quipped.

"Yes, I did." Abigail fell silent. Frank thought it best if she kept the diary's contents low key, too, for a while. It might be safer for her.

"What would anyone want with a kid's old diary anyway?" Martha couldn't help but pry.

"Beats me. A souvenir? Some people are strange." Abigail acted innocent.

"Creepy, if you ask me. Breaking in a person's home and taking worthless mementos like that.

"You know," Martha remarked, off handedly, "when the old sheriff was brought up in this last installment, it got me thinking. Cal Brewster *was* batty over Emily. Some say he shadowed her, in his squad car, for a while because she wouldn't give him the time of day. He stopped her every chance he got and flirted with her. And Cal Brewster was married, with three children. I vaguely remember him from when I was a kid. I always thought he was fat. Sloppy in his habits and in his duties. He had a reputation as being a woman chaser and also as having a really bad temper. Some cops do. It goes hand in hand, sometimes, with the monumental ego it takes to be a cop. Though, I do remember, Sheriff Cal got more mellow, became a better cop, as the years went by.

"He liked pretty women; liked younger girls, as well. I know. I used to stay out of his way, because he made me uncomfortable. I knew someone once who was a friend with Cal Brewster's children, lived next door to them, and overheard Cal's boy talking about his father's women and how Cal's infatuation with Emily drove his mom insane with jealousy. Maybe Cal was Emily's secret boyfriend? Have you ever thought of that?"

Hmm, and could be Cal Brewster, or his wife, had been Emily's stalker, Abigail speculated. Samantha had also written about Emily's stalker in the last story and was hoping to get feedback. Could be someone, who knew something, would come forward.

"Emily was beautiful, I remember," Martha went on, "but it gave her more grief sometimes than not. An abusive ex-husband, a crazy jealous boyfriend, a sister who envied and hated her, a town which didn't accept her…*and* a stalker. It sounds like a movie of the week. I don't blame her for wanting to leave. It's a shame she didn't make it."

"Was there anyone else who hated Emily–whom you can recall?" Abigail had mulled over who else could have been Emily's tormentor and, for some reason, she asked, "Was Mason married back then? You told me, once, he was eventually married to someone called Norma, right?" She'd remembered Mason might have been one of Emily's admirers. If the sheriff's wife was a possible suspect then Mason's wife could be, too.

"Why would you ask about Mason's ex-wife? Anyway, I don't think they were married yet in 1970. They were only engaged, I believe. They weren't married until later."

"Just curious. How long have they been divorced?"

"A couple of years, I guess. She was a loner, uppity, and knew how to spend money all right; nearly bankrupted him a couple of times. She kept ordering things over the phone from catalogs. But, heck, it was her money. I can't believe they stayed married as long as they did. He was no prize, mind you, but Norma was wacko. The last decade of their marriage she wouldn't leave the house, was petrified of everything. She used to send people hate mail, out of the blue. He finally had enough of it. The divorce was his idea. There'd been rumors he beat her and that's why she never went out. Rumors he only married her to get the store and daddy's money. Once he had her, though, he couldn't stomach her crazy behavior. Who knows? Marriage. Glad I'm not handcuffed to anyone anymore. Life is too short to be miserable, I say."

Martha's eyes had a sly shine. "Hey, you're not interested in Mason romantically, are you?" There was open disbelief in her voice. "He's way too old for you."

Abigail nearly choked. "God no, I'm not interested. Just curious. I've heard people talking. And, yes, he is way too old."

"Good. Besides I happen to know Frank–who is an excellent catch–is nuts about you. Who'd want old moldy hamburger when they could have filet mignon?"

Abigail glared at her. She knew Frank liked her. She wasn't naïve. Yet, having him nuts about her was something she hadn't seen coming. "Frank and I are just friends, I keep telling you. Friends. I don't want any man right now. All right?"

"Whatever you say. But, you can't grieve a dead husband forever, Abigail."

Martha, having finished her ice cream, got up and collected her briefcase. "I have to run and show a house. I hope the boys I hired to clean it out did their job. The last owner left a mess. I couldn't wade through the trash and empty beer cans. The mice were having a party. Yeck."

Abigail remembered Frank's party. "Are you coming Saturday night to Frank's barbeque?"

"I wouldn't miss it. It's the social highlight of my month. Music, food, good company. A card game. I love cards. I might even be bringing someone."

"Oh," Abigail gave back the same as she'd gotten, "someone you're interested in?"

"Oh, he's interested. Don't know if I am yet. You'll meet him Saturday. Name's Ryan."

"What are you bringing? I'm baking fudge brownies."

"Potato salad deluxe. Brownies sound fattening but bring 'em on, I say. The more desserts the better. My hips won't thank you, but, hey, who's asking them? See you there."

Abigail watched as Martha walked out of the ice cream shop and down the sidewalk, heat shimmering around her. She knew she couldn't put off getting groceries any longer. Her cupboards and refrigerator were bare. A girl had to eat. She could go to the supermarket the next town over, but she needed to go to Mason's. Between her commissions, she'd been painting watercolors of the town, sections of Main Street, and wanted to display them in his store to sell. She had to face the store owner to do it.

Why was she finding it so difficult? Was it because he'd been one of Emily's boyfriends all those years ago and he'd lied to Abigail, point blank, about it? He'd lied about even knowing them. Why would he have done that? Or was it because Mason so obviously liked her? So what if he was twice as old as her. Lots of older man liked younger women. He still made her uncomfortable and she still needed to deal with him. Her physical, and financial, survival won out. She returned to her car, unloaded the framed watercolors and lugged them into Mason's store.

He met her at the door. "Here, let me help you." His hand brushed her shoulder as he took the pictures, and she inwardly cringed.

"Well, if it isn't our town's celebrity sleuth. I've read every word of those stories on the Summers' murders and I'm as intrigued as the rest of the town. I can't wait until the next installment. See what else you've unearthed. Any idea, yourself, who killed them? Any hot suspects?" he pried in a deceptively nonchalant voice.

She hadn't caught any sarcasm, or underlying meanings, and chided herself for the way she was behaving. Paranoia wasn't like her. He was just a lonely, old man who was trying to be friendly with his customers.

"No, none so far." Frank's advice whispering in her head, she played it dumb. "It was so long ago. The whole newspaper thing has gotten out of hand. You know reporters? Samantha simply wants to sell papers. Everything's fodder for her stories." She shrugged. "We'll probably never know what really happened to them."

Mason laid the stack of watercolors on a counter, but avoided her eyes. "Probably not."

Before she realized what she was doing, she inquired, "Did you know Emily?" Then it was too late to take back the words. Stupid, stupid.

An awkward pause. "No. Like I told you." He seemed to rethink something and added, "Oh, I saw her and her kids around town all right. They shopped here sometimes. I knew who she was. That was about it."

Abigail guarded her expression, so he wouldn't know she knew he'd lied again. Last time, she was sure of it, he'd said Emily and the kids were before his time. Why was he lying at all unless he was hiding something?

He'd spread the pictures across the counter and studied each one. "These are lovely. Excellent."

His mocking gaze met hers. "You have an eye for details most people don't see. I love your use of colors. You are truly an artist, my girl."

"Thanks. Do you have room for me to display them?"

"I'll make room." He was observing her in a peculiar manner, or that could have been her imagination.

She tried envisioning what he'd looked like thirty years ago. He might have been a heart breaker, might have been handsome, but his looks had matured into an old man's. Behind his constantly charming smile, Abigail saw hints of discontent and of his life's disappointments. She couldn't see now, what any woman might have seen in him then. But time changed everything, and everyone, no one stayed young and good-looking forever. People got old, their bodies and minds aged. It was inevitable.

"I might buy one myself," Mason was saying, bringing her out of her reverie. "This one which has my store in the corner of it." He tapped one of the pictures. "I love the way you used the lights of the sunset to bathe the store fronts. Delightful. The price is more than fair. All the prices are. I'll put the pictures out today. They'll sell. And here…you said you weren't that good." His words were flattering, and he was staring at her again. "You underestimate your own talent, Abigail. You underestimate yourself." He smiled, and he was almost nice looking…for a moment or two.

Why was she being so ungracious? Mason was merely trying to be nice to her. He was trying to help her and she needed help. She could at least be nice back. She returned his smile.

"I need to pick up some groceries. I'll be back." She edged towards the shelves, aware his eyes followed her every move. She gathered what she needed and paid for it; then got out of the store as quickly as she could, feeling guilty for not being more grateful to him. He still made her nervous. Relieved to be away from him she drove home.

That night she pushed all thoughts of dead people and murderers out of her mind and worked on her paintings. It was hard, but she did it. Snowball kept trying to prance across her illustration board and she had to shoo her off more than once. The kitten had to be in the middle of everything. When Snowball stuck her nose into the swirl of red paint on the palette, Abigail ended up locking her in her bedroom. Then there were pitiful meows from above.

Abigail was still working when the noises began outside. It sounded as if something or someone was roaming around her yard but, each time she looked, there was no one there. Just the warm darkness and the silent trees.

Yeah, she was getting way too paranoid. Time to go to bed. Maybe sleep would help.

Chapter 12

At ten minutes after six on Saturday Abigail arrived at Frank's cabin. Louisa and her husband, Michael O'Neal, and Martha and her friend, Ryan Sutcliffe, were already coffee klatching on the front porch. They introduced each other and Martha told Abigail that Frank was inside playing cook.

On her way to the kitchen, she bumped into Frank's son, Kyle, who was lurking in the living room sitting on the couch with a laptop computer on his knees. His long fingers clicking away as fast as a magician's. "Hi, I'm Abigail. You must be Frank's son, Kyle?"

"Guilty."

She put her hand out. He just looked at it and returned his attention to his computer. She waited for him to say something else, but he didn't. Kyle, olive-eyed with a hairless face and short cut hair, was so unlike Frank that Abigail couldn't believe he was his son. His clothes were the standard college uniform of T-shirt, blue jeans, and tennis shoes and he didn't look like a future doctor as he hunched over his laptop, his thin face serious. He looked like a kid.

Frank's voice boomed from the kitchen. "Kyle, you need to get the fire started for us, Son."

"Okay, Dad. Doing it." Kyle got up, shambled past her like a brontosaurus, and headed for the deck.

"Nice laptop. A Macintosh," she said to his

back. “I used to work all the time on Macs doing ads for the newspaper. If you’re an artist, you need a Mac. Yours is a pretty shade of green.”

The boy paused a second in the doorway to look at her, as if he was seeing her for the first time. “Thanks. It’s a good computer. I like the color, too. An artist’s computer, huh?” He smiled slightly, then went into the kitchen.

Abigail followed and found Frank busy preparing the steaks for the barbeque grill. The rear door slammed as Kyle exited to the deck.

“Are any of Kyle’s friends coming for dinner?” She put the plate of brownies on the kitchen counter. “I don’t see any other young people hanging around.” The kitchen was overflowing with brought food. Frank was supplying the meat and drinks.

“No. He insisted he didn’t want them over tonight. Too many grownups. He’ll see them tomorrow. I think he’s ashamed of us.” Frank chuckled. “I didn’t argue. Count yourself lucky. Have you heard the music they’re listening to these days? Rap or hip hop. I can’t understand a word they’re singing. Drives me wild. It makes me want to pull out *their* hair.”

“I know the feeling. Rap isn’t one of my favorites, either. But my parents didn’t like the Beatles much, if I recall. They said they sounded like a bunch of off key girls.”

Frank glanced upwards, pursing his lips, and a smile slid out. “Neither did mine. Care for the Beatles, I mean.”

Abigail sampled the potato salad, her

stomach growling. "Samantha couldn't make it?"

"No. Something about going home to see her parents for the weekend. She said to say hi and let you know she's working on the next chapter of the Summers' saga. Told me to tell you there's some letter from some woman, marked personal, waiting for you at the newspaper. You should come by Monday and she'll give it to you."

"I can't read it until Monday? Darn. What else is new?" She watched him salt and pepper the meat before he stacked it on a plate.

He turned to Abigail. "I made a call to the sheriff this afternoon. He's gotten complete forensic results on the bodies you found. As well on the two elder Summers."

"The medical examiner said it'd be a while for the results. Whew, they sure got it done quickly."

"I pulled some strings is what happened, because being a big city ex-detective has its advantages."

"And?"

"According to the forensic anthropologist, someone whose specialty is osteology or the study of bones, the three bodies were an adult woman in her late twenties to early thirties, and two children, around ten to twelve years old, a male and a female. They're Emily, Jenny and Christopher all right. I have little doubt of it."

"Could they tell how they died?"

"When dealing with bodies dead three decades, forensic anthropologists can only assess age, sex, stature; analyze trauma or disease with the bones that are left. Without any soft tissue death, by other means, is hard to pin down. It takes longer. We got a break from the adult female body, though. Her bones showed she most likely died by strangulation. Her neck was broken. That was the probable cause of death.

"The two kids had no obvious traumas or injuries. They weren't in any kind of accident. Car or otherwise. Though the bones did show possible signs of poison, which permeates into the marrow. The same with the old people. They're going to run more tests but they wanted us to know what they'd found so far."

"Broken neck and poisoning," she echoed. "Jenny wrote in her diary how sick Christopher was that last week, or so, and that her mother was also missing. If Christopher was being poisoned it would explain his mystery illness. And it'd explain how someone was able to get away with poisoning them so easily. No one was watching out for them."

"That could be a possible scenario." Frank had known those three piles of bones when they'd been walking, talking and feeling human beings with problems and dreams. His expression was hard to read, but Abigail suspected his memories were torturing him.

"Since you've found those graves, Abby. I can't stop thinking about them and how wonderful, but fragile, life is. It makes me grateful for this moment in time, with good friends, on a lovely summer's evening with a terrific meal ready for us to enjoy." His smile was bittersweet. "I'm a lucky guy." He nodded, then went to put the steaks on the grill.

She trailed after him, thinking of what he'd said about cherishing the good moments in life when they came and realized he was right. This was one of those times.

"You did a fine job with the fire, Kyle. Thanks." Frank's face softened when he was around his son. He put down the plate of meat, threw his arm over the young man's shoulders, and gave him a hug. Kyle tolerated the show of affection but made a face over his dad's shoulder.

"I have to get something from my room." Kyle grunted, sweeping his gaze across Abigail. He acknowledged her with a quicksilver grin and a friendly hand gesture as he moved past. She'd been accepted. His shuffling footsteps made their way up the stairs to his room.

"He's a good kid," Frank said as he worked over the grill. "I only wish he were more outgoing. That he had more friends. He's so darn smart, so in a world of his own most of the time, there's no room for anyone else."

"He'll grow out of it." She voiced the observation and felt comfortable enough to make another one. "And that I-don't-give-a-care-about-anything attitude? It's a façade to protect him from being hurt. He'll open up to people in his own time. I think he misses his mother."

"He does. He took her death real hard. I think he blames himself for the car accident. Jolene died on the way to pick him up from a party one night. A party she didn't want him even going to, but he'd badgered her until she took him. I was on duty and wasn't home. Weather was bad with icy snow. She ran off a bridge. Kyle locked himself in his room for days and wouldn't talk much to anyone, even me, after it happened. He seemed to pull himself together, though, when he went off to college. So I thought he was on the road to recovery. He's not entirely, but he's working on it."

"Given more time, space, and your love, he'll eventually heal.

"By the way, while we're alone. Who is this friend of Martha's, this Ryan fellow?"

The smell of the sizzling meat curled around her nose. It made her eyes water.

"I was going to ask you the same question. This is the first time I've met him. All Martha told me was he was another realtor from Chalmers she's known for a long time. He's recently divorced. Seems like a nice enough guy. Except, as all salesmen, he talks too much."

"Then Martha and he are perfect for each other."

Frank laughed.

"I met your sister's husband on the front porch. Now he's not all that talkative, is he?"

Frank made a funny noise in his throat. "No, he isn't. They've been married fifteen years, and I don't think we've exchanged more than a handful of words. He works in a mortuary, sells cemetery plots and stones on the side. I guess that explains it. His clients don't talk much so neither does he. My sister, though, loves him and he's been good to her, so I put up with him."

"Oh, you're a good brother."

"I am," Frank affirmed with a mischievous grin. "Let's join the others on the porch. I can hustle back here, every so often, to check on the steaks. They won't take long."

"Hey, how's your novel going?" she inquired as they reentered the house.

"Done, and in the hands of my agent."

"You promised you'd tell me what it's about, once it was finished."

"I'll give you a synopsis before you leave tonight, I promise. Now comes the waiting. My agent told me not to dwell on it, but move forward and start another novel. I'm thinking, if it's okay with you, of doing it on Emily, Jenny and Christopher. My agent thinks it would make a good story."

Abigail wasn't surprised. The newspaper had gotten such an amazing response to the articles, so Frank putting the mystery into a book made sense. "Okay with me. It's quite a story, especially if we can find out who killed them and why."

"Hopefully if we keep digging, we'll solve it. Or, at least, get more answers. I won't give up and I know neither will you. Emily's counting on us."

"Spoken like a true detective," she muttered, trying not to let her uneasiness show. Then she returned to the earlier topic. "I'm going to hold you to that promise of a synopsis on your book tonight–even if I have to camp out on your porch. I won't go home until I have it."

"Hey, now that could be fun. I have extra fluffy sleeping bags, and marshmallows we could toast over a fire. We could have a porch camp-out. You know, it's not supposed to rain."

She let out a laugh and thought how good a friend Frank was becoming. He could make her laugh, which was rare. They joined the guests on the porch. The seven of them sat in the rocking chairs, got to know each other, or tried to, and discussed trivial or important matters. The main themes of the night were the Summers' mystery, and Frank's book. They even got a few words out of Michael.

Ryan turned out to be a friendly man. Martha seemed smitten with him. They held hands and smooched when they thought no one was looking. They were so cute together, comparing notes on their work, and making eyes at each other; though Ryan did talk a lot.

Which balanced out Michael's muteness and Kyle's holding back in the shadows.

They were waiting for the steaks to cook. Louisa was perched on the porch railing bathing in the warm twilight. "Abigail, I have a story to add to the Summers' folder. Something I've never told my brother, about Jenny and Christopher. I'm younger than Frank. And though I was a deal older than Jenny, we hung around together some that last summer. I hadn't thought about her, that house, that strange family, in years and years…until Frank gave me copies of those newspaper stories the *Journal*'s doing, When I saw their pictures. It all came back."

"You knew Jenny and Christopher?" Abigail was interested. Here again, another coincidence.

"I did. I met Jenny one day in the park. She and her brother were on the swings, and she asked if I was Officer Lester's sister. I said yes. As I recall, my brother had been kind to them after a car accident where Christopher was hurt. She wanted to be instant friends and tagged around after me for weeks. I liked her but she was younger. She was a pest. They were peculiar kids, always daydreaming, drawing pictures; yakking about stuff like aliens coming to earth and…ghosts.

"Jenny believed there was a ghost living in her basement. Her grandma. She believed the ghost talked to her all the time. One night I was foolish enough to spend the night with her. We slept on the front porch on cots. Jenny, Christopher, and me. We ate popcorn. Drank soda pop from cans. It was sweltering that summer night. So hot we couldn't sleep. The katydids were noisy. The dark was spooky.

"I remember that night very well. How sweet Jenny's mom was to me before she left on her date. She asked if we needed anything else for the sleep over. She made us a supper of cheese macaroni and oven-baked fried shrimp, the frozen kind you get from a box. She was so happy Jenny had a friend staying over. I remember thinking that she was so pretty for a mom. She put on make up like a movie star, teased her lovely blond hair, and wore lots of jewelry. Her perfume smelled heavenly.

"I also remember how much fighting was going on in the house between their Aunt Edna and their mother before their mother left for the night. I was a child and didn't take notice of what they were arguing about…something to do with a man…with the house. Something. But, it was terrible, the hatred between the women. I was glad to be out on the porch; relieved when the yelling stopped and Jenny's mom left. We didn't have that kind of arguing at our house. Our parents were happy and rarely raised their voices at us, or anyone.

"That's one of the reasons I didn't remain friends with Jenny and Chris. Their Aunt Edna was a mean spirited witch. She had this malice towards her niece and nephew which was so strong you could feel it. Jenny told me she found glass in her breakfast cereal one morning and was sure her Aunt Edna put it in there. Lucky for her, she saw it before she put the spoon to her lips and tossed the whole bowl away. There were other times her Aunt tried to hurt her and Chris, she said. But, I guess, when she saw the look of horror on my face about the glass in the cereal, she kept those other stories to herself. I never knew whether to believe Jenny or not. She was always making up things."

Louisa looked at her brother. "Those two kids made me feel guilty because I had so much and they had so little. The clothes Jenny and Chris used to wear were not much more than rags. Her mother got them from the church donation boxes. Jenny didn't mind. Can you imagine a kid, these days, not caring how they looked? Kids today want designer labels, their own cell phones, and computers. Jenny and Chris had nothing.

"At midnight, after Aunt Edna and Chris were asleep, Jenny dared me to go into the basement to talk with her dead grandma. I didn't believe in ghosts so I went. I thought it would be fun to show her up. That and I didn't want her to think I was a scaredy-cat."

Martha was unable to stand the suspense when Louisa paused. "Well, did you see the ghost?"

Louisa's profile was faintly outlined in the fading light. "I'll never know if I did or not. That's the weird thing. Jenny and I went into the basement with a candle. She said her grandma always liked candles. It was eerie down there. So dark. You know how scary basements are when you're a kid? And there *was* something down there…a pulsating shadow…which I never could quite get a focus on. A presence. I heard a voice, not mine and not Jenny's. It called Jenny's name. Then something, like fingers, gently stroked my cheek. I began shaking so badly I ran out of the basement like it was full of snakes. Later, of course, back up on the porch, I told myself I'd imagined all of it. I almost believed it.

"Here's the clincher. Jenny claimed her grandma's ghost was sad because her daughter Edna poisoned her and her husband. It gave me the creeps. I never went back there and avoided Jenny afterwards. It was a short time after that they left. Or so we believed. Sad to think they've been dead all these years, not away." She shook her head. "Sorry Abigail, I know it's your house now, but I think it's haunted."

"It could be," Abigail replied good-naturedly, "though I don't really believe in ghosts."

Frank announced the meat was done.

Martha stood up. "Now that I'm thoroughly creeped out, let's go eat. We can have more ghost stories later, when it's dark, so we can really get the full effect. I'll even run out in the yard, hide somewhere, and make spooky noises."

After dinner, everyone sat in the kitchen playing cards. Abigail talked Kyle into joining them and, she thought, all in all, he had a good time. Later in the evening everyone ended up on the porch again, rocking in the chairs and talking, except Michael and Kyle, who rocked and listened.

The night was soft dry velvet and the moon above a huge white medallion which cast an ivory glow over the porch and yard. There was a faint breeze as Frank exposed the plot and the story behind his novel.

Louisa rocked her chair slowly, seemingly in thought. "It sounds intriguing. It'll sell, Brother. Soon, I bet, we'll be seeing your novels in the book stores, seeing you on the talk shows acting the big shot writer."

Frank's laugh was spontaneous, yet humble, at the same time. "Spoken like a baby sister."

"I like the title," Michael surprised everyone by blurting out loud. Everyone laughed.

Michael and Louisa left first, then Martha and Ryan. Abigail, Kyle and Frank remained on the porch chatting about their favorite horror movies. Kyle had let down his defenses, behaving like a normal human being, as he entertained them with tales of his college classes and his teachers. The evening had been so much fun Abigail didn't want it to end.

"Thought I'd warn you early, Abby," Frank spoke as she was leaving. "Next week there's another town picnic. No crafts, but homemade chili, ice cream, rides, and a bonfire later."

Leave it to her to relocate to a town which celebrated something every other week of the year.

As Abigail steered her car home her mind wasn't on the upcoming festivities. It was on Emily and the kids, what had happened to them, on the bodies' forensic results, what Brown and then Louisa, had said about them–and whether there really was a ghost in her basement.

Chapter 13

Early Monday morning Abigail arrived at the newspaper's office. All day Sunday, as she'd kept busy, and finished Frank's watercolor, she hadn't been able to stop speculating about the letter Samantha had for her; and obsessing about the possible ghost in her basement. She hadn't ventured into the basement since she'd cleaned it, and was miffed at herself for being a silly nitwit. *There was no such things as spooks.*

"Good morning, Abigail." Samantha was poised at her desk, camera and purse dangling from her shoulder. "You caught me on my way to a story. I can't chat. Here's the letter." She thrust an envelope at Abigail, dashed for the door where she paused, turned, and spoke as fast as she'd moved, "I didn't open the letter. Let me know later what it says. I'm d-y-i-n-g of curiosity. See you later." Then she was rushing out the door, and gone.

"Nice to see you, too, Samantha!" Abigail yelled after her. There was no answer but the slamming door.

Abigail plopped down at Samantha's desk. She read what was on the outside of the envelope: *Urgent and personal for Abigail Sutton!* She tore it open, and began to read.

Dear Abigail Sutton,

I live in Orchard, about twenty-five miles from Spookie. I was a friend of Norma Mason, who lived here in Orchard the last few years since her divorce. We were neighbors. Norma used to live in Spookie, and was married to the John Mason who runs the general store. Recently, she was sent copies of your newspaper stories about the missing Summers family by an old friend who still lives in Spookie. I'm writing you because Norma had something very important to tell you about the Summers. But three days ago she died, under circumstances I believe were suspicious, before she could contact you. As she confided in me before her death, I feel it's my duty to tell you what she told me. If you're interested call at the telephone number below. We'll arrange a visit face to face. Alone, please. I think that's best.

Yours truly,
Lorna Henreid

Abigail didn't think Samantha would mind if she used the newspaper's telephone, so she dialed the number at the bottom of the letter. A few minutes later she was on her way to Orchard to meet the letter lady.

***

Lorna's home was a small brick house, yet well kept, the grounds immaculate, and landscaped with bushes and flowering plants. Abigail walked up to a porch, where there was a white trellis covered in miniature roses. White wicker furniture was on the right of the porch, a glider swing was on the left. An attractive woman, looking to be around sixty years old, dressed in an apricot pants suit, opened the door. "Abigail," she breathed. "Come in."

Abigail stepped inside. "Thank you for letting me talk to you like this. For sending the letter." The living room was a pale pink. It was filled with expensive looking oak furniture. The plump woman in front of her had dark cropped hair, and warm gray eyes.

"Ah, honey. I was Norma's friend. I have to do something." Smiling, she gave Abigail's shoulder a motherly pat. "Come on into the kitchen. I made us some tea. Rolls."

"You didn't have to do that for me, but thank you."

In her sunny kitchen, Lorna poured a cup of tea for Abigail, then offered her a roll from a porcelain plate with a pretty rose pattern. "Since Norma passed away it's been lonely. She used to come for breakfast most mornings, and we'd go to neighborhood yard sales, to the mall or putter around in our gardens together. I'm going to miss her so much. She was a good friend."

"I'm sorry." Abigail took a bite of a roll. "When did she die?"

"When I wrote the letter it was three days after Norma's death. We'd just buried her. Let's see, that was…four days ago. She's been dead seven days. The coroner said she fell down her basement steps. An accident. I wrote you that letter because I don't think it was an accident."

If it wasn't an accident, then what was it? Abigail's inner voice brooded. "Why would you think that?" She added sugar to her tea, finished her roll, as she admired the cozy kitchen. The whole house was so clean, organized, and so different from Brown's dingy place.

"Because Norma had become afraid of someone from her past. She wouldn't tell me who. Ever since her old friend sent her those newspaper articles, especially after the one where you found the graves, Norma was behaving strangely. One night, before she died, she knocked on my door, and asked if she could speak to me. She had something to get off her chest, she said. Frightened, she kept jerking every time there was a noise outside.

"She spoke about her old life with John Mason. Those newspaper articles, she claimed, had revived unpleasant memories about Emily Summers; the affair John Mason had had with the woman thirty years ago, when he was engaged to Norma. Norma hated Emily Summers with a passion. She confessed she nearly killed Emily herself, she was so worried over losing John to her. Norma was obsessed with John in those days. You have to understand, as Norma put it, thirty years ago, Mason was a dreamboat. He had a wit, and a smile, which thawed any woman's heart. He was sensitive, smart, and had this smoldering animal magnetism that was so sexy. He had, when he was young, great potential. A real passion for life. Women threw themselves at John all the time–when he wasn't drinking. Ha, that was the catch, Norma said. When he drank he was a brute, a monster.

"Anyway, Norma and John were supposed to be married in October, but she'd felt him slipping away more each day that summer. Rumors were John had a woman on the side. Emily. He was in love with Emily, but he was to get the store from Norma's father, and a lot of money. Norma had a good-sized trust fund which would kick in when she finally married. So, according to Norma, John lied to her about Emily, and kept seeing both. Emily was poor, she had two kids John never warmed up to, but John wouldn't let her go. Greedy, he played his women against each other to get what he wanted. And, by what Norma said, it all ended badly.

"She never knew how badly until she learned you'd found Emily, and the children's, graves…and the pieces fell into place for her. She'd always believed, like everyone else, they'd just moved away. She figured out, she thought, what might have happened. The guilt was eating at her. Mostly about what she'd done to Emily all those years ago."

"Norma was Emily's stalker, wasn't she?" The second Abigail said it, she knew it was true.

"I think it was Norma. Norma hinted she was the stalker, but never really admitted it." Lorna sighed. "The stalker was alluded to in the last newspaper installment, but no one knew who it was. The Norma I knew was a quiet, simple woman. Thirty years with that womanizing ex-husband of hers had worn her down. It was a miracle she had the courage to leave him. She was much happier divorced, and living here, alone. She must have been a firecracker when she was younger, though. She told me she'd loathed Emily Summers for trying to steal her man, blamed the woman for everything, but she never actually hurt her, or the kids. She just tried to scare her off."

"She left the hate notes in the mailbox?" Abigail wanted it clarified. "She killed their cat, burnt down their shed, and injured Christopher with her car?" *And killed Emily?* –because a spurned woman's jealousy could be deadly? Abigail wanted to ask, but didn't.

"She practically confessed to most of that, she wasn't proud of it, but Norma adamantly denied being the person who ran Christopher over. She'd never hurt a child. Only wanted to frighten them so they'd leave town. She swore she had nothing to do with any of their deaths."

That didn't mean Norma hadn't killed one, or all, of them, Abigail mulled the possibility over, merely she'd lied about it. As Frank said, most murderers were accomplished liars.

"Norma regretted her treatment of Emily, and the children, more than anything else in her life. Well, except for marrying John Mason, especially when she found out years later John had had other girlfriends, on the side, at the same time, not just Emily."

Oh, now that was interesting. "That cad. But…back to the other thing, why was Norma afraid?"

"She never actually said, but she *was* scared of something, or someone. The last time I saw Norma she told me the story of the night she threatened to call off the wedding. She and John had an awful fight. He went off to see someone afterwards, but the following day he came begging Norma to take him back. He had scratches on his face, behaved oddly, and told her he'd had an accident in his car. He drank in those days, had blackouts, and sometimes was violent. So Norma thought little of it. He swore to her he was done with other women forever, and reported Emily was planning on leaving town. Good riddance to her. Two months later, Norma and John were married. Their marriage was awful, to hear Norma tell it, with his controlling nature, tight fingers on her money, drinking, and running around on her. Years later, she wished he had taken off with Emily Summers–or any one of the other women. She would have been better off.

"Anyway, Norma had all that, and more, on John's relationship with Emily. She was going to send it in a letter to you. She'd been getting threatening phone calls, feared someone was targeting her. She ranted about vengeful ghosts, being haunted, if she didn't tell what she knew. Not like Norma, at all, who usually didn't believe in such things. She was so frightened those last days. So, when I found out she'd died by falling down the stairs, it got me thinking: Something's not right. She was always careful going up and down those steps. She had terrible arthritis in her legs, so she took her time, and always held the banister tightly. She wouldn't have fallen. I know it.

"So I sent the letter to you. If someone pushed Norma down those stairs, and it was partly because of your stories, you needed to know. That someone is still out there." Lorna's face was serious.

"You're saying someone could have killed Norma? That someone might now want to hurt me, so I should be careful?"

"That's the sum of it. I'm positive Norma wrote you a letter the night before she died, but didn't, I don't think, have time to mail it. I wish there were some way we could find it. It's probably in her house somewhere."

The plan formed before Abigail could stop it. "Norma lived next door in the white house on the left? Is it empty now?"

"Yes, just sitting there empty. Norma and John have a son and a daughter. They're putting it up for sale, but haven't cleaned it out yet. No one's been there since the funeral. They asked me to keep an eye on it for them." There was a glint in the woman's gaze as her lips curved upwards. "But I often kept an eye on the place for Norma, too. I have an extra key, so I can't see the harm in going in, and looking for that letter. If it is addressed to you, it's lawfully yours. Right?"

Abigail kept a straight face. "Right. It's lawfully mine." Then she grinned. "And if you have legal access to the house…."

Lorna took a key off a wall hook. Abigail followed her outside to the rear door of Norma's house. Lorna unlocked it. Once inside they stood, in shock, gawking at the piles of debris strewn everywhere. The floors were covered with stuff. The cabinet doors were open, and their contents had been tossed all over the floor. The place was a mess.

"My, my," Lorna whispered. "I don't think the police, or her kids, did this. The kids are neat freaks like their mother was. Someone's broken in here."

Deja vu, Abigail reflected, looking around. Was a curse following her or what?

"I imagine," Lorna moaned in a meek voice, "we need to report this to the police."

"We will. After we find my letter. Unless someone beat us to it. Any idea where it might be?" Abigail didn't want to spend any more time in Norma's house than necessary. "Also, let's not leave any fingerprints if we can help it. I don't want the police to think we did this."

"Good idea. Norma had a couple of secret hiding places for money and such. Let's look in them first. Maybe your letter wasn't found. One place was behind her bathroom medicine cabinet, and another was in a secret compartment in her desk. I'll show you."

The medicine cabinet, emptied of everything, was on the floor. It had been ripped from the wall. Well, scratch that hiding place. She hoped the letter hadn't been hidden there. They made their way through the wreckage to the bedroom. They checked the desk.

"Got it!" Lorna exclaimed as she pulled an envelope, with a stamp and Abigail's name on it, out of a crevice of the desk. She handed it to Abigail. "I knew she wrote you a letter."

Opening it, Abigail scanned the sentences, her breath an ice cube in her throat. She finished, and recapped what she'd read for Lorna. "Norma suspected John strangled Emily, during a lover's quarrel, the night they had their big fight. He got drunk one night years later, and blabbed some things to her which made her think that. Confessing

Emily had wanted to leave him, wanted to sell the house, escape town to be with another man–not her ex-husband–Mason was so enraged he attacked her in a fit of passion. Unfortunately, John passed out and stopped talking, before he could actually incriminate himself. But, after that, Norma feared he might have killed Emily; that he'd spent the next three decades covering up the crime. To Norma it made sense. That's why, after he'd broken up with Emily that summer, he'd come begging to get her back. He'd killed Emily, saw his life and freedom slipping away, and, in the end, didn't want to also lose the good life marrying Norma would have brought him. It'd been damage control. Norma believed he did it, but had no proof. Not even verbal."

"Does it say anything about Emily's kids?" Lorna asked.

"Only that, as Norma remembered it–and I'd wager she was watching Emily's house plenty–Emily and the children weren't seen for weeks. It was the end of that summer. Then Edna, Emily's older sister, announced one day they'd driven away for a fresh start. And no one questioned it."

"You think Mason was the one who broke in here because he knew about the letter, and was afraid of what might be in it? Could be he remembered what he said to Norma during their marriage, that night he was drunk in particular, or what she might lie about to get him in trouble?"

"Could be." Abigail couldn't imagine charming Mason breaking into anyone's house. On the other hand, she couldn't imagine him doing any of the other things Norma's letter said he might have done, either. The paper felt funny in Abigail's hands. The woman who'd written it only days ago was dead. Suddenly, she was uneasy standing in the middle of a vacant, vandalized house. "Where are the steps Norma was supposed to have fallen down?"

"This way." Lorna forged ahead. Abigail trailed behind her through the rubble.

The basement was as untidy as the upper floors. Someone had been frantic to find something. What? Yet the basement stairs looked sturdy, the banister heavy, and the steps were carpeted. It would have been difficult, but not impossible, to tumble down them. People fell all the time. She wished, not for the first time, that Frank had been with her. She could have used his expertise. The best Abigail could do was examine the scene. Nothing looked suspicious, to her anyway. The banister was intact. There weren't any scuffs, or rips, in the carpeted steps. Lorna said Norma had died of head trauma, of some kind, and the casket had been closed.

Making the sign of the cross, Lorna held back from the stairs. "I can't bear to look at where poor Norma died. It makes me sad. She'd turned her life around the last few years. Each Sunday she went to church. She had friends. The funeral was magnificent. There were so many flowers." The woman was weeping, dabbing at her eyes with her sleeve. "She didn't deserve to die like that, alone at the bottom of the steps. Poor Norma."

"Let's get out of here." Abigail had seen

enough. "It's time to call the police." She was thinking about the letter, about Norma and Mason. Norma's accusations made no sense. Had she lied to try to hurt her ex-husband? Mason was such a pillar of the community, although a boring pillar. And hadn't Frank offered Mason a beer the day of the picnic? He'd turned it down, saying he didn't drink. Yet, Norma claimed he'd once been a violent drunk. Interesting.

Well, well. Norma thought Mason had killed Emily. But, in Abigail's mind, there were also a fistful of other possible candidates.

Norma, not to speak ill of the dead, had had more than enough motive to want to hurt the woman, and years later, to put the blame on her hated ex-husband.

Todd Brown had had his own reasons to harm his ex-wife.

Then there was Sheriff Cal.

And Edna, of course.

Who else had hated Emily enough to kill her? What about the twins…who'd killed them? Abigail's head hurt. Sherlock Holmes she wasn't.

The two women left Norma's house. They returned to Lorna's kitchen. Lorna then made the call to the police. She simply said she'd noticed lights on in Norma's house, had discovered the mess, and thought they should check it out. Soon after, thanking Lorna for the refreshments, and her help, Abigail headed home. With the letter safe in her purse, her mind full of questions she couldn't answer, she drove straight to Frank's house.

Chapter 14

Abigail banged on the front door until Frank answered. He was in exercise shorts, bare chested, dripping in sweat, with a towel around his shoulders as if he'd been drying himself off. "Why, hi, Abigail," he welcomed her, short of breath, his face flushed.

"You'll never guess what I've found out," she said, sweeping by him into the living room.

"Nice to see you, too, Abby. You lucked out, I just got back from my daily run. You caught me as I was heading to the shower. Can it wait until I get out? I won't be long."

"It can. Don't let me stop you, Frank." She went back outside and sat down on the top porch step. "I'll wait out here."

"Soda, beer, in the fridge. Help yourself. Or I'll make coffee when I get out." He left the front door open.

Abigail fished the letter out and read it again as she waited. The day was cool for August and some artist had feathered the sky with wispy clouds. The smell of burning leaves made her nostalgic for fall. She sat there, thought about Norma, Emily, Mason and the past; trying to put the new pieces together.

Frank emerged, clean and dry, from the shower, in blue jeans and shirt, and made them a pot of coffee. He brought her a cup along with his, then settled in one of the rockers. "It's supposed to rain by tonight. We need it," he casually commented, studying the sky. He'd blow-dried his hair. Shaved. He looked good. "What's up?"

Abigail presented him with the letter. After he read it, she filled in the rest, telling him about Norma's death, her neighbor Lorna's suspicions and the vandalized house.

He took the contents of the letter with skepticism. "Nah, I can't imagine Mason had anything to do with Emily's death. By what he says, he didn't know her very well back then. Besides, everyone in town knows Norma loathed Mason by the end of their marriage–and she was off her rocker.

"I heard she used to max up the credit cards, call women out of the blue to accuse them of having affairs with her husband; used to throw things at him. She even put him in the hospital once. Martha told me about it when I lived in Chicago. Their divorce was so hostile. One scandal after another. John was the one who wanted it, not Norma. So I wouldn't put it past her to write a pack of lies and throw herself down the steps. If you have any doubts about her death, I know Orchard's chief of police, so we can go visit him. Ask some questions. I'm sure he'll help us out."

"You know Orchard's chief of police? Do all cops know each other?"

"Most do," he drawled. "Oscar Tannebaum is the chief. I went to the police Academy with him when we were young. Good hearted guy. Smart cop. We're both widowers, both own Gold Wings; both enjoy fishing. We've kept in touch over the years. I'll give Oscar a call." Frank put the letter in her hand, went into the house, and returned a few minutes later.

"Did you reach him?"

"Sure did. He was thrilled to hear from me. He's invited us down for supper. Said he'd tell us all he knows about the Norma Mason death when we get there. Bribe, if I ever heard one.

"By the way, I bought a new motorcycle yesterday, another Gold Wing, and brought it home. I was going for a ride today anyway, so how about us taking one to the Orchard Police Station? I have an extra helmet. And rain's not supposed to come in until later tonight. The bike is ready to go. I spent this morning tuning and cleaning it. It'd make a nice jaunt."

She didn't know what to say. "A motorcycle, huh?"

"Yeah, a form of transportation with two wheels, windshield, and saddlebags."

"I know what they are. I just didn't know you had one. I haven't been on a motorcycle in years." With a pensive look on her face, she folded the letter and put it in her purse. "Joel and I had this old Eleven Hundred Yamaha. He fixed it up. We used to ride everywhere…years ago. But I'll tell you: I don't like going fast and I hate riding in storms. Sure it isn't supposed to rain until later?"

"I guarantee it. I don't speed, and if it storms, I'll pull the bike over until it stops. Promise."

"Okay. I'll go," she surrendered. Frank found an extra jacket for her, because sometimes, he said, it got chilly out on the country roads.

The Gold Wing, a full dresser, in all its pearl white iridescent glory, was waiting at the end of the curved driveway. It was clean and shiny and gorgeous. "She's a 1994 with low miles on her," Frank bragged, handing Abigail a matching pearl white helmet with a built in CB. "Oscar's going to be so jealous when he sees her."

"I bet." She put the helmet on her head, slid the half facemask down over her eyes; and after Frank did the same, she swung her leg over the seat and climbed on. He gave her brief instructions on how to operate the CB. Then they were on their way. It felt strange being on a motorcycle again. Strange being behind a man who wasn't Joel. It felt good, though, to be out riding the country roads with nothing between her, the trees and sky, but air.

The ride was smooth. Calming. The breeze was cool. They commented on the scenery over the CB and when they ran out of words, Frank switched on the radio. Soon they were pulling into the Orchard's Police Station. It'd been relaxing, sitting behind Frank skimming down the road, arms around him. She could have ridden for hours and never stopped. She'd forgotten how exhilarating it could be.

Slipping their helmets over the handlebars, they entered the building. Abigail had been in a couple of police stations exactly like it. It was modest-sized, full of desks, chairs and people in uniforms whispering to each other. A few glanced up when they came in. One officer rose from his desk and strolled over.

"Frank Lester, as I live and die!" A short, compact, man in a blue uniform with gray hair and a square face stepped up and slapped Frank on the back as if he were a long lost brother. "You haven't changed one bit, except for that straggly salt and pepper mop. The extra pounds around the middle. You need a haircut."

"Yeah, and you need more hair. Looks like you're in the army. I'm retired now. I can grow it to my butt, if I want." Frank had an easy way with the other man. He did with most people but Abigail could tell these two were old friends.

Frank introduced Oscar to Abigail. The officer greeted her with, "Any friend of Frank's is a friend of mine." He gave her a big grin. Standing beside Frank, she returned it, and noted, though Oscar's mouth was smiling, his eyes were the probing sharp eyes of a cop. Nodding, his gaze x-rayed her.

"Before we get to the reason we're really here, Oscar," Frank stated, "come outside and see my newest Gold Wing. It's a beauty."

Oscar and Frank went to drool over the motorcycle while Abigail went in search of a restroom to comb out her helmet hair. She caught up with them as they were reentering the building.

"That is a beautiful bike," Oscar was saying. "You got a heck of a buy. Almost as good as the deal I got on mine. I'll bring my cycle up one weekend and we'll do some riding."

"You got a deal. Anytime."

Oscar ushered them to his desk. He offered them seats. "I'm six months from early retirement," he said once they'd settled. "I'm pretty sure I'll pass on it and keep working as long as they'll let me."

"Early retirement isn't bad. It's great to do what you want, Oscar. Believe me."

"Ha, and you were the most gung-ho cop I've ever known. How's the fishing up by you?" Oscar was shuffling papers as he talked, putting things in order so he could leave for the day.

"There's this lake behind my property full of catfish. When you come for that ride you'll have to stay overnight. I have a guest room. We'll do some fishing. Fry what we catch."

"You got a deal. Now, you wanted to know about Norma Mason's death?"

"Whatever you can tell us. Norma was from our town before she moved here. We just want a little more information on how it happened. We heard she fell down some stairs?"

"I shouldn't be telling you this, Frank. But, since you're an ex-cop and a friend, keep where you got the information to yourself. I investigated the scene after Mrs. Mason's fall. The paramedics called me in when they noticed the irregularities. There was a large amount of prescription drugs in the house, and more opened empty pill bottles on the premises. The neighbor lady, a friend of the deceased, had said other than an arthritis prescription, Mrs. Mason took no other drugs. Yet, there were way too many pill bottles for my liking. The M.E.'s workup showed there was a large number of drugs in her bloodstream at the time of death. Much more than normal.

"I didn't find the stairs particularly unsafe.

Relatives and others thought Mrs. Mason had become increasingly paranoid lately. People were watching her, she said. She'd been calling here at the station and reporting intruders inside and outside of her home for weeks. We'd go out there and there was never anyone. So there were problems. Consensus is Mrs. Mason might have thrown herself down those stairs. Suicide. Out of her fears or by accidentally taking an overdose. It's the only thing which made sense. Since we can't prove it, and it doesn't make a difference to me, I let the coroner put down the cause of death as accident. For her family's sake."

"Accident…but it could have been suicide?" Abigail gently shook her head.

Frank seemed to listen, but kept his thoughts to himself.

"That's the official verdict," Oscar finished, coming to his feet. "Case closed. I wish I could have had better news for you. I've told you what I know."

Abigail was about to blurt out about the house break-in, when Frank, apparently sensing what she was going to do, shushed her silently, a finger to his lips, shaking his head. *It wouldn't do any good,* his look warned. *He's told us all he knows.* So she kept silent.

"We appreciate it, Oscar. Now, how about we go to that steakhouse you crowed about and get us some supper. I'm about to die of starvation." Frank stood up.

"That sounds good to me. Let me finish with my people here, sign out, and I'm with you." Oscar attended to last minute business before the three of them went to eat. Once or twice they touched on the subject of Norma Mason, but Abigail and Frank didn't learn anything more than what Oscar had already told them. The time they spent with Oscar was pleasant. Abigail got to hear stories about Frank's past which helped her understand him better.

"Abigail, did you know Frank used to shoot in competitions? He actually won trophies. He can also hunt with a bow like an expert; play the best game of chess I've ever seen."

"No, I didn't know that. But nothing he does, or can do, surprises me anymore." Abigail caught Frank's wink. "He has more sides to him than a Rubik's cube."

The sun was setting by the time they said their farewells to Frank's old friend and got on the motorcycle. While they'd been inside a sudden storm had begun to move in. Frank thought they could ride ahead of it. Wrong. On the road barely minutes the downpour overtook them, along with thunder, lightning and wind, and they pulled under a concrete viaduct to find a dry cubbyhole.

"So, Mr. Weatherman," Abigail confronted him as they hunkered down on the concrete, eyeing the downpour. "It wasn't supposed to storm until after twelve tonight, huh?" They were soaked.

"Not supposed to. Oops, guess those silly weathermen were wrong again. I'm sorry."

"Weathermen are wrong half the time, if you ask me. Heck, Frank, I could be a weather person for all the smarts it takes. Hey, everybody out there on the other side of the screen, it's either going to rain today or it isn't. Hey, the sun's out, which means it's sunny. All you have to do is look out the window, toss a coin, or take a guess. I'm right more than the weather people."

"You got a point there. But I *did* think we'd be back before this storm hit. Oscar and I got carried away with old police stories, I guess. It was so good to see him again. I haven't since Jolene's funeral. For a while, when we were first cops, his wife and mine, the four of us, were inseparable. We used to go on vacations, ride bikes or motorcycles together. The good old days," he muttered, peering at the rain. Lightning lit up his face, the earth around them, and then the absence of it plunged everything into darkness. "Ooh, it's bad out there. It's lucky we found this place for shelter, though it looks like this is a fast moving storm. It will let up here soon and we'll make a dash for it. We're only fifteen, twenty minutes away from home.

"I wonder if Norma really committed suicide?" Frank mused aloud as if he'd had it on his mind for a while. "What do you think?"

"Lorna doesn't think she did. Norma had been happy, her life good, except for her suspicion that someone was watching her. She wasn't suicidal. She was only taking arthritis medicine. Lorna was positive about that."

"More loose ends. It seems like someone wanted the police to believe Norma tossed herself down those stairs." Frank fell into silence as they watched the rain, which was slackening off. "You know, rain's let up and we're still not that far from

Norma's house. We could take a short side trip back there. I could look over the accident scene. See what I can find."

"And I could ask the neighbor to let us take a peek? She has a key and permission, of a sort, to enter Norma's house."

"That'll work. We won't be breaking any laws then." Frank dug his cell phone out of his jacket's pocket. He handed it to Abigail. "Give her a call. See if she'll let us borrow the key. Tell her we'll just sneak in quietly, look at what we need to look at, and be out in a wink. No harm done to anyone. We won't touch a thing."

Abigail didn't have to think about it. Frank would be able to ferret out clues she wouldn't have seen, if there were any there to see. "Okay, I'm game. Let's do it." It took a minute on the phone with Lorna and they had their permission. They only had to wait for the rain to let up.

There were cows nearby. Abigail heard them calling to each other. The scent of wet hay was heavy on the night air. She felt like she was in an episode of *Murder, She Wrote*, without a script.

They waited another ten or so minutes until the rain was a light drizzle, got on the motorcycle and rode. Abigail directed him to the street, they parked in Lorna's driveway, then got the key from her.

"I was just heading to bed," Lorna told them after Abigail introduced Frank and they'd said a few words to each other. She was standing in the doorway with her robe on. "When you're done just drop the key in my mailbox. I'll get it tomorrow.

Call me if anything comes up."

"We will," Abigail promised. They said goodnight. Quietly, in the dark, Abigail and Frank made their way to the back of Norma's house.

"We're in luck," Frank whispered. "Someone's left the lights on inside. Probably to make it look occupied."

"I still feel like a burglar, sneaking into an empty house in the middle of the night," she whispered back as he gently shut the door.

"It's not the middle of the night and we have a key. Show me the stairs."

She led him to the basement door. The house appeared the same as when she'd been in it earlier that day. It was still a mess. If the police had already been there, there weren't any signs of it.

The basement light was on. Frank inspected the steps and the banister, saying nothing. "Before we leave, Abby, I'm going to take a quick look around the house." He left her standing in the kitchen by the door. He reappeared a few minutes later. "One of the bedroom windows has fresh scratches on the sill. I suspect someone recently climbed in through it from the outside."

"Someone who might have helped her fall down those steps?" Abigail kept her voice low.

"Maybe. From what I've seen I don't think it was suicide at all. There are scratches on the underside of the banisters. Scuffmarks a step or two down. Oscar told me they'd found splinters under Norma's fingernails, attributed to accidental scraping as the body went down. But I think, doped up as she was, she fought her attacker; as well as digging her fingernails into the wood as she tried to stop her fall.

"I also noticed the list on the kitchen bulletin board of things Norma wanted and needed to do this week topped by the words: *My Maine Cruise...leaving Aug. 18!* That's next Thursday. Hand drawn balloons, hearts, all around it. Her closet, I checked, was filled with new dresses and handbags. Some still had the sales tags on them. There's brand new luggage on the floor. All bought for her trip. She was excited to be going."

Abigail got it. "Ah, so if she was excited about going on vacation, had bought new clothes and all, why would she kill herself? Though that doesn't rule out it being an accident."

"No, it doesn't. Time to go." Frank grabbed her hand. They left the house, dropped the key into the neighbor's mailbox, and trudged back to the motorcycle. They climbed on and headed for home. The rain had stopped, but off in the distance, there was a sky crowded with sheet lightning. Thunder boomed. "We're in a lull between storms but another front's moving in, so we should hurry."

As she clung behind Frank, her arms tight around him, she spoke over the CB. "Are you going to tell Oscar you don't think Norma's death was a suicide and possibly not even an accident?"

"Now I will. I'll call him tomorrow. Tell him what I think. I didn't want to drag him into it until I was sure. But he should know. He should talk to the neighbor."

***

At the cabin, Frank rolled the Gold Wing

into the garage as the second rainstorm roared in. They'd just made it. "Do you want to come in for coffee?" he asked as they were standing on the porch, protected from the rain.

"No, thanks. Snowball is probably wondering where I am. I need to feed her. So I'll scoot on home before this rainstorm gets any worse. I can see the fog moving in. It's going to be thick tonight."

"I had so much fun today, Abby…how about one day next week we go on another ride? There's this amazing scenic route I know. It winds around a lake up through the hills."

Abigail met Frank's hopeful eyes. "Okay. I'd like that. I'll bring a picnic lunch."

***

As she drove away, backlighted with a distant halo of lightning, she could see Frank waving. She didn't make it home before the full storm hit. The last stretch rain and heavy wind shook her vehicle so fiercely she could hardly keep it on the road. When she pulled into her driveway, tucked the car up close beside the house, she was relieved but still had to fight the wind to get into inside.

On her front porch she found a cardboard box. She lugged it into the house. The note on top said: *More correspondence from the Summers' story.*

Ah, so the box was from Samantha. It was full of letters. Oh boy.

After a shower, and making hot chocolate, with the kitten asleep in her lap, she spent the rest of the evening reading the letters as the storm raged outside.

Dear Abigail Sutton,

I knew Jenny Summers and her brother, Chris. My mother worked at the bakery (it was called The Chocolate Donut back then) and I helped her that summer. I remember those kids. I was older, but Jenny and Chris came in most mornings and bought day old donuts with pennies they'd found on the side of the road, in parking lots, or what they got cashing in empty soda bottles. Jenny bought glazed donuts, and Chris, jelly. Sometimes I'd give them the donuts free. They never had much money. We felt sorry for them. Jenny asked me if I liked horses. I said I did. The next time she came in she gave me this picture she'd drawn of a horse as a present. It was really good. They were sweet kids. Often, I'd see bruises on them. When I'd ask what had happened, they would say they'd fallen climbing trees, or skating. I knew that wasn't true.

Another letter said:

Dear Mrs. Sutton,

Jenny and Chris Summers were friends of mine. I used to see them out at Cooper's Pond on hot days and we'd swim together. Their mom was usually gone working. Their Aunt Edna was mean to them. I saw her hit Jenny once. Jenny didn't cry. Nighttime, they'd sneak out of their upstairs window; climb down the elm tree to get away from her. A bunch of us kids would play hide and seek, in the dark, in the field next to the house. Jenny had horse statues on a shelf. All kinds, colors and sizes. She loved horses. Chris loved those colored plastic dinosaurs. They were all over his bed. He carried the smaller ones in his pockets. He also liked spiders. Real ones. Jenny was scared to death of spiders. The two kids were close and were together a lot.

And one read:

Dear Abigail Sutton,

I was a nurse at Chalmers Hospital. I recall those Summers kids. I remember them because they were brought in with bruises, cuts and, once, a broken bone. Even though the woman, their aunt, I believe, maintained the injuries were caused by accidents of one kind or another, I never swallowed that. And those kids were sick all the time. Stomachaches, headaches; not being able to hold food down. They were malnourished. It wasn't normal. Before they left, or disappeared, or died (as the graves now show) I wanted their mother to come in so I could talk to her about the children's worsening conditions. I called twice in a week. The aunt said her sister couldn't come in and gave me some ridiculous story as to why. She said Emily was out of town for a time. I never saw any of them again after that. I've thought about those kids a lot over the years. It was so sad. I was a young, inexperienced nurse back then. I didn't realize what was going on. I've seen enough now to know those kids were probably being mistreated. I've often felt guilty, as if I should have done more, but didn't. I regret it more than ever, knowing they died that summer.

And there was a strange angry one, hand written in thick red letters:

A. Sutton,

You'd better keep your nose out of things which don't concern you, lady! Leave what happened to the Summers in the past; stop dragging up what you have no business in. You don't know what you're doing. I'm warning you this time. Next time you won't be so lucky. Pets can die. Houses can burn. Cars can have no brakes. Get the message? They're dead. Let it go.

When Abigail examined the envelope, there was no stamp, post date or return address. Just a plain white envelope with her name on the front. Someone had hand delivered it or dumped it in with the others.

Great. Now she was getting threats. She called Frank.

"So you made it home all right?" The storm as loud on his end of the phone as on hers.

"Yep. I got wet getting in the door, but now I'm snug and dry. Just me and my cat lounging on the couch, sipping hot cocoa."

"You give your cat hot cocoa?"

"Sure, she loves it," her voice mocking. She chuckled. "I called because Samantha left me more letters on the porch. Fan mail from the newspaper stories. I just got done reading one that wasn't so nice." She gave him a quick rundown on what the letter had said.

"I was afraid of this. It was only a matter of time before the weirdos came out of the shadows or perhaps one certain dangerous weirdo. Do you need company? Do you want one of my guns?"

"No, no. Anyway, no one's going to be out

in this tempest."

"Well, don't take chances. Get that wooden club of yours out, keep it with you. I'll talk to the sheriff about having his men put an extra patrol past your place for a while. I'll let him know about the hate letter. He'll want to see it."

Abigail released a weary sigh. "Tell him to stop by tomorrow. I'm going to bed in about ten minutes. And, Frank, I can take care of myself."

"Of course, Abby, tomorrow. Goodnight. Call me if you need anything. Promise?"

"I promise, Frank. Good night." She hung up, put the letters away, took the wooden stick from the closet and went to bed, Snowball at her heels. The house was shaking. The rain was a steady roar coming down. Every few seconds the house lit up from the lightning. It felt so good to be home, warm, dry and safe.

She dreamed she was walking in the woods behind her house through the storm and her nightgown wasn't getting wet. Her hair flew wildly about her head. Her hands came up to push the strands away from her face so she could see. Limbs tumbled around and past her. The lightning illuminated her way. Her feet were taking her somewhere she didn't know. She heard childish laughter. When she looked over her shoulder, there were two children dancing around her in the rain, their flaxen hair a corona around their small heads, their eyes sapphires in the dark. Their feet were bare, their clothes translucent. They were beautiful fairy children. Jenny and Christopher.

She followed them through the night woods

to the tree house as the thunder rocked the ground. The children ran to her, their grasp soft as a cloud and their touch made her smile. They were like her own children; she'd come to know them so well. Their eyes were melancholy and happy all at once.

"Watch and remember," they spoke together. Lightning spiraled down from the churning ebony sky, through the branches, and hit the ground around the tree house. The girl ran to the base of the tree, dug around in the muddy dirt, snatched up a glass jar. She showed it to Abigail as the rain cascaded around her. She smiled a ghostly smile. In the jar there were pieces of paper. The girl's form wavered in the misty air before it evaporated. The glass jar fell and burst into a hundred pieces of glass. The scraps of paper rose into the wet night then fluttered off like rain birds.

Christopher put something tiny, lumpy, into her hand. He smiled and vanished into his grave again. When she looked she saw one of his tiny green dinosaur toys lying in her palm. She closed her eyes for a moment, two.

When Abigail opened them again she was in her bed. It was morning. No storm, no rain. The sun was bright above. She got up, made coffee. Drank a fast cup, then dressed, pulled boots on and headed into the wet woods. She had no trouble finding the tree house in the daylight. Lightning had struck it. The tree itself was split down the center. She'd brought a shovel and begun to dig where her dream Jenny had dug. It took a while but she found a buried jar with the missing diary pages in it. Hurrying home, she washed the jar off. She opened it over the kitchen sink.

Inside there were the missing pages from the diary covering the children's last two weeks alive–and a tiny green toy dinosaur. She read the pages. Reread certain parts of them:

I caught mom on phone with a new boyfriend. They were fighting. She's afraid of him.

Aunt Edna and mom had awful fight about money mom said belonged to us that our Aunt stole. She's gonna call the sheriff. Mom shouted at her and said we were leaving soon as we could. She was gonna sell this house. Aunt Edna would be broke. No place to live. Aunt Edna was so mad.

Late last night I heard mom and someone, a man, I think, fighting outside. I went to the window, but saw nothing.

This morning Aunt Edna said mom went out of town. Don't know when she will be back. Mom out of town? Mom would never do that without telling me and Chris.

Mom has been gone three days. Aunt Edna says she's with our dad. That's strange. They hate each other. Chris has been sick and is worse today. He's throwing up and everything. Aunt Edna wont take him to the doctor or the hospital. Says she cant afford it. The phone has been turned off. She watches us all the time or I would get some help. Something is not right.

Mom has been gone over a week. I ask Aunt Edna when mom is coming home but she wont tell me. I cant believe mom would leave us alone so long with her.

Chris is really sick and cant eat now at all. He is so skinnie. His bones stick out. Last night he was crying because of the pain in his belly, so I snuck out of the house to get help from Mrs. Vogt. Aunt Edna caught me and locked me in the basement all night and wouldn't let me out until I promised not to do it again. She said us being sick is nobodys business but ours. We are proud. We don't need help from noone. We will get better soon. I cried and cried. Grandma sang to me and keep me company the whole night in the basement.

I am sick to my stomach again today. So tired. I think I have what Chris has.

Aunt Edna was talking to someone on the phone and she was real upset. I couldn't understand most of what they were saying, sometimes I don't hear too good.

Mom still not home...sheriff comes over to see aunt a lot. But he won't talk to us.

Today Chris wont wake up. I am going to sneak out of house when Aunt Edna goes to get groceries and try to make it to Mrs. Vogt's house again. But I am sick, too... so if I do not make it I will put these pages in a jar and bury it on the way in this hole we have under our tree house for mom to find when she comes home. She knows our hiding places.

And that was the last message. Obviously Jenny had not made it to Mrs. Vogt's.

Abigail phoned Frank, agreed to meet him at Stella's in an hour to hand the pages over to him, someone who could protect them. Frank had a safe. Lots of guns. Let that thief try to get into *his* house.

Chapter 15

Munching on an apple, Abigail walked into town. She needed exercise. The weather person swore it wasn't going to rain. She was going to meet Frank at Stella's for lunch. She was carrying a canvas bag full of paperbacks because she wanted to go to the town's bookstore, Tattered Corners, first. Martha had said it had a large collection of used paperbacks she could trade her old ones for. Which fit into Abigail's meager budget perfectly.

It was the first time she was visiting the bookstore. It wasn't much to look at from the outside. A narrow framed building squeezed between two larger businesses and two doors down from the general store. She ducked into Tattered Corners stealthily, her eyes on Mason's window. She didn't want to see, or deal, with him right now. She couldn't look at him without thinking of Emily Summers. She was afraid she'd give her feelings over everything away if she saw him. A few days ago she'd driven all the way to Chalmers to do her shopping.

Inside the bookstore, she made herself stop fretting about the Summers, the diary pages, and the hate letter. There was more to life than the past. The walls were crowded with wooden shelves of books from floor to ceiling. The air was filled with the aromas of polish and old book paper. There was a table stacked high with old paperbacks of all kinds. Abigail lost herself looking through them and had some picked out when a woman came up to her.

"Can I help you?" The woman was dressed in a soft cotton dress a watery shade of mauve. A silk scarf was tied loosely around her neck. She wore her hair long, loose, and clasped in a blue barrette. Her eyes were brown, expressive, her skin light and mostly unlined. Her teeth were perfect and white. There was a lot of money in that mouth, Abigail thought. The woman took care of herself. She had style and class; looked to be close to sixty if she was a day. But she was well preserved.

"I've been meaning to come in for weeks. I bought the old Summers' house."

"Abigail Sutton, I know who you are. I read the *Journal* every week and recognize you from that first Summers' story when they ran your photo. What a sorrowful mystery it's turned out to be," the woman purred in her husky voice, as she extended her ringed hand to shake Abigail's. "I'm Claudia Mathis, proprietor. It's nice to meet you. I wondered if you were a book person or not. I know you're an artist and most artists are readers."

"I love books. It's just that I've been so busy fixing up the house, and working on commissions, I've had no time to come in until now. I've picked out a few books." Abigail lifted up the paperbacks in her hands. "I brought in some of my own paperbacks. Can I trade them for these?"

"Of Course. That's how it works."

A boy in a Harry Potter T-shirt skipped into the store. He scanned the shelf of comic books by the door. He cocked his chin at Claudia as she acknowledged his presence by waving her fingers at him.

"How long have you owned the store?" Abigail queried, after the exchange had been made, and she'd tucked the paperback replacements in her bag.

"Over three decades. I've lived in Spookie my whole life. Third generation. And yes I knew Emily Summers and her family. Come back to the rear of the store and have some refreshments. We'll talk."

Claudia led and Abigail tagged behind as the bookseller paused before a wooden cart laid out with a silver tea set, china cups, saucers, and a plate of cookies from the bakery down the street. Abigail recognized the empty bakery box on the corner table. The bakery made excellent cookies.

"Please, sit down, Abigail, have some tea and civilized conversation." Claudia lowered herself onto a plush chair. "I think we have a lot to talk about, you and I."

Abigail liked Claudia right away. She made her feel at ease as they talked about the town and its people. Claudia was happily married to a local carpenter, had raised five children, all of whom had grown up and moved away to bigger towns and bigger jobs. She wasn't bitter her children lived in other places. Her life, she said, was full the way it was, with her husband, the bookstore, and their traveling. She'd seen most of the United States and some of Europe. Something Abigail had always wanted to do. Claudia was educated, intuitive, and had read every book in the shop. She loved to garden and had an orchard of apple trees.

"You know, Abigail, you're the talk of the

town with this mystery of yours. It's time I tell what I know." Claudia evaded looking at her. "I know who Emily's married lover was. I've always known that. And more."

"John Mason?" Abigail supplied softly, though they were the only ones in the store. The boy hadn't found what he'd wanted and had left. The bell above the door had tinkled as he went out. "We didn't feel it was necessary to put it in the newspaper, though."

"Oh, no. Well, I mean, he was one of Emily's conquests, but not the one she was afraid of. I was talking about Sheriff Cal Brewster. Emily and I were friends and she'd confided in me. She didn't have much money so she helped me here at the store after hours sometimes for cash or trade. I was just starting out. My bookstore was new. She'd taken accounting classes in high school. She helped me set up my books. Emily was a lot smarter than people gave her credit for. She taught me so much. Cal was crazy in love, obsessed, with her…and I think *he* killed her. I can't be sure but in my gut I feel it. Everyone wants what he or she can't have. And some will destroy what they can't have."

"But he was married."

"He was, but that didn't stop him from wanting Emily. She fought it, of course. She wasn't like that. She was a good woman. She was just lonely and way too beautiful for this small town. And…Emily loved someone else. She never told me who, I only knew she did.

"And yes, now you mention it, John Mason was involved with her a little, as well. But then most of us women were involved, or in love, with John back in those days." Her laugh was gentle. "You wouldn't know it from the way John is now. Life has embittered him. But he was handsome and exciting once. Charismatically passionate. He used to read three books a week. He wrote *poetry*. Every eligible woman in the county had her hat set for him. But he was trouble in capital letters. He drank too much, drag raced his cherry-red mustang into countless accidents, desired every pretty woman he saw, and he was the most ruthlessly ambitious man I'd ever met. Back then, anyway.

"Heck, even I'd loved John for years before Emily showed up that summer. I'd done everything I could think of to get him to marry me. That was before my husband, you see. But I was nothing. I had no beauty or money. John and I dated, but he'd moved on to other women after me. Always looking for something he couldn't seem to find. Oh, he wanted it all, John did. Adoration, wealth, and respect. He played his women against each other. He liked to see blood. Playing women off against each other was sport to him. He got off on it.

"Until he met Emily.

"He fell head over heels for her, real love for the first time, I think, that he'd ever felt in his life. He even risked his engagement to Norma. And Norma was his ticket to success, his way out of the wretched poverty he'd been raised in."

"Through the store and Norma's trust fund, right?" Abigail cued.

"Ah, you know it all. John was a nobody, an orphan without a future when he came to town.

He'd lived most of his life in foster homes. You have to understand that to understand why he was the way he was back then. Emily was so wrong for him. She was poor, but he met her, loved her, and nothing else mattered. Not me, not Norma, nothing. But here's the irony, Emily didn't love him. She dated him briefly and then dropped him just like that." She snapped her slender fingers. "It drove John insane that Emily didn't want him anymore. It made him mean. He drank more, which made him meaner, and even crazier. Though, in the end, John seemed to accept it. While Cal Brewster didn't."

"So you knew Emily really well, huh?"

"In the beginning, I sought Emily's friendship. Figuring if I got close to her, I'd stay close to John and eventually find a way to get him back. I tried to be like her, copy her. Thinking if he wanted a woman like Emily, I could become that. I went to night school and opened this bookstore. It made me what I am today." Her slow smile was self-mocking.

"But when I got to know Emily, I truly *liked* her. Emily's friendship began to mean more to me than John. One day I'd woke up and thinking of John hadn't hurt so much. I'd met my future husband by then. Things had changed." Claudia's eyes went to the store's front door. People were passing by in the sunlight; all in a hurry going somewhere or other.

"I knew about Emily's stalker, too. I believed, at the time, it was Norma, John's fiancée, trying to get rid of her…when she didn't need to. Emily was no threat to her.

"And I knew about Emily's sister, Edna, who'd been stealing Emily's inheritance money from their bank account. Emily was going to sell the house, leave town, and put Edna out on the street."

Abigail dropped cookie crumbs in her lap and brushed them off.

"Truth was, Emily was also leaving to begin a new life with the man she truly loved–the one she wouldn't talk about–somewhere else. She had her bags packed and everything. She came by one afternoon to say goodbye. She said she was sneaking away with the kids, fearful of what Cal, John or Edna would do if they found out. Yet, I believe now, coming into town was where she made her mistake. I watched her drive away and saw Sheriff Cal take out after her in his car. That was the last time I ever saw Emily or her children."

"You think Sheriff Cal caught up to her?"

"Now I do. You found their graves. I think John knew she was leaving, as well, because I saw him later that night. He was beyond distraught. I assumed it was because Emily had left him. He was drunk, cursing, and breaking bottles in the street. I followed him to his rented room and tried to console him. Not that I had designs on him, I was over him, but only because I felt sorry for him. He was rude to me, ordered me to leave, and told me never to bother him again. I left. That was the last time I talked to John for a long while. After that he avoided me. He still avoids me."

Abigail thought, as much as Claudia was talking about Mason, she might still have unfinished business of some kind with the man. Sometimes love and hate rode side by side.

"Anyway, John married Norma soon after that. I married a year later. End of story. The point is, I think either Sheriff Cal had something to do with the murders, or Edna. She also had a crush on John, did you know that? She never had a chance, of course, she wasn't near pretty, rich, ambitious, or smart enough for him. But how she tried. I think she hated her sister, besides for the inheritance problems, even more for her having captured John's heart."

A couple had come into the shop. They were milling around, taking books off the shelves and paging through them. They looked like buyers.

"Just thought you'd like to know all this. I have to take care of business now, but perhaps you'll visit again. We'll talk some more. On other subjects. It's been nice finally meeting you, Abigail." Claudia rose and excused herself.

Abigail stood up as well. It was time to meet Frank. "Thanks for the books, the tea, and the enlightening conversation, Claudia. It was nice meeting you, too. I will be back." She grabbed her book bag, slung it over her shoulder, and walked to the front of the store. Out into the hot sun, chewing over her exchange with Claudia, she wasn't paying much attention to anything around her.

She didn't see Mason come out of his store until it was too late. "Abigail, I caught you!" he exclaimed, placing his hand on her arm.

He'd startled her. Unsettling to have just been talking about him and, suddenly, there he was in the flesh. "Mr. Mason, what do you want?" She tugged her arm away. Retreated a step.

"Didn't you see me waving my arms at you through the window?" He was staring at her, smiling. He seemed so happy to see her.

"No, I didn't." Plastering on her own smile, she made herself behave. So he'd been a player in his younger days. So what? So he'd known Emily. So he'd lied about it. She couldn't meet his gaze.

She tried to imagine what he'd been like when he'd been young; she couldn't. All she could see was an aging man who'd long ago lost his looks and himself.

"I wanted to tell you. I've sold three of your watercolors. I bought one, the one I admired with my store in it, and two others sold to townsfolk who really loved them. I have the money, and was about to call you, then here you are. I thought you might need the seventy-five dollars."

She looked up. Mason was trying so hard to be nice, it made her feel guilty. "Thank you, Mr. Mason. I do appreciate it. I could use the money."

"Then come inside. I'll get it for you." He took her hand and pulled her into his store. It was empty. The last thing she'd wanted was to be alone with Mason, yet she didn't have much choice. What was she afraid of anyway? He wasn't about to make a pass at her in broad daylight in his own store, right? Right.

He gave her the money and a receipt. "I listed what amount you received for each picture. We have a good thing going here, hey? We're both making money. Everyone who sees your artwork, Abigail, loves your pictures. They rave about your use of color and how exquisitely you recreate inanimate objects. Bring in more pictures. I suggest, you push up the price at least a third. They're worth it. Gretchen Stickley promised she'd come by on payday to buy the large picture of the farmhouse surrounded in sunflowers." Mason made a hand flourish towards the farmhouse picture propped against the wall. It was an old picture she'd had forever. It had a price tag of one hundred dollars on it. That, plus what Abigail had in her hand, would pay her utilities for a month. She was thrilled.

"I also talked to other storeowners in nearby towns," Mason said, "and some of them are ready to take your artwork on consignment, as well. Same commission split. Isn't that marvelous?"

The praise, the money, and the promise of more sales flustered Abigail, but she didn't feel at ease around Mason. It was hard to pretend she did.

"It is, and that's kind of you."

"Abigail?" She was aimed for the door when Mason demanded, "After all this time, why are you digging up that stuff about Emily Summers and her kids? Can't you let the dead rest in peace?" There was more than irritation in his tone, there was suppressed anger. Gone was the amiable man from a minute ago. This was what he'd really wanted to talk to her about.

Abigail's feet froze, then she pivoted around. Mason was so close behind her she could see the desperation, the sorrow in his face, which hadn't been there before. He must have really loved Emily, she thought. All her stories were bringing back sad memories. They were hurting him. And, surprisingly, her heart softened towards him.

"It just happened, Mr. Mason. If you've read the newspaper stories, you know that. The notes and stumbling on the graves the way I did. They were all accidents. I never set out to disturb the dead at all. They disturbed me."

Mason lowered his voice. "You need to let it drop. Now. Spreading her life, her death, and her dirty laundry all over the newspapers serves no purpose. Stop the digging, the articles. They're just sensationalistic claptrap anyway. There are things in the past best left there. Secrets that don't need to see the light of day. Believe me, I know."

She couldn't tell if the words were a threat or friendly advice.

"I don't think I have anything to say about it anymore. An official investigation into the murders has already begun. Once the bodies were found, it was inevitable."

The word *murders* made him recoil. There was suddenly a controlled fury in his eyes. "You started it and you're the one keeping it going. Don't think I don't know that."

Then, he seemed to catch himself, changed tactics, and gave a resigned sigh. "Just remember I advised you to stop. For your own good…your own safety," he whispered.

She was about to ask him what he meant by that when, unexpectedly, Frank was standing at the door. "Abigail, there you are! I got worried about you. You were supposed to meet me at Stella's at twelve, remember? So when I saw you dash in here, I thought I'd mosey on over and see what was taking you so long."

"Frank." Mason greeted the other man, his face reverting to a blank expression.

"John." Curt. No other banter, but a coolness in his manner Mason must have sensed because he didn't add to the conversation.

She spoke to Frank, "I was just leaving." She plucked Mason's hand off her arm and walked out the door, Frank behind her. She didn't look back.

"What was that all about?" Frank questioned the moment they were outside.

"I think he tried to bribe me. Or threatened me. I think. I'm not sure."

Frank took her arm and swung her around to look at him. "Do you want me to go back in there and break his neck?" he said with a hint of humor.

"No. I'm fine. He freaked me out, that's all. He's disgruntled over this whole Summers' thing. If I didn't know better I'd say he had something to hide."

"You need to stay away from him, Abby. He was involved with Emily, we know that. Could be he does have something to hide, and a cornered animal is a dangerous animal, don't forget that."

"Don't I know it." She let out the breath she'd been holding. "I hadn't planned on making nice chitchat with him, but he ambushed me as I came out of the bookstore. He dragged me inside on the pretense of giving me money…because he'd sold three of my pictures. One to himself. He talked about putting my watercolors in other stores. Then, out of nowhere, he asked me to drop the Summers' investigation. When I didn't give him the response he wanted, he turned a little weird. Thanks for rescuing me."

They went into Stella's. The usual lunch crowd was there, including an elderly woman, and an elderly man who was dressed in frayed bib overalls. He had stringy white hair, was missing a front tooth, and his glasses had a band of adhesive tape holding the bridge of the frame together. The two were bickering over who was going to pay for the food they'd eaten.

"What else did Mason say?" Frank interrupted her people watching. "Your face is still flushed."

Abigail told him as Stella came over to take their order. Frank ordered the day's lunch special. She only wanted coffee.

"We're going to have to be more careful from now on with Mason. As well as I thought I knew him, I don't know him at all these days. We used to be friendly. But lately, he sidesteps me on the street and is barely civil when I'm in his store. He's not himself. Something's going on, I just don't know what. Those articles have affected him. I'm wondering why."

"I think he hates us dredging Emily's life up. The woman who broke his heart and got away. He really loved her, according to Claudia at the bookstore. Anyway, I'll stay away from him for a while. Let him cool down."

"Good idea. Now let me see those diary pages you found out by the tree house." Frank held his hand out. "So strange you had that dream. Then you go out there and find the missing pages for real. As if the ghosts of those kids were speaking to you. Spooky, if you ask me." He wiggled his eyebrows until Abigail laughed.

Abigail rummaged through her book bag, found the pages, and handed them over. He read them, a frown on his lips. "Whoa, this isn't absolute proof Edna poisoned those two kids, but it's pretty close. I've been thinking about that old lady so much the last few weeks. Thing is, I still can't see a cold-blooded sister and child murderess. She was eccentric, selfish, antisocial, and had few friends, if any. But, on the other hand, I've known people to kill for less than jealousy, a house, and an inheritance. You just can't tell."

"Murderers and people who do bad things are born with black souls." Abigail gave her opinion. "No conscience. On some level they're evil and sometimes can't help themselves."

"So you think some people are born evil?" He folded the pages; returned them to Abigail. "Intriguing theory." He opened his notebook and began scribbling. "What else did you find out from Claudia?" His pen was poised, as if he knew Claudia had revealed something else of interest.

She updated him.

"I never knew this town was such a Peyton Place of smoldering passions." He huffed. "I remember Claudia from those days. She was shy, her nose in a book most of the time. She was cute, but not flamboyantly pretty like Emily was. Really smart. She went to college, I know that, yet ended up marrying a man who worked with his hands. Go figure. I never had a clue she was in love with Mason, too–which, if you think about it, could make her a suspect as well. She had a motive. Ha, but as I remember both of them, John wasn't her type at all."

"Or so you thought."

"I guess I was young and didn't always see things, or people, the way they really were," Frank conceded. "Abby, you have more information, so what are you going to do with it? Take some people's advice, drop the whole thing, or print what you've discovered and keep digging?"

"I'm going to give the information to Samantha for the next story."

"You wouldn't!"

"I would and I will. Though I won't let her use any names of living people. Jenny and Christopher would want me to continue. They'd want me to find their killer." Abigail was solemn. "I'm not going to let anyone scare me off. I'll just have to be more careful–and have stronger locks installed on my house. I'll go see Samantha after I leave here. The sooner I do this the better, before I chicken out. She's going to flip when she sees these missing diary pages."

"Back flip probably. Don't worry, I'll keep an eye on you. I'll be your bodyguard if I have to be. I'll protect you."

"I feel safer already. Thank you."

"You're welcome. I always take care of my friends." After Frank finished his lunch he accompanied Abigail to the *Journal*'s office where they had a nice long chat with Samantha.

Chapter 16

Samantha was thrilled with the diary pages. Abigail spilled everything about their trip to Orchard, seeing Brown, Norma's death, the hate letter, finding the missing pages, and some of what Claudia had confided about the old sheriff and Edna.

"Our readers have been begging for more of this hometown whodunit," Samantha confessed. "I have more photos that came in last week of Emily and the kids. I can use them to fill another page.

"And I'll be careful how I write it. Without proof, using names of living people as possible suspects, is unethical."

And unsafe, Abigail thought.

"It's great we have this hand written stuff, these diary pages, from Jenny herself. The letter from Norma, though, I can't use any of it because it's unsubstantiated. All that, along with what Brown recollected about a stalker…wonderful! This mystery has been better than a Sherlock Holmes serial. That Emily's mysterious lover, whoever he was, out of jealous rage, *may have* strangled her to death in a fit of passion because she was leaving him. Classic. That someone, or Edna, *may have* poisoned the children to have free and clear title to the house and the inheritance, and Edna *may have* been blackmailing someone…for thirty years…is so juicy. What a story."

"Yeah, what a story. A sweet woman is maybe murdered by her abusive boyfriend and two innocent children are maybe killed for greed." Abigail couldn't deny the uneasiness which had settled over her. She could still see the pain and anger in Mason's eyes when he'd confronted her over Emily's life being smeared throughout the newspapers. Was she doing the right thing?

"It's horrible enough to think of how Emily died, but it's worse to think someone killed the children, and that it took place in the house you live in now. It must be eerie, I imagine." Samantha must have sensed Abigail's disquiet. "To think Edna might have done that and no one ever suspected. You never know another person as well as you think is beginning to be my new motto."

When Samantha had everything she needed for the next article, Frank walked Abigail home.

***

Three days later Abigail awoke and got ready to go after a copy of the newspaper. She didn't have to go far. Someone had sent her the edition special delivery wrapped around a rock. It had smashed through her front window, landing in her living room.

Outside on the porch, she stepped on splatters of blood, and looked up. There were tiny bleeding birds stuffed in the openings of her birdhouses. Real dead birds. Their beady eyes glazed, and motionless, their feathers smeared with red; limp beaks hanging downward. Blood dripped down on the wood.

Groaning, covering her mouth, she slid onto the swing. The message was clear. Someone was warning her to stop what she was doing. Stop chasing the Summers' mystery. Was the person responsible watching her from a distance at that very moment? She'd been in a trance, but the thought snapped her out of it. She'd be safer inside. *Where was Snowball?*

Abigail launched herself from the swing, ran inside, and was relieved when she found the fur ball sleeping behind the sofa. She scooped the kitten up and hugged her until she meowed in protest. Picking up the phone, she dialed Frank's number.

"I'll be there in ten minutes. I'll call the sheriff before I go," he said before he hung up.

Over coffee, Abigail read the article which had sailed in with the rock. Samantha, as always, had written a fine piece, including everything, every new clue, every new development–and all the contents of the found letter and diary.

The problem, Abigail realized, was the reporter had made hypothetical cases for Edna either being the murderer, or of a mystery man behind the scenes who'd been dating, or wanted to date, Emily. The ex-husband had also been offered up, or the dead sheriff, the sheriff's wife or someone perhaps married, or engaged, to someone else, as possible suspects. That was hitting close to home. If a person had known Emily and the people involved in town at the time, it's possible to imagine who the murderer might have been. The real murderer, if he or she were still alive and in the area, would be livid, Abigail thought, rubbing her eyes. People would start to point fingers. It was in their nature.

"Samantha, what have you done?" Abigail asked aloud. Not that Samantha had meant to point fingers. No one knew for sure who Emily's or the children's killer had been. Not for sure anyway. But someone had tossed the rock and killed the birds. Who had they angered that much with the stories? Someone who knew, or was trying to hide something, and was afraid of being discovered…perhaps the killer themselves. Frank was right about one thing; she'd better be careful. She was obviously a target these days.

She collected a trash bag, paper towels, and a pair of metal tongs, unable to bear the thought of those dead birds in her birdhouses one second longer. She was about done plucking broken feathery bodies from birdhouse holes when Frank roared up the driveway in his truck. Sheriff Mearl pulled in behind him.

"Original way of getting a message across." Frank stood in the sunlight and watched Abigail put the last two bird bodies into the trash bag. "If you sing like a bird, you'll end up a dead bird?"

"Something like that," Abigail retorted sarcastically. Finished, she shoved the trash bag off the side of the porch to be dealt with later.

"You know, if I didn't know better, I'd say you have your very own stalker. Hate letters, broken windows, and dead critters on your porch." Frank leaned against the post.

"Maybe the same stalker Emily had?"

"Not if it was Norma. She's dead."

"If Norma had really been Emily's stalker…or only stalker. Emily seemed to have had a lot of enemies."

"That she did."

Frank exchanged a silent nod with the sheriff who'd come up onto the porch.

"Lady," Sheriff Mearl grunted, "trouble follows you like a trained dog. As often as I come out here, you should provide me with my own monogrammed coffee mug."

"Funny, Sheriff. I guess that's a hint you'd like a cup of coffee, huh?"

"Wouldn't mind having one, now that you offer. I haven't had my quota yet this morning."

"The pot's in the kitchen. You know where that is, Sheriff. Help yourself. Cups in the top right cabinet. Cream and sugar on the table. We'll be right behind you."

The sheriff sauntered into the house towards the kitchen, his gun belt and holster squeaking, and his boot steps echoing loudly across the floors.

"I don't know why you called him," Abigail said to Frank. "He's not going to be any help. He never caught anyone the other times. There was never any evidence left behind. And I'm sure whoever did this was also as clever in covering their trail."

"I had to call him in. He's the sheriff. A report has to be made. Just be careful what you say to him," Frank muttered. "We have to remember it was Mearl's father who investigated the original disappearances in the first place. Mearl's father who had a thing for Emily and might have been involved in her death. Let's not forget that. Could be why Mearl's been so attentive to you and this situation from the beginning. Could be Mearl knows more than he's letting on."

She hadn't thought of it that way. It took her off guard. "Nah." She dismissed the warning. "Sheriff's here for the free coffee and any gossip he can glean. That's all."

"You have gossip?" Frank grinned and was rewarded with the tiniest of smiles. "See, I knew I could make you smile if I tried. I'm sorry about your bird massacre. But, when you opted to run those stories, I did caution you it could cause repercussions. Well, it did."

"I know, my fault. What kind of person butchers little animals to make a point?"

"Someone who's frightened he, or she, is going to be exposed. Someone who took a lot of trouble to get all these birds dead and here. All their little necks are broken. A pretty personal touch, that."

"I'd say. Wonder where the person got them from?" She shook her head. It didn't matter. "I'd like to get a hold of whoever did this and wring *their* neck."

"I bet you would." Frank opened the door for her. "Let's get some coffee, then get the sheriff out of here. Afterwards, I'll fix that broken window for you." She tried to talk him out of it, but he insisted. "What are friends for?" He followed her into the kitchen.

The sheriff, now reclining in one of her

chairs, focused his eyes on Abigail after she'd said her say. He asked if anyone had seemed unhappy with her over the articles. She told him of her run in with Mason three days before. "Humph, well, all I can tell you, Mrs. Sutton, is to keep your doors locked. And I'll let you know if I find out anything." He had a toothpick between his lips he kept moving around. He said he was trying to quit smoking for about the hundredth time; the toothpick was a placebo. "Do you want me to stake out your place for a day or two and see who shows up?"

"You could do that, Sheriff," Frank interrupted gently. "But I have it covered." There was a firmness in his eyes the sheriff couldn't argue with.

"Have it your way, Frank. Just keep me posted on anything further that develops. I'll go and take care of the paperwork for this incident." He looked at Abigail with cool eyes. Today his manner had been strictly business. He wasn't acting like his usual fawning self. What a relief. "You're gathering quite a file, young lady. Somebody doesn't like you much."

Abigail wondered if the sheriff was one of them. He couldn't be happy about what had been written in the newspaper, about his father-the-womanizer and how he'd taken advantage of Emily all those years ago. At the least, it had to be embarrassing.

After the sheriff left, she and Frank cleaned up the broken glass. He made a trip to the hardware store for supplies, and when he got back, he put in a new pane of glass for her.

"When I was in town," Frank said as he was finishing the job, "I tried to see John. To have a word with him about the way he treated you last time; what he said to you. But his store was closed up. In the middle of a weekday. Very unusual. He's always there. I went by his house, rang the front door bell, and peeked in the windows. There was no one around. His car's gone. No one's seen him today. I asked."

"Now that is strange." It bothered her that Mason wasn't at his store the day the newspaper came out and someone left slaughtered birds on her porch. What was that about? Ever since their run in she'd had an odd feeling about Mason. Claudia had said he'd been in love with Emily all those years ago. Suddenly, everything he'd ever said to her, the way he'd look at her, was interested in her, had a different meaning. If she looked so much like Emily, it made sense now. Perhaps Mason thought she was Emily come back? To haunt him? For revenge? Now that was almost too spooky to contemplate.

"He could be away on a trip or a vacation. People do leave town for one reason or another, you know," Frank offered.

"I know. I'd feel better, though, if you'd been able to see him, to gauge his reaction to what happened this morning. See if he acted guilty. I don't like his vanishing act. He's been lying. You know, as well as I, he knew Emily back then. Really well. Maybe he knows something more." Or, perhaps, he knows Edna killed all of them. But why would he hide that knowledge?

"I'll keep checking his business and home until I can speak with him.

"And I've been thinking, Abby, about Brown. Since our visit with him, I've come to the conclusion that something about his reaction to the deaths rang phony. We need to speak to him again. He's hiding something. I know it. He could be your thief and vandal… except…he lives so far away. Quite a distance to come just to scare you. The person who threw the rock and killed the birds only meant to frighten you. Make you stop prying into the murders. They could have hurt you, just as easily, but they didn't."

"Instead, they hurt defenseless, innocent little creatures. It's despicable."

"I agree. Terrible."

Frank stayed for sandwiches, and later, tired of discussing her troubles, Abigail asked if he'd heard anything more on his novel.

"No, nothing yet. I called my agent the other day and she reminded me, it takes time, especially for a first novel. An editor's looking at it and you can't push an editor. They'll read my book as soon as they can get to it. My agent was polite about it but I sensed she was a little peeved at me for bothering her again. So I wait.

"By the way, when I was in the hardware store, the owner wanted to know why I needed the glass, so I told him. He's been following the stories in the newspaper and admires you for searching for the truth. He didn't charge me a penny for the glass. Says you're a town heroine. He has kids and can't stomach anyone who'd kill children. He said he never cared for Edna. Called her a cold fish. Oh, and he wants you to paint a picture of his family when you have the time. One of his customers has been raving about the picture you did for her. Wow, your reputation is growing. Maybe, someday, I'll know a famous artist," he teased.

The news, along with the fixed window, helped pull her out of the dumps. "Another picture. If my freelancing keeps going this well, I'll never have to work a real job again."

"I'm happy for you," Frank said. "I have a proposal. Let's go for a motorcycle ride. The fresh air will do you good. I'll throw in a hot fudge sundae later in town. My treat. I'll go home and get the Gold Wing. I'll pick you up in about twenty minutes?"

"You fixed my window, so how can I refuse? A ride will do me good. Twenty minutes will give me time to grab a shower and get ready. Thanks, Frank. For everything."

He left and Abigail took a quick shower. Quick not only because Frank was coming back soon, but because she was so sure the sound of the water spray was masking the noises of someone breaking in. She kept turning off the water, listening, her heart hammering. It was the fastest shower she'd ever taken. Then, when she was dressed, ready to go, she sat on the porch swing breathing in the fresh air. Her eyes stayed away from the birdhouses. She was glad Frank would return any moment.

The day was a hot one, the sun blazing. It'd started out balmy, now it was hotter, and humid.

Sweat trickled down her collar along the sides of her face. She was tired of the heat and wanted cooler fall weather to come. It was the end of summer. Labor Day was the following weekend and, so too, another holiday picnic which Frank kept bragging about.

Time. How quickly it went. She'd been in town over two months but felt as if she'd always lived, and belonged, here. She thought, her present problems and petty vandalisms aside, Spookie had become her home. If someone was tormenting her, he or she would grow weary of it eventually, or the sheriff, or Frank, would catch them. Abigail had confidence in Frank if not in the sheriff. If anyone could solve this thing, Frank could. This too shall pass.

Abigail gazed out past the trees and the road. Maybe there shouldn't be any more Emily Summers newspaper stories. Frank was right, it'd become too dangerous. Let the past stay dead and buried. What ever happened to those three would probably never be known. The mystery never solved.

The sound of the engine preceded the motorcycle, its throaty growl rushing through the woods to prompt her to her feet. A soothing ride, breezes in her hair and on her face, was what she needed. To be free. Hopefully, she'd outrun the dead bird images stuck in her mind.

Frank rode up, a big smile behind his clear facemask. "I see you're ready. Jump on." He didn't ask if she'd locked the house up and that gave him points with her.

"Where are we going?" She climbed behind him, placing her feet on the foot pegs. In a yellow T-shirt, blue jeans, tennis shoes, and her hair in a ponytail, she'd dressed for comfort.

"Remember the scenic route I told you about which curves around the lake behind my property?"

"Uh, huh." She put the helmet on he'd handed her.

"That's where we're going. A wonderful ride. I've ridden it twice. It takes about three hours but it's worth it. The panorama is lush. The lake is lovely. Afterwards, we can get ice cream or a meal, if you want. Is that all right with you?"

"It's all right with me. Lead on." Touching him on the shoulder, she grinned behind her mask. Picturesque beauty, open roads, an azure sky and no storm clouds in sight, she mused, here we come. She'd planned on painting her future art studio but it could wait. Frank was trying to cheer her up and she was going to let him. After the newspaper story, her shaky morning, perhaps it was best if she were gone for the day. If she was gone no one could get to her.

Riding the country roads around the lake they enjoyed the cooler air. They made small talk over their helmets' CBs, cherishing the scents and resonance of the summer day.

They stopped to stretch their legs, sitting by the edge of the lake on a broken length of tree trunk. "I love it out here." Weaving and playing with a blade of grass between her fingers, Abigail's eyes scanned the horizon. "It's so peaceful; makes you feel close to God. It makes it hard to believe anything bad can happen in a world so beautiful or that humans could harm other humans."

"You're brooding about Emily and her kids, again, aren't you?" he scolded.

"I can't stop. We all love a good murder mystery, don't we? However, if you think about it all, it really boils down to one human being killing another. It's gruesome."

"I feel the same way, Abby, and it's one of the reasons I don't miss being a homicide detective. I don't miss the crime, the brutality and the murders. Oh, I miss helping people; finding a killer, bringing him or her to justice. I know it gives a closure, a sort of peace, to the victims. I don't miss the rest of it."

"You don't?" Abigail tilted her head in the sunlight, her eyes on Frank's suntanned face.

"Well, I might miss the challenge of piecing the clues together. Solving cases. Like an intricate puzzle, it takes patience, and attention to details. It's exciting at times. I'm older now, and I sure as heck don't miss the kind of scum, idiot, or brilliant, I had to deal with. Evil does have a face. Unfortunately, sometimes it's human. You talk about the innocence of nature, yet it's the absence of man which makes nature so beautifully pure. That's why I love being out here among the trees, water and sky, just like you."

"You're too deep for me, my friend." Abigail cradled her helmet in her arms, staring at the pearl whiteness of it, and mulling on human evil and Emily Summers. The killing of children.

Frank picked his helmet up off the ground

where he'd laid it. "Now you're thinking about the Summers again, those kids, aren't you?"

She made a face at him and shrugged. "Are you a mind reader or what?"

He smiled. "Nah, I'm only perceptive. You had that unhappy look again on your face. You had to be thinking about the Summers."

"I have this feeling," she hesitated, for a moment, as if looking for a way to put her thoughts into words, "call it a premonition, that there is something important we're overlooking."

"We could be. Nothing is ever as simple as it appears. I'm still going to talk to John when we get back tonight, if I can find him. I want to talk to Brown again, too, see where he was this morning…and have another conversation with the sheriff. I'm going make a couple other calls."

"Thanks, Frank, for all your help. Thanks for this ride today. It's given me time to clear my mind. To remember I'm alive and the Summers are dead. And I don't want to end up that way. Their lives and deaths are in the past. Like Joel. My life is now. I have to remember that."

"No one's going to hurt you. I'll protect you."

She didn't need to answer because she knew he meant it. It was just the sort of man Frank was. She felt safe with him. They climbed back on the motorcycle, continuing their ride, and afterwards stopped at Stella's for cheeseburgers. Stella was off for the night. Her grandson waited on them. He had extra copies of the article. He had to sit down to give them his theories on who might have done it.

"I think old lady Edna killed those kids," the boy voiced his opinion. "Most people can't imagine her doing such a thing, but I can. In the summers, I worked part time at the grocery store when old lady Edna was still alive. I used to run groceries out to her about once a month for Mr. Mason. She was the only customer he did that for. I had to make sure she received the food in person, and that she gave me a hand-written receipt back, that she had. I got paid five bucks each time so I didn't complain. I don't look a gift horse in the mouth.

"Anyways," Stella's grandson went on, "old lady Edna never once asked me to come in, or gave me a drink or even thanked me, no matter how terrible the weather was. She was one unfriendly old bat. She had these squinty eyes. Always acted so grouchy, complained and crabbed about everything. As if I cared. I was only delivering her groceries. Oh yeah, I can believe she killed those kids. What a witch."

***

Dusk came as Frank rode Abigail home. They left Main Street and were moving along the gravel road which led to her house when the car came up behind them. At first, Abigail thought nothing of it. Cars were supposed to use roads. Frank was running at a slow speed, eyes ahead on the treacherous gravel; his vision probably hindered by their helmets and the shadowed road. With the car on their tail, he slowed down, edging over to the shoulder on the left, expecting the vehicle to pass. Traction wasn't good. Abigail could feel the wheels slipping.

That's when the car speeded up. It tapped the rear bumper of the motorcycle. The first tap was a light kiss and the second was a shove. Abigail grabbed Frank's waist as the machine bucked or she would have turned and shook her fist at the car. It was a miracle they didn't go down.

"What is that idiot doing!" Frank shouted as the Gold Wing swerved. He fought to keep it upright. They'd gotten back on an even keel when the third, and final, shove came. The car's engine revved. Its front fender hit them hard. The Gold Wing jumped into the air, flew about ten feet, and went into a skid in the gravel alongside the road.

Frank held on, struggling to lay the motorcycle down without hurting them or wrecking it. He managed to barely hold on as they went down. Abigail wasn't as lucky. She was thrown from the bike into the air.

The car roared past them and sped off into the night.

"Abigail!" Frank yelled as he got up from the ground, looking bruised and shaken but otherwise unhurt, and turned to look for her, not seeing her right away.

"Here!" She let out a groan from the ground about fifteen feet behind him. "I'm back here."

Frank stood the motorcycle upright and rammed the kickstand down. The machine was scratched, the rear fender slightly dented, but it was in one piece with both wheels still attached.

He ran to where she was sprawled in the gravel, holding her left arm, and trying not to cry out or moan in pain.

"Are you okay?" He went down on his knees beside her and hovered, afraid to touch her, but wanting to comfort her in some way.

"No. I think I broke my arm. It really hurts." She fought to keep the tears from falling. "I flew off the motorcycle and came down on it. I heard it snap. I probably need to go to the emergency room."

"My cell phone is in my saddlebag. I'll call 911 and get an ambulance. Don't move or you might make it worse." He made the call, returning to her side in minutes.

"They're on their way from County General in Chalmers. It won't be long. Oh, Abby, I'm so sorry. I feel responsible. I couldn't get away from the guy. I can't believe he actually struck us." His distress was changing into anger.

"Did you see who it was, or the make and model of the car?" she asked weakly. The pain was worse. She was dizzy. Her stomach was rebelling at the same time she was fighting to remain conscious.

"Not really. The car came up behind us so quickly and stayed too close. Its headlights blinded me. After the car rammed us and drove away, I only had time to notice it was a newer model light colored Chevy. The license plate was mudded out. No numbers or anything.

"Mason has a dark blue Camaro, so it couldn't have been him."

"I don't have insurance," she said.

"Don't worry, I do, and it'll pay for your hospital bill no questions asked. Oh, Abby, I'm so sorry."

"It's okay, Frank, it wasn't your fault. It

could have been worse if you hadn't handled the bike as well as you did. We could both be here on the ground, whimpering, or we both could be dead. Lucky you have insurance, unlucky I couldn't keep my seat. I should have held on tighter, but it just happened too quickly."

In the distance, a siren increased in volume until it was ear splitting as Frank held her in his arms. They loaded her into the ambulance. Frank rode the bike, which still ran, behind it to the E.R.

Four hours later, Frank brought her, left arm in a cast, home. He'd ridden the Gold Wing to the cabin and had returned to the hospital with his truck.

"I'll try not to hit any bumps."

"Thanks, but they gave me pain pills. I don't feel anything. Speed. Get me home. All I want to do is sleep. Forget this happened. I've never had a broken bone in my whole life," she muttered. It was dark outside. She could hear crickets chirping. No one had fed Snowball her supper.

"Then you've been fortunate. I've had plenty of broken bones and I know they can hurt like hell. Again…I'm so sorry."

She waved her good hand on her good arm at him. "It's not your fault. Just get me home."

He pushed the gas pedal down as she leaned her head against the seat and shut her eyes.

"Do you think the same person, who threw the rock and killed the birds this morning, also slammed into us in that car?" she asked in a drowsy voice. The pain pills were really kicking in. Everything now had a dream quality about it.

"I don't know. Possibly. It could have been someone else mad at you over the articles, or mad at me, for heaven knows what. I was a cop for a long time, you know.

"Or–it could have been a totally random road rage incident which went too far. Some people don't like motorcycles."

***

She hadn't heard him, she was asleep, drooling against the window. Frank got her home, into the house and tucked into bed, clothes and all. He fed the cat, locked up the house on his way out and left a note for her saying he'd check in on her in the morning. He got as comfortable as he could on the porch swing, in the dark, as a restless sleep claimed him.

He didn't believe their being hit on the motorcycle had been an accident for one Chicago second. Someone had been trying to give them a warning–or kill them.

With the first rays of dawn he awoke, careful not to make too much noise and wake the woman sleeping in the house. He inspected the premises, the yard, and then drove home; returning a couple of hours later with something to eat for both of them.

He hung around most of the day and into the evening, under one pretense or another, until Abigail kicked him out or believed she'd kicked him out. Instead, he haunted the area, guarding her house from the front seat of his truck, on and off, for a couple of days until he was fairly sure she was safe.

One night sitting there, it brought to mind what Abigail had said about Sheriff Cal Brewster doing the same thing all those years ago, but for Emily. The squad car parked outside Emily's house all those nights…had the sheriff been harassing her or had he been trying to help her? Now that was a good question. One Frank didn't have an answer to.

Chapter 17

Abigail covered her eyes, pushed her head against the glass, and squinted against the general store's window. She was careful not to let her plaster cast touch the glass. It'd been four days since she'd broken her arm. It was the first time she'd gotten out. Her arm was sensitive, and any pressure at all, even jostling the cast, made her wince. She'd driven one handed into Chalmers for groceries, grateful, as she'd been since the accident that she'd broken her left arm, instead of her right, because she was right handed.

On the return trip, she'd swung into town to see if Mason had reopened his store. He hadn't. It was locked, empty, dark and silent. Her watercolors were inside and she wanted them back. He'd picked a heck of a time to go on a long vacation, which according to the hardware storeowner next door, was exactly what he'd done. He'd be back next week. Maybe. The least he could have done was left someone in charge of the store and kept it open. The town needed it. Wasn't there a law against closing a store which was the only one in town, without any advance notice, like that…like there was a law against a hospital, or a police force, going on strike or something? Nah, maybe not. It was his store. She guessed he could do what he wanted with it.

She'd decided she didn't want her artwork in his store any longer. The way he looked at her, the lies she'd caught him in, and the way he was behaving since the last newspaper article had finally convinced her to cut her losses and run. He wanted something from her she wasn't able to give. But he'd slipped away and she hadn't been able to retrieve her artwork. She wanted her pictures back. There were two other businesses offering to showcase and sell them for her and she needed the money.

Walking away from the closed store, her arm hurt more than it had when she'd gotten up that morning. It was probably time to go home. Rest. Pop a few more of those pain pills. She couldn't take them when she was driving, or walking, or…awake. They knocked her out. From now on she'd have more sympathy for anyone who had a broken anything. Every chore took twice as long to do and people thought you were an invalid, as if you couldn't take care of yourself.

Frank had been a pest since the accident. He blamed himself, and no matter what she said, he bent over backward being sweet to her to assuage his guilt. He'd brought her homemade soup, stew, and had baked a cake. *He had baked a cake.* Washed her dishes. Watched her house at night when he didn't think she knew. He had driven her nuts with helpfulness and protectiveness until she had shoved him out yesterday. She'd told him she appreciated his concern, but she needed her privacy back. She was going to be fine. He'd finally gone home with his puppy dog face, his head lowered.

As she was trudging to her car, she spied Myrtle with her wagon in front of Stella's. Her curiosity was too much for her, she had to talk to the old woman, hurting arm or not. She hadn't seen Myrtle since that bizarre night in the woods.

"Abigail Sutton!" Myrtle yelped, looking over at her. "It's been awhile, hasn't it?" Her print housedress, yellow with white flowers, looked about five sizes too large and hung, practically touching the ground, on the old woman's frail frame. A thick belt kept it from falling off. Her hair had been dyed raven black, re-permed into tight ringlets and it looked so odd with the tiny wrinkled face. Yet Abigail would never tell Myrtle that.

"Myrtle, yes it has. How was your gambling excursion?"

"Lousy. I lost fifty bucks. That's my limit, then I come home. Except I didn't come home straight away, as you know. Us women went on a joy ride across the state visiting relatives. We even stayed at a bed and breakfast with the best homemade vittles I've ever had. We watched the eagles fly in Alton. We stayed away much longer than planned. I had a good time, though, and at my age that's a feat. I take it where I can get it these days.

"Unlike that rock of a sister of mine, who refuses to leave that mausoleum of hers for any reason. I get so angry with her. She never wants to go anywhere. The whole world's out there. If you're alive and can still walk, ya need to go out and enjoy it." She spread her stick-skinny arms out wide and did a little jig right there in the street.

Abigail laughed.

"Sorry about your broken arm there." Myrtle

gently patted Abigail's cast. "I heard about your accident. Better be careful. Those motorbikes are death traps. I hear you've been busy. The rock saved the newspaper articles on the Summers' family for me. You found graves and missing diary pages. You're unraveling the mystery, ha, and you being a stranger. It was so long ago, but I still can't fathom they've been dead all this time. You want to know what I think?"

"Give it to me."

"Emily's mysterious boyfriend killed *her* and Edna killed those kids, or they did it in cahoots. I've always thought Edna had done something terrible, but conjecturing and knowing are two different kettles of fish. Most people can't tell who the bad ones are. I can. I can see behind their masks." She winked. "Now, dearie, tell me about those dead birds the other day."

Abigail did, positioning Myrtle and her in the shade of Stella's Diner and off the hot sunny street.

"Whoa, someone's pissed at you." Myrtle tittered. "You hit someone's raw nerve." The old woman peered into Stella's window with a yearning look on her face.

"Were you going into Stella's for some lunch?" Abigail asked.

"I was thinking of it. I got a terrible craving for a piece of Stella's banana cream pie. It's the best in the county. I love banana cream pie, but I forgot my money, so I have to pass." Her mouth fell into a mock frown. Her face was pathetic. She sent a sly glance towards Abigail.

"I have money, Myrtle. How about we go in and, my treat, have pie and coffee? You're the reason I found those graves and Jenny's diary. I've never had a chance to thank you. We can catch up on everything. It's hot out here and my arm is giving me a fit."

Myrtle agreed without protest and the two went into Stella's, which was already decorated in stars and stripes bunting for the coming weekend festivities. Frank was right, holidays were a town obsession. Abigail, though, had decided she liked it. She reminded herself to put the flag, Frank had bought her, on her front porch when she got home.

When they'd settled in a booth, the wagon parked beside them because she refused to leave it unprotected outside, Myrtle broadcasted, "I can't wait until the Labor Day picnic this weekend. I always eat a bowl of chili and sample every pie in every booth." Her expression clouded. "Last year I got pretty sick. Threw up all over one of them pie booths."

"Perhaps this year," Abigail suggested kindly. "You ought to limit the pie, to be safe."

"I can't. I love pie. I got to eat every one I see. I steal pie. Sometimes I…steal things."

Her manner reminded Abigail of a simple child. The old lady was worse than she'd ever seen her. She flinched every time there was a noise, her eyes darting here and there. One minute she'd be conversing as if she knew where she was, and who she was with, and the next minute her mind and attention would be wandering, or completely gone, and nonsense would tumble out of her lips. Then

Abigail remembered Frank had told her most of Myrtle's senility was an act. Hmm. The old lady was a lot smarter than most people thought.

Abigail tried not to chuckle when Myrtle suddenly sang out Perry Como at the top of her lungs. *Hot diggity, dog diggity, look what you do to me!* The older people in the back of the diner joined in, laughing and acting as if the sing-a-long was a normal occurrence. Maybe it was.

Stella came over to take their order. "Myrtle, a little off key today aren't we?"

"Mind your own business, you music Nazi!" Myrtle pouted, turning her head away.

Stella ignored the old woman and spoke to Abigail, "I read that latest story, Abigail. Whew, it's been better than my soaps. I heard about you and Frank's accident the other evening, too. Sorry to hear about it. Good thing the only injury was your arm. It could have been worse. Motorcycles are unsafe. You couldn't get me on one if I was dying.

"What can I get you guys?"

Myrtle sang until their pie came. Then she was too busy stuffing her mouth to do anything else. She wanted a second piece. Abigail indulged her, but stopped it at two pieces, using the that's-all-the-money-I-have-on-me excuse. It worked.

"I've been trying to get my artwork out of Mason's store," Abigail told Myrtle. "But it's closed and has been for a week. No one's seen John Mason at all."

"I have," Myrtle announced. "I seen him slinking around town. He don't want nobody to know, but he's here. He hides behind the trees." The woman turned wide eyes on her companion. “Not fat trees, the skinny ones, because he can make his body into a stick. He can fly sometimes, too.”

“You’ve seen him?” Abigail played along. Myrtle was agitated. She didn’t want to upset her more. The second piece of banana cream pie must have gone straight to her brain and shorted it out. Too much sugar. Myrtle met her gaze. The old lady’s forehead creased as if she were trying to recall something important.

“I saw him yesterday, down behind those trees around the pond, by the courthouse.”

“Oh, then I’ll be sure to watch out for him.”

“Be careful,” Myrtle admonished. “He’s really mad at you. You found the graves. He was Emily’s boyfriend. When Emily was still alive, that is.”

“You’re right, he was one of them anyway. How did you know that?”

“I saw them kissing once, many years ago. I liked Emily. It was all such a pity. She had all that money and your house. Now she’s dead.” Myrtle must have seen many people come and go in her life. She carried a lot of ghosts with her. That must be what it was like to be old.

Martha came into Stella’s, and spotting them, hurried over. “Hi, Abigail. Myrtle.”

Myrtle sprung from her seat. “Gotta go! The white wolf will gobble me up if I stay one more second. He’ll find me for sure.” Aside to Abigail, “Thanks for the pie, dearie. Remember what I said.” And she was gone out the door, into the sunshine, her wagon bumping along behind her.

"Myrtle doesn't believe in long goodbyes," Abigail remarked, "does she?"

"No, she doesn't much care for me, is what it is. Since she caught me making fun of her one day behind her back, she's avoided me ever since. Nutty old woman."

Martha sat down and, seeing the empty pie plates, sniggered. "She played that I-don't-have-any-money-on-me-can-you-spare-me-a-piece-of-pie con on you, didn't she?"

"She did."

"That old broad is a tilt-a-whirl trip." Martha examined Abigail's wounded arm with her eyes. "Okay, enough about crazy old women, how are *you* doing?"

"My arm hurts."

"I can see that by your pained mien. Can I sign your cast?"

"No. I prefer my plaster uncluttered and creamy white, thank you."

"Alrighty. You're no fun. When I was a kid I broke my leg by falling out of a tree. All I recall was how god-awful it hurt and how the cast itched me to death the whole time it was on. Believe me, after that I never climbed another tree. I heard you did that on a motorcycle?"

"Does the whole town know about everything that happens to me all the time?"

"Yep. That's a small town for you. Now tell me the entire story of what happened from the beginning. And don't leave out any of the juicy details."

Abigail gave her a condensed account of the

accident, and of the rock and dead bird incidents.

Martha flagged Stella down. She ordered a hamburger and coffee. Someone in the rear of the diner yelled hello to her and she yelled hello back, afterwards returning her attention to Abigail. “I’m worried about you. I don’t think that accident was an accident. You should come and stay with me for a while, or, at least, until they catch whoever it is playing those dirty tricks on you. Next time, you might not be so lucky to get away with only dead birds on your porch or a broken arm.”

“Thanks, but I don’t need to hide. I have Frank. He doesn’t know I know, but he’s been staking out my place playing secret sentry. Even after I told him to stop.” She peered out the window, a slow smile forming. “It wouldn’t surprise me to see him sneaking around outside somewhere right now. Talking of men…how’s Ryan?”

“Ryan wants us to get married,” Martha mouthed between bites.

“Really?” Abigail tried to focus, but her arm was aching. She wanted to go home.

“I’ve been having so much fun dating him, he treats me so well, I’m afraid to say yes. A man will give you anything, do anything, until he gets a ring on your finger. Then–boom–you’re his slave and he starts treating you like a wife. Do this. Do that. They stop treating you like, well, a lover. I’ve been there, done that.”

“All marriages aren’t like that, Martha. Mine wasn’t. Joel and I were lovers and friends first. There wasn’t a day that passed when he didn’t leave me a love note, a flower, or a gift with an *I love you* attached. It got better each day. If it's real love, marriage won't spoil it." The lump in Abigail's throat threatened to surge into tears, feeling sorry for herself. It was a combination of missing Joel, pain from her broken arm, and a growing dread of something unknown rushing at her.

"You truly loved your husband, didn't you? The story book kind of love?"

"Yes," Abigail spoke with a soft sigh. "I loved Joel more than anything in the world. One of life's cruel jokes: it uncovers what you love and need the most and then takes it away from you."

"You were lucky to have had him as long as you did, Abby." There was envy mingling with compassion in Martha's smile. She, too, had begun to call her Abby. "True love. Most people never have that. I know I never have."

Martha paused. "I hear John Mason has up and gone, without leaving a forwarding address, or saying any goodbyes, and he did it about the time of the last Summers' newspaper article. What do you think that's all about?"

When speaking to Martha, friend or not, Abigail had learned whatever she told her today, everyone in town would know tomorrow. There were things with the Summers' story she didn't want to get out. Not yet. "I don't really know why Mason left town, or why. Someone told me he went on vacation."

"That's a good one. This weekend is the big Labor Day celebration. The town merchants make a pot of money. John Mason has never missed making money. I think something in the stories scared him off for some reason. I'd sure like to know what it was."

Martha had gobbled her lunch. "I hate leaving good company, but I have paperwork to do. I'll see you at the picnic Saturday. I'll drag you to the best chili and pie booths. I know them well." She glanced at her thighs with a frown. "Now take care of that arm and stay out of traffic. Ciao."

"I will to both," Abigail promised. "Bye." She watched her friend leave money and exit the restaurant.

Her pain had become a silent shadow, constantly there, so Abigail paid her pie bill, bid farewells to Stella and to her grandson cooking in the back, and drove home.

After making sure the house was locked up around her, she downed pain pills and fell asleep on the sofa. Snowball was snoring on her chest and the wooden club was tucked in the crease of the sofa on her left side.

***

She slept through the afternoon, evening and night, and dreamed Joel came to her back door. She was so happy to see him, she ran into his arms, and into nothingness. Standing in the open door, she glimpsed Joel at the end of the yard. It was dark and there was barely a faint sliver of moon, yet Joel was encircled in a globe of glimmering light, so he was easy to see. Oh, how she'd missed him! He was gesturing her to follow. So she did. She followed him through the woods, among the sleeping trees, to Jenny's and Christopher's tree house. The tree was still intact, untouched by lightning; towering, hulking, dark above them. Joel halted at the graves, which were aglow in a soft blanket of radiance.

There were nine graves with wooden headstones when she remembered there being only three. Joel was hovering behind the first one. She walked towards it. It was Emily's grave.

"What do you want me to do?" she asked Joel. "Why have you brought me here?"

The dream Joel had only smiled grimly and moved on to the next grave. She followed him. It was Jenny's grave. The third grave was Christopher's. Abigail, sick sensation clawing in her chest, went to the fourth grave. Edna Summers was scratched on it. The fifth grave Norma's. The sixth, and seventh, graves were Emily's parents.

Abigail was terrified of going any further. She didn't want to look at the remaining two graves but Joel insisted. In life, she'd never been able to deny Joel and in the dream it was the same. The eighth grave was Joel's. As she watched, tears welling in her eyes, her throat closing with uncried sobs, her husband threw her a kiss as he sunk through the dirt into his grave. He was gone. At that point she wept. Joel was truly dead. She'd known it for months but for some reason it hurt more at that moment, for the truth of his death had, finally and forever, come home to her.

The ninth grave was open, waiting, and as she stared into the hole, footsteps in the leaves behind her alerted her someone was there. When she swung around it was a man or a woman. She couldn't make out the face because the person was in the shadows. She couldn't tell if the person was short or tall because the image flickered like a flame.

"I've dug nine graves. The ninth has been waiting for *you*," the husky voice rasped. Without warning, the shadow person shoved her into it. She screamed, struggling, but no one heard her. She tried to climb out, yet she couldn't. Her body was a frozen lump stuck in the fresh earth. The shadow cackled above her and shoveled in the dirt as her world went black.

Abigail woke up screaming, until she realized she was on her couch in her house. Safe. She'd been dreaming again. The pain pills gave her the most awful nightmares. It was morning and someone was knocking. Putting on her robe, she answered the door.

It was Frank, a box of donuts in his hands. "I knew you were awake. I heard the screaming. Nightmares again, huh?"

"I don't want to talk about it," she groused, pushing her uncombed hair off her face. She let him in. "I'll go make coffee." She padded off to the kitchen.

***

Frank slumped down on the couch, took a donut out of the box and stuffed it into his mouth. Snowball bounced up beside him, begged for a piece, which he gave her. The kitten liked the chocolate iced ones, especially the icing. Exhausted from the nights he'd spent in his truck, at the end of Abigail's driveway, Frank appreciated the softness of the sofa.

He didn't know how much more he could take. Stakeouts were a young cop's pastime. Sleeping in a truck. Drinking cold coffee. Staying awake all night. Catching cat naps during the day. He was getting too old for all that.

But listening to Abigail in the kitchen, he had the feeling, as he had for days, she was in danger. He had to watch over her for a little while longer. Call it his cop's instinct…and his instincts were rarely wrong.

Chapter 18

Frank arrived in good spirits the morning of the Labor Day picnic to escort her to town. The day was warm, cloudy, though no rain was expected until late that night. She hoped it would hold off at least until the picnic was over.

"Did you hear from Kyle?" were the first words out of her mouth when she saw Frank. Kyle was supposed to come down for the weekend and go to the picnic with them.

"He's coming. He won't be here until around two, though. He's got to drive down from Chicago. I told him he could find us lingering along Main Street."

"Breakfast at Stella's first, I presume? Bacon, eggs, biscuits and hot coffee?"

"It's tradition." His earring sparkled in his ear. Today he'd tied his hair into a short ponytail. There were sandals on his feet, his blue jeans were faded, and there was an American flag on his shirt. He looked comfortable and a lot younger than his years.

She was wearing a brimmed straw hat, so her face wouldn't burn, with a blue scarf tied around its base. Her blouse was white and her shorts were a patriotic crimson. She'd begun to feel almost normal because her arm didn't hurt as much as the day before. She'd stopped gulping the pain pills because she couldn't tolerate the nightmares.

Dreaming about graves, and faceless shadows, had scared the pain right out of her. The last time she'd taken the pills she'd dreamed of Edna poisoning her coffee. Afterwards, as she'd laid on the couch, unable to move or speak, Snowball meowing pitifully in the background, the shadowy ghosts of Emily, Jenny and Christopher had taken turns coming and sitting with her, waiting for her to die.

"Come with us. We're waiting for you," Jenny had begged in her child's voice, small hand stroking Abigail's arm. "We'll help you find Joel…he's here somewhere."

A see-through Christopher had pleaded, "I'll teach you how to roller skate. It's not hard." Then, a pale translucent streak, he'd left the room on his skates.

"I don't belong with you," Abigail told them. "I don't want to die. I have a lot of life ahead of me. Why did Edna do this to *me*?"

"Because you've been digging up her business, all the dirt; putting it in the newspaper. She'll never forgive you for that," Emily's ghost murmured before she'd drifted away.

In the dream, Abigail had shut her eyes as her spirit left her body. She'd awakened. The dream had been so real she thought she'd died. Instead, it was as if she'd been given another chance, another life. That was the last time she'd taken the pills, because it was easier to take the pain.

Entering Stella's Diner, Abigail thought on how things had changed. People recognized her now, sympathized about her broken arm, and kidded her about wanting to be a Jessica Fletcher clone in a Murder She Wrote episode. They wanted to talk about the graves she'd found and the diary. They all had theories of who killed who.

"What's your next case, Jessica?" a middle-aged bald man solicited. "My Aunt Ester can't find out what happened to her investment money. You want to look into that for us?"

"The stock market has fallen. That's what happened," Abigail joked back.

"We have a family mystery," another customer joshed. "Cousin Mary Ann Stoebel went to Montana seven years ago. No one's heard from her since. What do you think became of her?"

"She's running a cow ranch, out in the middle of nowhere, and she has no phone?" Abigail responded good-naturedly.

And on and on. Most of it was friendly ribbing, which was the townspeople's way of showing acceptance. Frank merely smiled and said nothing.

Breakfast was ordered and came and Martha, Ryan and Samantha joined them. Samantha was chattering about going out of town in two weeks for editorial classes. "Frank," she initiated after a gap in the conversation. "Was there ever any conclusive proof in Edna's parents' autopsies to what they actually died of?"

"The medical examiner found traces of long term poison in their bone fibers. It had soaked into the remnants of their clothing. The same kind of poison he found in the children's bones. So most likely, whoever killed the old people, killed the kids as well."

"That's terrible, but fantastic for the wrap up story I have planned." Samantha turned to include Abigail in the conversation. "I know you've been plagued recently with warnings from someone unhappy with the stories." She was looking at the cast on Abigail's arm. "I'm really sorry. I feel responsible, being it's my articles which have gotten you both in trouble and put you in danger. If you want me to, I'll stop writing and printing them. No matter what the publisher wants." She was serious.

"And let whoever's been doing these awful things win?" Abigail spoke first. "No way. We'll be careful." She glanced at Frank and he nodded. "So don't muzzle the truth because of us. You just go ahead and do that wrap up story. Freedom of the press, remember?"

"At least we're safe today with all these people around," Frank pointed out.

"You're a brave pair, you are." Samantha smiled. "I thank you both from the bottom of my heart. Our circulation has gone through the roof since we've starting writing about the Summers and it's made my publisher, and me, so happy. The mail and reader participation alone has been astonishing. Finding the graves, the contents of the diary, its missing pages, and printing about all that put us over the top. People love an intriguing who-done-it.

"I'd like to speculate who might have been the poisoner of those four victims and what might have really happened to them. My boss is pressuring me for closure.

"And I'd love to be able to serve up the

killer, but with no positive suspect, and too many possibilities…it ain't gonna happen. The late Sheriff Cal seems likely. Myrtle thinks Edna killed all of them." Samantha dropped her voice so only Abigail and Frank, could hear. "We know from Norma's letter John Mason was one of Emily's boyfriends…but we can't be sure he was the only one or even if it's true given Norma's state of mind at the end and her hatred for her ex-husband.

"So we can't use names because we don't have the proof to be pointing fingers. Ruining reputations. It leaves us open for libel. Between you and me, as I know John and don't believe he'd do anything so heinous, the ex-husband looks guilty as sin, horrible as that would be. But who knows?"

"Right, we can't prove anything," repeated Abigail. "People can speculate to their heart's content, play detective, but we may never find out who killed them. We're at a dead end."

In the beginning, she'd wanted so badly to solve the mystery and then the murders, but slaughtered birds, a smashed up motorcycle and a broken arm later, she wasn't so sure any longer. It wasn't worth Frank's life or hers she'd decided. The dead were still all dead; nothing would change that.

"No matter," Samantha said. "It's been amazing. It has made everyone rethink how they should treat their neighbors–with more compassion and understanding–and brought the town together, reliving some of its history. That's worth something."

Abigail's mind wandered, pondering on the secrets of the town and the past as Frank ended the discussion by offering his prediction of who would most likely win the chili contest.

"What sort of chili do you fancy, Abigail?" Martha was holding hands with Ryan.

"The kind with crackers."

"I'm sure there will be some of that kind, as well." Martha giggled.

Abigail and Frank sampled the carnival rides stretching up Main Street, enjoyed the summer day, strolled through the park and around the courthouse's lake where miniature paddleboats waited for passengers. Abigail did all she could to put those graves out of her mind.

It wasn't easy. It was as if Emily's ghost was around every corner. The ghost was dressed in flowered bellbottoms, her eyes black outlined like Cleopatra, and she was hand in hand with her children as they haunted the streets they once walked so long ago.

Around three o'clock Kyle slipped out of the crowd and caught up with them. Along with a grin, he gave Abigail a hug, careful not to jar her cast. His warm welcome touched her.

"How's the sleuthing business going?" he teased. When Abigail gave him a curious look, he explained, "Dad's been keeping me updated on your adventures via telephone. I heard a car tried to turn you, Dad, and the bike into a metal pancake. I heard about your broken arm. That'll teach you to ride with him." He thumbed back at his father and chuckled.

"I'd ride with your dad any time. It wasn't his fault. But let's not talk about that. It makes my arm throb." Her face frowned and Kyle let the subject drop.

"Your hair's getting long, kiddo." Frank tousled his son's hair

"Yeah, I look like a hippie. Like my dad. Now I just need an earring. Or two. A nose ring."

A smile curved Abigail's lips. "They might look good on you. Buy gold."

"Well, now that Kyle's here," Frank looked at everyone, "how about we get some chili and pie, and then take a leisurely paddle around the pond to work it off?"

"Sounds like a plan," Abigail seconded as they headed for the food booths.

Later, the six of them paddled in circles around the lake and, laughing, taunted the other boaters. The water was no deeper than four feet at any spot. The boats were small fiberglass tubs. It'd been years since Abigail had been in a paddleboat, the cast made it awkward, and she got a little sunburned, but she had fun anyway.

At five o'clock the chili winners were announced, the prizes given out. Frank talked Abigail into going on the Ferris wheel and they watched the entire town from the top of it. He held her when the wind swayed them and she laughed as he pointed out people and things below. "Look, there's Myrtle and her wagon over on Plum Street coming this way…the country band is setting up on the bandstand…see where the bonfire's going to be…there's Stella's grandson talking to that Sarah girl again. I think he likes her." Frank was enjoying himself. He'd gone on every ride at least two times and sampled half the food at the booths. That Kyle had showed up made the day perfect.

After the rides the gang listened to the band. Abigail sat the fast ones out, because her arm was sore, but danced a few slow ones with Frank. As the day wound down the evening twilight crept in and brightened the tiny twinkling lights strung along the streets. The band got louder, and more clouds drifted in darkening the shadows, but no rain.

Abigail didn't want the day to end, she'd had such a good time, but since the accident she tired easier and knew she'd be home before they lit the bonfire. She'd taken a break and was sitting by herself at the picnic table. Martha and Ryan were dancing, Frank and Kyle getting drinks, when an unsettling thought occurred to her: Were her pictures still safe inside Mason's store? Just because he was irritated over the stories didn't mean he would have done anything to them? Did it? She should check to be sure. Mason was out of town, so it had to be safe if she just snuck a peek in the store windows.

The idea nagged her until she acted on it. It was only a short ways down the street. The sound of the music followed her.

The store was dark and empty inside, the closed sign hanging on the door. Trying the doorknob, she found it locked. She peered through the window, face pressed against the glass. She couldn't see her pictures, couldn't see a thing. Much as she hated the thought, she'd have to wait until Mason returned to town and the store opened again. Sighing, she was about to go back when she caught a glimpse of something moving behind the glass. *Someone was inside.* She slid up against the wall. Froze. Her inner voice told her to leave, but her common sense said if there was someone inside, all she had to do was run and fetch Frank–or yell. There were people all around her, so she was safe.

Hesitating was her mistake. The door swung open, a hand darted out and snatched her good arm, physically dragging her into the store. She screamed and fell to the floor as the door slammed shut, trying to keep the cast from hitting the hard surface. As her eyes adjusted to the murkiness, someone hissed, “Don’t scream again. I won’t hurt you.”

Even in the dim light filtering through the windows, she recognized John Mason. “Mr. Mason?” Abigail squeaked as he helped her to her feet, keeping a grip on her, but he was careful not to jar her bad arm any more than he already had.

“It’s me. The man whose reputation you’ve ruined. I was just gathering some things before I left town. It was nice of you to drop by to say goodbye.”

She could see he was upset. Not himself. “I’ll be missed quickly,” she warned him.

“I’m not going to hurt you. I just want to talk to you.”

“Why?” She tried to keep her body from trembling. He was behaving so strangely.

“To set some things straight. It won’t take long. I’m sorry you broke your arm.”

Abigail gritted her teeth and mumbled, “Things happen.” For the first time with him, she was frightened. She never should have checked out the store alone. So stupid. But, she calmed herself, he only wanted to talk to her. No danger there. And because she was a normal person, who couldn't believe someone would want to harm her over printed words, she believed that.

"I'm sorry you think I ruined your reputation, Mr. Mason. I don't think I did. I suppose you're referring to the newspaper stories on the Summers? Your name was never mentioned."

He nodded, his eyes shining in the faint light. "You didn't use my name, no, but you didn't have to. Innuendos and the other clues pretty well pointed a finger *at me*. Anyone who lived here in those days can make the connection…make assumptions. What was printed was as good as branding me a murderer! After that last story, I had to go into hiding. I can't show my face without someone staring at me, whispering behind my back. Life as I knew it, everything I worked so hard for, is over. I can't stay here any longer." There was a hostile desperation in his voice.

The words spilled out before she could stop them: "Did you kill Emily?"

He didn't answer. In the background, Abigail heard the picnic, muffled and far away.

"You *were* Emily's secret boyfriend, weren't you?"

He must have comprehended he couldn't lie. She had him. "One of them, but I was in love with her. I wanted to marry her. You make it sound sordid," he breathed. "Made it sound sordid in those stories."

"Because you were engaged to Norma and

you were abusive to Emily and those kids?"

He didn't answer her.

"Did you throw the rock through my window? Did you kill those birds on my porch?" she suddenly demanded. "Send me that threatening letter?" Now she was getting mad. If he wanted to set the record straight, why not all of it. "You ran Frank and me down on the motorcycle, too, didn't you?"

"You didn't listen!" There was harsh resentment in his accusation. "I warned you to stop prying."

Her skin had gone chilly. She was in trouble here and she finally knew it. "I couldn't stop searching for answers once I found the graves. *They* wouldn't let me. I was living in their house, John." His first name just slipped out, an attempt to temper his growing anger. "They'd waited a long time for the truth to be known…for their justice. In a way, *they* led me to their graves. *They* begged me to help them."

Mason's shadowy tormented face drained of color when she'd used his first name. He stared at her as if she were a ghost. Emily's? She'd triggered something and he was losing control. Lowering his head, he mumbled hoarsely, "I loved Emily…she was the love of my life. That wasn't in your exposés, was it? Unfortunately, I didn't know that truth until years later and it was too late. Life went on. I grew older and unhappier, every year. More alone. I stare into the mirror and wonder who is this old man? Where has my youth, my life, gone? The happiest days were when I loved Emily…but she didn't love me. She left me for another man. A younger man."

He continued to study her with that odd expression. "You look so like her. Same eyes. Same smile. You're an artist. She was an artist. You could be her twin or Emily reincarnated. Has anyone told you that? The first time I saw you in this store, you gave me quite a shock. I feared she'd returned to haunt me."

"Because you killed her?"

"You think if I had, I'd be stupid enough to tell you? Tell anyone?" There was a crafty rasp in his voice.

She mutely shook her head. Mason shoved her into a chair. She had to get away from him. He was unbalanced. He'd hidden it well…until now.

"I'm leaving town today. You've chased me out. Ruined my business–and my life!" He stared around at his store with grief stricken eyes. "People believe I'm a murderer. I'm not! I'll tell you the truth…*Edna* killed Emily–her own sister–*and* those kids…*with poison.*

"Yeah," he whispered, his eyes glittering with paranoia. "Edna did it! Her parents? She murdered them, too. Poison. They betrayed her. Left the house and the inheritance to Emily and the kids, not Edna. What a joke on her. Edna was the oldest, but she was stealing their money. Emily's money. Ha, that did it. Emily caught her.

"So Edna got rid of all of them. She buried them by the tree house. She hated Emily; hated the kids. She wanted me, you see. But, ha! Me have anything to do with that lazy, plain as a grapefruit, hypochondriac–no way! I wouldn't give her the time of day," he uttered contemptuously.

Abigail was horrified. Mason was lying. The final forensic results didn't support Emily's being poisoned. The kids, yes, not Emily. Emily was strangled–probably by a pair of strong angry hands. Hands like Mason's. It'd been a crime of enraged passion.

"But I couldn't get rid of Edna."

"She was blackmailing you, wasn't she?"

Mason seemed startled. He shut up, glaring down at her. Abigail's eyes had accustomed themselves to the dimness. She could make out Mason's unshaven face hovering above her like an evil moon. It was a face tired, beaten, and old with a twisted, feral expression. His clothes were rumpled. He appeared nothing like the debonair man she'd met three months ago. The past had caught up with him. Guilt had undone him.

Because, though he'd blamed it on Edna, Abigail knew in that moment–whether crime of jealousy or insanity–*he'd killed Emily*–and not Norma, Todd Brown, or Sheriff Cal Brewster. It explained everything. "How do you know about that?"

"Remember, I found Edna's ledger? It was one of the things you broke into my house to steal, yet didn't find." Abigail shrunk into the chair. There was a sudden threatening in his manner that scared her. She'd gone too far this time and knew it. She should make a run for it, but he had too firm a grip on her arm. So, whenever he let his guard down, she'd better be ready to run.

"You got to understand," he whined. "Emily told me she was going to Chicago to start a new life and to be with *him.* I'd had a horrible fight with Norma and told her it was over. I was sick of her plain, nagging face…I'd been drinking…I couldn't bear the thought of someone else having my beautiful Emily. I'd lost *everything*. I went to Emily's house…it was dark…she was packing her car. The children were upstairs…they hadn't been feeling well for a long time…I begged Emily not to go…told her I'd give up Norma, the store, everything…all I wanted was *her.* I was weeping, on my knees, shameless. Seeing her leaving made everything so clear. I was nothing without her. I'd even marry her!

"I was too late. She wouldn't listen. *She was in love with someone else.* And suddenly my hands were around her neck. I didn't know what I was doing!" His fingers opened and closed, clenching, his eyes reflecting some horror he alone was remembering, then they narrowed. "It was the booze. It made me do it. That's why I quit drinking. After that night I hardly ever drank again.

"Afterwards I saw my life spilling away. I'd be disgraced and humiliated. I'd go to *prison.* I couldn't face it. *And Edna saw it all from the window,*" his voice broke, his eyes glistened with tears.

"But…she helped you bury Emily in the woods and promised not to turn you in, if you gave her money every month. If you'd go along with her story that Emily and the kids had left town? But she poisoned them, didn't she?" Abigail pressed gently.

"She got the house, the money and then...she blackmailed you for the next thirty years. She kept track in the ledger. Right?" It was a calculated guess and by the way Mason reacted, it was either the truth or close to it.

"Ah, yes, Edna's ledger. That woman was so greedy. Every year she wanted more. With my ex-wife already draining me, I had to do *something*. What a shame, someone helped Edna into the next world. Did you know old Edna was dying of stomach cancer? Poor soul. Just not fast enough. Someone, I have no idea who, added a few lethally doctored pills to her monthly medical prescription. *Tsk, tsk.* It must have killed her. No one asked any questions when she died. They all just thought it was the cancer. I figure I did her a favor. Thirty years of blackmail was enough. Hell, I couldn't stomach paying *one penny more*."

But, how did he know about the drugs in Edna's system, she thought, unless he did it? "*Who* killed the children?" Soft, low. Careful. Careful.

"It took me thirty years to get it," spoken in another whisper. "That Edna poisoned them, too, like she'd poisoned her parents before them. For the inheritance. Irony was, that until you discovered their graves beneath the tree house by Emily's *I never knew they were dead*. I never went back to the grave after we put Emily there. I swallowed Edna's story that she'd sent the kids back to their father two weeks later when she caught up to him. I never checked to see if he had them. Why would I? And throw suspicion on me if there was ever a murder investigation? I thought I was being smart." But he didn't seem to realize by saying those words he was incriminating himself.

"*Imagine* my surprise when I read in the newspaper that *three* graves were found, not one. What a fool I'd been! Edna blackmailed me decades for killing Emily when *she killed four people herself.* All that money I was forced to give her for nothing! I could have blackmailed *her.*" A sour laugh emerged from his throat. He was behaving more like a mad person every second.

"And your ex-wife, Norma? Did you also kill her?" Abigail was in so deep, why not plunge deeper?

"Well, I did give her the pills, and she did kind of stumble down the stairs trying to get away, too doped up to know what she was doing. Oops, I opened the wrong door. Humph! I merely wanted her to go to sleep on the sofa so I could look for that letter she'd written. Talking to her earlier, I figured she'd write you. Norma blabbed too much. She had a big mouth, always did. Yet, she wouldn't tell me where she'd hid it. One thing led to another.

"Well!" He threw up his hands in a reckless gesture. "*Imagine* my astonishment when I found her at the bottom of the steps, dead as a doornail. *Tsk, tsk, tsk.*"

Abigail's mind was spinning. Mason had killed Emily, Edna, *and* Norma, and was justifying it. Strangling Emily, living with it all those years, and then having to dispose of Edna, and Norma, had finally driven him over-the-edge *insane.* What should she do? Her arm throbbed, her head hurt, and she was beginning to be truly scared.

She had to get away from him.

She noticed people walking past the windows. Maybe, they were missing her at that very moment and were searching for her? She could hope. Her eyes, now fully adjusted to the murky store, spied a knife lying on the counter behind Mason. He'd said he wouldn't hurt her, so what was the knife doing there?

He'd stopped talking. Seemed confused. He'd let go of her arm, his hand had fallen on the knife, was caressing it, and with an odd glimmer in his eyes, he turned slightly to stare at it. "I…guess I shouldn't leave any…loose ends."

"You almost killed me and Frank," Abigail reproached him in a soft voice, stalling for time, so she could find a chance to bolt. She slowly began to stand up. "Were you really trying to kill us?"

"It wasn't me. I don't have a white Chevy. I have a red Camaro."

How would he have known it was a light colored Chevy, she brooded? Another lie.

"But, believe me, I'd have good reason for wanting Frank Lester dead." He snorted. He'd picked up the knife and slowly brought it to touch the skin at the base of her neck.

Abigail had to fight to keep from reacting. Screaming. *Stay calm.* "Why would you want Frank dead?" she pressed gently, trying to distract him; trying not to panic at the feel of the blade pinching her flesh.

"Because last time I saw Norma, she spitefully informed me of what I'd never known. Frank Lester was the younger man Emily left me for all those years ago. Emily had told Norma that the day before she was going to leave when Norma had a run in with her. Emily was going to Chicago, to be with *him*, and start a new life. Frank!"

Frank? Abigail's mouth fell open. Nothing could have shocked her more. She didn't know what to say, but didn't get a chance to say anything, because she felt his arm come around her shoulder as he firmly grabbed her. The knife dug deeper into her skin. The air felt heavy. She couldn't breathe.

"He loves you, as I once loved Emily, I think. You look so much like her…the cause of my heartache, my despair–" He stared at her with confused eyes. "*Emily…I killed you once…why are you back?* Do I have to kill you again to finally be rid of you?"

He thought she was Emily. He was going to kill her. Again. He dropped the knife and reached for her neck with swift hands, and instinctively, she threw her cast backwards, suffered the pain and slammed it into his face. With a yelp, he released her, and fell to the floor. And she bolted for the door. It was locked.

Mason didn't chase her, though, because, all of a sudden, there was a crowd of people at the glass, peering in. There were voices calling her name. Abigail recognized Frank's voice. They'd come looking for her. *Thank God!*

"Abigail!" Frank yelled, pounding on the door. "Are you in there?"

"Yes, I'm in here!" She glanced frantically over her shoulder at Mason, still on the floor, in the gloom behind her. He was scrambling to his feet.

The knife was nowhere to be seen. It was most likely with the dust bunnies under the counter somewhere.

"I'm going to go now…never meant to hurt you, Emily, I swear…so sorry. *Just leave me alone, for God's sake,*" she heard him sob. Then he was gone.

There had to be another exit in the rear of the store. Mason had been prepared for this.

Abigail moved out of the way as the front door crashed open. She fled into the sunlight, squinting, and there was Frank with open arms. "I'm all right," she announced, her eyes on his worried face. "I was…talking…to John Mason. He killed Emily, Edna and Norma–and he's getting away! He went out through the rear of the store somewhere."

The look of relief that she was okay on Frank's face turned to anger. "Which way did he go?"

"I don't know. He said he's leaving town for good. He must have a car, packed, and ready to go somewhere nearby."

"There's an alley behind the store. He could have parked his car there." Frank ran down the sidewalk to the alley between the buildings and around to the rear, leaving Martha, Samantha, Ryan, and Kyle with Abigail.

Martha put her arms around her friend. "Are you really all right, Abigail? What happened?"

"I'm fine, thanks to you guys, and I'll tell you all about it, every bit, as soon as I catch my breath." A smile crept over Abigail's face. It was over and she was okay. She was so relieved she could have wept. She turned to the newspaper editor. "And Samantha, now I have that final wrap-up, the answers you wanted so badly on the Summers' murders."

"He got away," Frank exclaimed, when he returned to the store. "You were right, Abby, he had his car, a brand new white, but muddied up Chevy Impala, crammed to the ceiling with suitcases, out back. He was driving off as I got to the alley. I just missed him.

"I'd swear it was the same car that hit us on the motorcycle the other night. Right down to the dirty license plates."

Frank called the sheriff to come pick him up and the police joined the chase, but Mason was long gone. He must have detoured the town, the picnic revelers, and headed straight for the main highways. The sheriff put out an APB on him.

Abigail collected her watercolors from the abandoned store with the help of Martha and Ryan and lugged them home. It was her artwork; she had the right to take them. Outside, the picnic was going strong as music, and sweet aromas, wafted on the air mingling with the evening breeze. It seemed as if she'd rode the Ferris wheel with Frank so long ago.

A gentle rain had begun, but Abigail didn't care if she got wet, or if her arm hurt. There was nothing like a close call with death to make a person feel alive. And her brush with death, she knew now, had been close. Mason would have killed her if Frank and the others hadn't shown up when they did. She was as sure of it as she was sure she'd been extremely lucky.

Frank caught up, later that night, with Abigail at her house and she repeated everything for the second time that Mason had said. She downplayed the part about the knife and the attempted choking, but Frank wasn't fooled. He put his arm around her and held her tightly as they stood in her kitchen. She was happy to be alive, but worried that crazy Mason was still on the loose.

"Mason believed there, at the end, I *was Emily*. Imagine that?" she said to Frank. "All his scheming, killing, and guilt must have finally shoved him over the cliff."

"As far as I'm concerned, he was already over the cliff and out in space somewhere. We just didn't know it until we started bringing the past out into the light. I'm glad you're okay and, don't worry, we'll catch him. Everyone's looking. Local. State. County. Federal. It's only a matter of time before they track him down. He's not thinking clearly. He'll make a mistake, then we'll get him."

Abigail shivered. "I hope they catch him. Until they do, I'm going to lock my doors and keep my stick close."

"You do that." Frank smiled, said goodbye, and when Abigail thought he was gone she looked out the window and saw him snuggled down for the night, in his truck, in front of her house. He wasn't leaving her alone, unprotected. Not until Mason was caught.

Chapter 19

When Abigail told Frank that Emily had been going to join him in Chicago the night she died, it had staggered him. They were talking, sitting side by side, on the front porch swing. The afternoon had passed into the hour which was half day and half night.

"You have to believe me. I never knew she was going to follow me to Chicago. Or that she felt *that way* about me. Sure, I was in love with her, like I said before, a puppy-dog sort of love, but it wasn't reciprocated–or so I thought back then. We were friends who enjoyed spending time together. I cared deeply for her. I adored her kids. I'd asked her out many times, but she'd always said no. She thought I was too young for her, and by being with me, she'd ruin my future."

"She thought she wasn't good enough for you, was the truth of it. That's what I think. She was divorced with two kids, an abusive ex-husband, jealous boyfriends, and a stalker. She had a lot of dangerous baggage. While you were just starting out on your way up in the world, headed for Chicago and a prestigious police career; she was trying to escape a bad past. She was trying to have a better life.

"It could have been Emily *was* in love with you, Frank, but denied it to herself, until–poof–one day she looked at how lousy her life was here and resolved to begin fresh in Chicago, too. Or try to. With you, if you let her. No matter how much older than you she was. Only she didn't have time to tell you any of that before she died. Maybe, she was going to take her chances and surprise you in Chicago. She was just going to show up and hope for the best."

"You could be right. It was so long ago and by my memory Emily did react strangely to the news I'd gotten the Chicago job. She was happy for me, yet from the moment I told her, she'd avoided me. I thought she was mad at me for leaving, or had other troubles in her life. I was so excited about the new job, running back and forth to Chicago, and preparing to leave town, I never gave it much thought. I was young and foolish. I couldn't see what was right in front of my eyes."

"Emily might have loved you, and avoided you, because she was afraid she'd show her true feelings." Abigail studied Frank's profile in the moon's light. He must have been handsome thirty years ago and he still was. He had a rugged face which age often matured, but didn't actually change too much. She could imagine an older woman falling for the younger him. And, in truth, Emily hadn't been that much older than Frank back then. What was eight years difference anyway?

"It floors me Emily could have loved me and I didn't know it," the words were spoken with sadness. "Lost chances. Roads not taken. I keep wondering how different my life might have been if I'd known. If she'd shown up in Chicago and wanted to be with me."

"Would you have spent time with her, dated her…married her?"

"I don't know. I might have dated her. I really had a crush on her. But, I was so young. And I met Jolene that first year in Chicago and she *was* the love of my life. No doubt about it. She gave me a beautiful marriage and a son I adore. I wouldn't change any of that for the world. What would have happened if I'd been involved with someone else that first year in Chicago? I don't know." Since he'd learned of Emily's secret love for him, and how she'd died, he'd been retrospective, and more than a little melancholy.

"What hurts most is, if Emily wouldn't have loved me and wanted to move to Chicago to be with me; if I wouldn't have been the reason she broke it off with Mason that night…she might still be alive. I can't bear I might have been the cause of her death, indirectly or not, and I never had an inkling of any of it. It's been hard these last few months, remembering Emily and that time, then learning she and her children have been dead all these years, murdered. That she'd actually loved me. It's all been so hard."

"It must be a shock." Abigail laid her hand tenderly on his arm. Their eyes met. A leaf had fluttered down from the trees, finding a home on his shoulder. "Frank, it wasn't your fault. Emily would have broken off her relationship with Mason anyway. Any reason she may have given for leaving him, or this town, would have pushed him over the edge as easily, I'm sure. He killed her because he'd lost her, and was jealous, was unstable even then, not because she loved *you*."

Abigail believed that and hoped Frank

believed it, too. Breathing in the chilliness of the September evening, she could taste fall. For once, her cast didn't itch. They were on her porch swing soaking in the night and each other's company, light seeping out from the house's windows illuminating their faces. Frank had needed someone to talk to, and she had let him.

*****

A few days later, Abigail and Frank once again were on the porch swing discussing things. The finale of the Summers' murder saga had come out the day before in the newspaper, and now everyone in town knew the whole truth. John Mason had strangled Emily Summers and, with Edna's help and silence over thirty years, had buried her in a shallow grave. Edna Summers had poisoned her parents long before Emily's death and then poisoned her niece and nephew to get them out of the way, for the house and the inheritance money. Mason had killed Edna thirty years later because he was sick of the blackmail and he'd sped along his ex-wife's death because she would have exposed him as Emily's long ago lover and, thus, possibly tied him to the old murders.

"What a monkey's paw of deceit, greed and murder. Now we know what befell all of them, as heartbreaking as it is. Abby, you solved the mystery. You are Jessica Fletcher. A younger Jessica anyway."

She laughed. "Oh, I solved it all right with a lot of people's help, yours included, and Mason's actual confession."

The police had caught John Mason getting

on a plane, at the airport, a day after he'd tried to hurt Abigail. Coming out of hiding, he'd made a beeline for Mexico. Living was cheap down there. He hadn't made it and was now in jail. Once in handcuffs, all the years of guilt, Edna and Norma's recent murders, must have broken him. He'd confessed; was resigned to paying for what he'd done.

"After all he did to hide his crime over the years. The blackmail and lies. And killing two more people. To just come clean like that was a surprise," Abigail said.

"Emily told him to confess, I heard he told his lawyer that from his jail cell. Yep, he's nutty as a peanut." Frank shook his head. "At least it's over. I pray Emily, her two children, can rest in peace.

"It's also time to get on with our own lives, Abby. We need to move on. It's been an interesting summer."

"Hasn't it?" she remarked. "I found a new town, new home, new life, friends, a new career– and we helped three restless spirits find peace in their graves. Well, really five restless spirits. Oh, then there was Edna and Norma." She was counting on her fingers. "Seven. Not bad for a summer's work."

"Okay, you can quit patting yourself on the back."

"Will there be a trial, you think?"

"It's doubtful. Mason's lawyer says he'll probably cop a plea. Mason doesn't want to go on trial. He doesn't want to be put on display as a murderer, even if he is one. He can't stand the humiliation. And it turns out he isn't well. Once he was behind bars, they discovered he had a bad heart…as well as seeing and talking to people that aren't there."

"Now that's ironic, isn't it? A bad heart?"

"That's a fitting description of the real John Mason, I'd say." Frank shifted on the swing, and as Snowball ran across his lap, he caught the cat and began to pet her.

"Good as any, I suppose," Abigail said, taking the cat from Frank and placing her in her own lap. The kitten had grown to twice its original size since Abigail had taken her in. She'd learned to scratch at the door when she needed to go out, and would throw herself at the outside screen door when she wanted in. Her idea of knocking.

"I could almost feel sorry for him. He's got to live with what he's done and he'll most likely be in prison for the rest of his life."

Frank shook his head. "I don't feel sorry for him. He got what he deserved, albeit three decades late, but better late than never. Emily and her kids will be dead forever and they didn't deserve to die like that. Killing Emily directly led to those two poor kids being done in by their aunt. Edna might never have had the nerve to poison them if their mother hadn't already been dead. It left them vulnerable. No, Mason's got a lot to atone for. I hope Emily pesters him for the rest of his miserable life. In prison. In the dark. With no windows. Like a grave."

"Yeah…and I hope Emily, Jenny and Christopher leave me alone. But, I haven't dreamed of them since the day I learned the truth."

"That's good, isn't it?"

She released a deep breath. "It's good. Though I did rather enjoy solving their mystery. Following the clues. Doing something worthwhile. It was exciting and I'm going to miss that. Now everything has gone back to normal. The usual. Cleaning house and paying bills. *B-o-r-i-n-g*."

"Nothing is boring in Spookie, Abby. You know what they say…life is full of mysteries."

"And murders? Heaven forbid. I've had enough of graves, dead bodies, and hidden murderers. Besides, I have my new commission to keep me busy."

"The job from the town painting a picture of the courthouse?"

"Yep, and for big bucks. If they like it, I'll get a second commission to draw the City Hall, as well." Abigail's face, in the shadows, was smiling. "The money will keep me in groceries and pay my bills for months. I won't have to take a job at the local Wal-Mart for a while. I'm ecstatic."

"I bet you are. And I'm ecstatic for you. I like my friends to be successful and prosperous. Makes me look better."

The swing's chains creaked, punctuating the moaning of the wind. "Frank, talking about successful friends, have you heard anything else about your book?"

"I have. I was just going to tell you. My agent called this morning and she thinks she might have it sold to a small publisher. There's not much of an advance. It won't make me rich, but it's a start, and I'll be published. Saying it out loud is hard because I still can't believe it. I wasn't going to talk about it yet, but–"

Abigail threw her arms around Frank in a hug. "I knew you could do it! I'm proud of you. I want one of your first copies, hot off the press. Signed, of course."

"You'll get it soon as I get mine."

"You'll have to learn how to act like a published author and start going to those writers' conventions and everything. I can't wait. Road trips! Can I go along?"

"We'll see. It hasn't been published yet. Then I'll need lessons on how to autograph, how to look humble, and how to escape from droves of fans. That's the important parts of being an author, or so I've been told."

They both laughed. Frank leaned over and when their lips met the kiss just happened. She found herself kissing him back then pulled gently away. She couldn't mistake the feeling between them. It was love. New, fragile, and promising. A little too soon for her, she thought. Or was it? Joel had really been gone to her for over two years. Two years was a long time. She kissed Frank again, in the twilight, and afterwards they held hands.

"We've been invited to Martha's house Saturday night to play cards. Listen to music," he said. "Snacks provided. You busy Saturday night, Abby?"

"Now I am." She hadn't forgotten Joel. She'd always love and remember, him. It was just that she had to embrace this new life of hers, leave the past, some of it, the sad and unchangeable parts, behind. She wanted to fall in love again. She wanted to be alive again. Because life was short, precious, and a person had to live it every moment. Every moment they had.

The silence which settled between them was comfortable as they pushed the swing. After a time, they talked about taking a motorcycle ride the next day, if it didn't rain. Snowball was sleeping, a purring ball of fur in Abigail's lap, and the night had become chillier.

Beyond the dark trees, Abigail thought she heard Jenny and Christopher's laughter. She hadn't told Frank, but yesterday, she'd found another scrap of paper tucked in a crack deep in the corner of the kitchen cabinet, where she stored her dishes. She couldn't understand how she'd missed it earlier. Unless she hadn't been meant to find it until then. The only words on the note, in red crayon, had been:

Mom says were leaving. No more mean boyfriends, no more mean Aunt Edna. Me and Chris are so happy. At last. Goodbye bad times! Hello, happiness and posterity!

And it'd been signed with a large J and a C.

The note had made Abigail sad and happy at once. It must have been written before Emily had been killed and the kids had become so ill.

But, it was the last time she'd feel sad for the dead children and their mother.

For now, surely, the ghosts were at peace.**

****

The End

****

If you'd be so kind…I would deeply appreciate it if you could leave a review of this book for me on Amazon and Goodreads – thank you, the author.

And if you'd like to read more adventures of Abigail, Frank and Myrtle in Spookie…be sure to read ***All Things Slip Away****, the second in the series,* ***Ghosts Beneath Us****, third in the series,* ***Witches Among Us****, fourth in the series and the fifth in the series* ***What Lies Beneath the Graves****, and out in 2020* ***All Those Who Came Before****; all available not only in paperback but in eBooks and Audible audio books.*

And if you liked this murder mystery series be sure to check out my other two stand-alone murder mysteries ***The Ice Bridge*** *and* ***Winter's Journey****…or any other of my 27 novels or 12 short stories.*

****

Links to the other 4 sequels of the Spookie Town Murder Mystery series:

~ **(Book #1) Scraps of Paper**:

~ (**Book #2 All Things Slip Away**:

Tiny URL: **https://tinyurl.com/y3nlcdhx**)

~ (**Book # 3 Ghosts Beneath Us**:

Tiny URL: **https://tinyurl.com/yxc5lgpa**)

~ (**Book #4 Witches Among Us**:

Tiny URL: **https://tinyurl.com/y4ud9h97**)

~ (**Book #5 What Lies Beneath the Graves**:Tiny URL: **https://tinyurl.com/y4afpuqb**)

And SOON, in 2020, there will be a Book #6: **All Those Who Came Before**.)

About **Kathryn Meyer Griffith**…

Since childhood I've been an artist and worked as a graphic designer in the corporate world and for newspapers for twenty-three years before I quit to write full time. But I'd already begun writing novels at 21, over forty-eight years ago now, and have had twenty-nine (nine romantic horror, two horror novels, two romantic SF horror, one romantic suspense, one romantic time travel, one historical romance, five thrillers, and eight murder mysteries) previous novels, and thirteen short stories published from various traditional publishers since 1984. But I've gone into self-publishing in a big way since 2012; and upon getting all my previous books' full rights back for the first time in 36 years, have self-published all of them. My Dinosaur Lake novels and Spookie Town Mysteries (Scraps of Paper, All Things Slip Away, Ghosts Beneath Us, Witches Among Us, What Lies Beneath the Graves, and All Those Who Came Before) are my best-sellers.

I've been married to Russell for forty-two years; have a son, two grandchildren and a great granddaughter and I live in a small quaint town in Illinois. We have a quirky cat, Sasha, and the three of us live happily in an old house in the heart of town. Though I've been an artist, and a folk/classic rock singer in my youth with my brother Jim, writing has always been my greatest passion, my butterfly stage, and I'll probably write stories until the day I die…or until my memory goes.

2012 EPIC EBOOK AWARDS *Finalist* for her horror novel **The Last Vampire** ~ 2014 EPIC EBOOK AWARDS * Finalist * for her thriller novel **Dinosaur Lake**.

***All Kathryn Meyer Griffith's books:** http://tinyurl.com/ld4jlow ***All her Audible.com audio books here:** http://tinyurl.com/oz7c4or

Novels & short stories by Kathryn Meyer Griffith:

*Evil Stalks the Night, The Heart of the Rose, Blood Forged, Vampire Blood, The Last Vampire (2012 EPIC EBOOK AWARDS*Finalist* in their Horror category), Witches, Witches II: Apocalypse, Witches plus Witches II: Apocalypse, The Nameless One erotic horror short story, The Calling, Scraps of Paper (The First Spookie Town Murder Mystery), All Things Slip Away (The Second Spookie Town Murder Mystery), Ghosts Beneath Us (The Third Spookie Town Murder Mystery), Witches Among Us (The Fourth Spookie Town Murder Mystery), What Lies Beneath the Graves (The Fifth Spookie Town Murder Mystery), All Those Who Came Before (Sixth Spookie Town Mystery), When the Fireflies Returned (Seventh out in December 2020), Egyptian Heart, Winter's Journey, The Ice Bridge, Don't Look Back, Agnes*, *A Time of Demons and Angels, The Woman in Crimson, Human No Longer, Four Spooky Short Stories Collection, Forever and Always Romantic Novella, Night Carnival Short Story, Dinosaur Lake (2014 EPIC EBOOK AWARDS*Finalist* in their Thriller/Adventure category), Dinosaur Lake II: Dinosaurs Arising, Dinosaur Lake III: Infestation and Dinosaur Lake IV: Dinosaur Wars, Dinosaur Lake V: Survivors and Memories of My Childhood.*

Her Websites:

Twitter: https://twitter.com/KathrynG64

My Blog: https://kathrynmeyergriffith.wordpress.com/

Facebook Author Page:

https://www.facebook.com/pg/Kathryn-Meyer-Griffith-Author-Page-208661823059299/about/?ref=page_internal

https://www.facebook.com/kathrynmeyergriffith68/

https://www.facebook.com/pages/Kathryn-Meyer-Griffith/579206748758534

http://www.authorsden.com/kathrynmeyergriffith

https://www.goodreads.com/author/show/889499.Kathryn_Meyer_Griffith

https://www.pinterest.com/kathryn5139/

https://www.smashwords.com/profile/view/KathrynMeyerGriffith

https://tinyurl.com/ycp5gqb2

Made in the USA
Middletown, DE
14 May 2020

94941145R00179